THE CALLING
of
MOTHER ADELLI

A Novel

Zoe Keithley

ZOE KEITHLEY

DEDICATION

To my mother, Isabelle Byrne Marhoefer, grandmother, Mary Prior Byrne, sister Martha Isabelle Marhoefer Abbate, her daughter Francesca Abbate, and our cousins Nancy Nosek Williamson and Mary Nosek Harrington, all Lake Forest Sacred Heart/Barat College alums; and to the religious who labored so mightily for and with us. Like our nation's flag, 'Long my we wave!'

HOW IT HAPPENS

A place gets a hold of you like a person does sometimes. Just so, the building that housed the Madams, their *Soeurs*, students and helpers commanded my heart and imagination over the years. Still, it was a surprise to meet again with that building, its grounds and wild growth, as I began a journal entry in writing class at Columbia College, Chicago, more than thirty years ago. I saw myself in the chapel of my boarding school, in sixth grade and waiting to go to confession.

Alas, the building, old beyond repair, is torn down now. But the ravines, trees, squirrels, birds and other wildlife hold the place for it still, alive and blessed in memory. Months later, in a different writing class, I found a young nun had replaced me in that same pew. Still later, looking for the nun, I found instead a nervous father at the front door of the boarding school and a red headed girl with a suitcase in tow. And the story had started.

1948. A father brings his unwilling and motherless daughter to boarding school outside Chicago while he tours Italy on medical business. The young nun, Mother Adelli, in charge of the girl, becomes caught in a Gordian knot of the Church, her religious order, privileged society, family, and the world of the arts as well as her own conscience struggling with the heartbreak and fury of the student, Helene, left in her care. That young nun is Mary Agnes Adelli. This is her story.

I.

Chapter of Faults

"Then a spirit passed before my face;
the hair of my flesh stood up;
It stood still, but I could not
discern the form thereof;
an image was before mine eyes,
there was silence, and I heard a voice
saying, "Shall mortal man be more just
than God? Shall man be more pure
than his maker?"

Book of Job 4: 15-17 KJV

ZOE KEITHLEY

One

The floors had just been waxed that September afternoon when Michael Rhenehan brought his ten-year-old daughter Helene to the Convent of the Sacred Heart for school. Before dawn, on their hands and knees, six Working Sisters had spun out the thick amber paste until a golden ice flowed everywhere.

Closing the door to his convertible, the heart surgeon saw old sagging brick, crawling ivy and milky windows. He took a deep breath and jabbed the doorbell. "God," he thought, "I hope this is going to be all right." It was September 14, 1948, and exactly three o'clock.

At the sound of the buzzer he passed into the narrow stone vestibule, through the inner door, its glass panes frosted and etched, mounted the worn wooden steps and strode out into the foyer where his heavy physician's sole sailed out from under him. In a rush of air, the fluted wall lamps, European side tables and antique vases sprang away; the ornate ceiling reeled downward and the gleaming floor delivered a hammering blow to his backside that emptied his lungs.

He lay there gasping. Ahead loomed the chapel doors with the oversized mahogany hearts he had seen pictured on the front of the brochure. Everywhere about him stretched the gleaming lake. And why in hell would anyone bring floors to such a high polish that nobody could walk on them? His hangover gonged behind his eyes. He could have shattered an elbow. He heard the anxious tippy-tap of portress feet and held up a hand. "I'm fine thank you, Mother." He strained the words through his teeth, found his knees, straightened his jacket and smoothed his hair while his right buttock throbbed. The redheaded daughter, dawdling up the stairs behind him with her night bag banging at her knees, froze at the banister and gaped until she saw the father stave off the clucking nun.

The Portress steered them into the parlor where the French windows let dollops of sunlight splatter over everything and the lace curtains sighed with the changeling wind. The nun murmured some words in French and disappeared. Why is it *she* never slips, Michael Rhenehan wondered sourly.

Father and daughter sat near the windows. Michael Rhenehan looked around. He saw solvency. If his dead wife Mary Helen were alive, she would be pleased. Why, the Order ran the best Catholic girls' schools in the world--everyone said so--and with nuns from the most prominent Catholic families. Well, they must all be royalty; the place was costing a fortune.

Past Superiors bossed the walls showing disapproval of a father who would bring his only and motherless daughter here like a dog to a kennel so that he could gallivant around Italy's major hospitals for six months lecturing on surgical procedure. Very well, but was he supposed to remain hog-tied in Chicago while those with less talent rushed past him to pick the fruit?

The stubborn odor of fresh wax mixed with that of his alcohol-driven sweat, his liver doggedly processing drinks from the night before while he wished to hell he could unzip his skin. Had that nun gone for someone or were they supposed to sit here all day guessing what to do next?

He stole a glance at the motherless daughter beside him busy rummaging in her nose. He let an elbow fly.

"Use your handkerchief," he hissed.

From under the wild copper of her dead mother's hair, she frosted him with startling robin's-egg blue eyes. She was tall for ten and thick, with square shoulders and a pan-shaped face all freckles.

"I've told you a thousand times to always bring a handkerchief. Your father is a physician, for God's sake.

Here." He rolled onto one ham, winced, and dug a square of white from a rear pocket.

She slid the finger in and out of her mouth, grinned.

"I don't need it now."

His blood simmered. Lately she found a million ways to defeat him. The two had argued the thirty miles north from Chicago while Lake Michigan flashed in sapphire bits behind thickets of woodland trees and sprawling stone mansions. Well, these nuns were famous for polishing off rough edges.

He pulled the drape aside and let in a blare of light. "But what a beautiful day." Out the window, columns of clouds marched toward them. He dropped the curtain. "Nana should see this place." He ran an index finger over the coffee table. "I could do surgery."

"You can put me in any school you want to over there. I'm all packed."

He saw the tiny muscles that shut off tears tighten around her eyes.

"You don't speak Italian, honey. Besides, what will I tell them here? And there's your uniforms, they're made to order; we can't send them back. We've been over this."

"I'll learn Italian. I'll wear the uniforms. Look at the windows. It's a jail here."

He had not noticed the elegantly curved iron security bars. For the hundredth time he forced himself to picture her scuffing along behind him down the streets of Rome, her lower lip in a pout. No, it would be hell. "You'll go to Nana's in New York for Thanksgiving--and you'll come to Rome for Christmas! You're making too much of this, Helene. It's only six months. Lots of kids do this." Where in God's name was that nun?

"It's too long. And you promised you'd never leave me." She turned upon him her eyes of righteousness. "You promised!"

They'd had their ritual down the years since the mother passed. "I'll never leave you," he'd reel her into his big bear hug. "Never ever?" she'd test.

"NevERRR," he'd growl again, hugging until she squealed.

But now he met her eyes, then looked away. Some promises couldn't be kept.

Just then a square of black boomed through the parlor door. Michael Rhenehan leapt to his feet. Reverend Mother Gregory, in perfect command of the floor, and with veil flaring like elephant ears, crossed with an outstretched hand.

"Dr. Rhenehan, of course. A pleasure to meet you at last." The woman had a handshake like a sea captain. "With school a week underway, I'm happy we can give you a bed. Sometimes a golden opportunity knocks for professionals, and we understand they must answer."

He judged her to be sixty-three or four, some seventy pounds overweight, built like a freighter and with a man-shaped head and an unnervingly wide mouth jammed into the tightly fluted bonnet. He nudged his daughter.

"And this is our new stieu-dent?" the Superior swiveled. "'Helene', isn't it?" Back to the father. "I know ours will be a splendid association." She clasped her hands as if she had caught a moth, swiveled to the girl again. "And you are going to learn and learn here, young lady."

Helene's face darkened. She climbed back onto the settee and stared across the room at the piano.

Michael Rhenehan waited for the nun to arrange herself on a chair, noted the bunion bulge in the left shoe and her small eyes taking in like an estate appraiser his shoes, suit, tie, cuff links, haircut, and then move to his girl's bearcub body, fly-away shirttail and sagging socks.

"The Portress mentioned the floor--" she gestured toward the foyer. "We apologize. Normally I would ask if we should call a doc--."

"I'm fine, thank you." His hangover banged away.

Outside, birds quarreled among the juniper berries and a north wind began to pull cloud trails across the sun. The light in the room sobered and brightened in a game of hide and seek.

The Superior straightened her back, opened her gunwales and began firing: The mission of the Order to educate women, the educational philosophy of its founder, Madeleine Sophie Barat. Michael Rhenehan counted the Persians floating like exotic postage stamps atop the polished wooden floor, then traced with his eyes the luminous ring of the antique magnifying glass on the coffee table while the pebbles of the Superior's voice scrubbed his face.

"Spare the mind and spoil the child is our experience here, Doctor. We take Ignatius of Loyola as our model."

Over the pendulum of her feet, the daughter gnawed her cuticle.

But what if Helene got sick or began her period? Well, but these were experienced women here; and he could always be reached by phone. This was for her future as well, after all.

The parlor door sang. The Superior leaned back, turned to look.

"Ah, here is our Mother Adelli now."

She came to them across the shining floor, a young woman not much taller than the girl but in the black cape and whispering floor-length skirts of the Order, her rosary beads chattering lightly carrying her body like a dancer. Transfixed, Michael Rhenehan rose.

Reverend Mother Gregory did the honors while the father watched his daughter inventory the new nun to a cold count of five.

"Mother Adelli is Mistress of the Third *Cours*," Reverend Mother Gregory leaned toward the girl and then deferred to the father. "'*Cours*' is French for 'course.' We were founded in France. Your daughter will learn French with us." She beamed all around.

"Oh, you'll be able to help me order when we go to *Amour's*." The father made a menu of his hands. The girl tisked and threw her head.

"I notice from your application your daughter has not made her First Communion. But she is Catholic?"

"Her mother had her baptized, and I keep her in Catholic schools. I know where to get the best education available." He watched pleasure flare in the woman's eyes.

"And all my friends are in the public schools," Helene announced and began pounding her heel against the leg of the settee while Reverend Mother Gregory's eyes widened and the young nun's body stiffened.

"You're going to break that!" Michael Rhenehan reached a hand to the girl's leg. She slid onto her tailbone and latched her arms over her chest.

"Now, do I understand that you prefer she not--."

"I am a man of science, Reverend Mother. I am not strong on religion. I want Helene to make up her own mind about such things. So, nothing further of the religion at this time, but your cultural atmosphere will be good for someone like my daughter who lost her mother at four years, and whose father is much too busy, I'm afraid."

"Oh, but saving lives, doctor. I recall the article in the *Tribune* last year about your work. Astounding, truly." The Superior hung upon him a momentary look of reverence, then recollected herself. "You choose wisely, for the Church is the cradle of Western civilization and the mother of our culture. " She paused, then added brightly. "Mother Adelli here will be going to Rome herself this summer, to make Final Vows."

"Oh?" Michael Rhenehan forced his eyes to open wide. But wasn't that what she was in here for? Something about the way the young woman sat, one hand upon the arm of her chair and eyes cast down, made him see a Renaissance madonna.

"You must stop at the *Trinita*, to view the miraculous fresco of *Mater Admirabilis*," the Superior went on as if seeing into his mind. "The color actually comes and goes in the cheeks; I've witnessed it myself. Each of our convents displays a replica. You'll see our own life-size *Mater* during our tour of the building."

The young nun would have been pretty, Michael Rhehehan decided, if it weren't for the slight under-bite. The dark-fringed eyes, now softly taking his daughter in, though set a bit wide, were wonderfully bright beneath black brows shaped like twigs in a Japanese print; and the chocolate mole riding the lower right cheek was out and out seductive. He never had understood forcing the soft rounds of the female form into these strange-looking and harsh constraints: the wrapped forehead, hemmed-in face, sleeves to the wrists, black wool to the floor. Odd the neck is left bare.

"Mother Adelli is really new here herself," the Superior went on. "She came to us from Omaha when our Mother Boreman took ill last March. You might be interested, a rupture of the left ventricle."

"Oh?" Michael Rhenehan nodded, pursing his lips professionally. He strained not to look at his watch. The Superior's wide mouth filled him with revulsion.

"Your classmates are having *Goûter* now." Mother Adelli leaned toward the girl who twirled the down on her crossed arms into peaks with her tongue. "Just downstairs."

"*Goûter*. Another French word." The Superior shot Mother Adelli a sharp look. "I have ordered *Goûter* for you here in the parlor. I'm sure you both can use a little refreshment after your trip."

"The students have been excited all day to meet you," Mother Adelli began again, but brought herself up short and dropped her eyes. It was against 'the Rule'--protocol-- that, Superior being present, a common religious speak up except invited by her Superior. Mother Adelli's cheeks heated. That had been twice now she'd spoken without permission.

The father wondered why the younger woman kept her voice so low; but then recalled from his daughter's Catholic school in Chicago the strict pecking order of religious institutions; not that different from the medical world, really. Probably the young woman was more forceful when she was not under such close supervision.

The Superior asked Mother Adelli if the student's uniforms had arrived. The girl bleated that she saw those things in the catalogue and wasn't wearing them. And she wasn't wearing that funeral thing either. She laid a look upon her father as if he owed her money. The father colored. His daughter had worn uniforms five years at Cathedral. What was the uproar? The Superior did not seem amused. White uniforms were for feast days. There were also the sports uniform, the brown oxfords, white gloves and white veil. No need for other clothes unless a student was going into the city. The daughter glared at the father and re-packaged her arms.

Thinking the new student might feel better knowing she had a place for her things, Mother Adelli mentioned the uniform was already in her alcove, and then widened her eyes: a third breach of protocol. Oh, her own room, the father rebounded; and here she'd been afraid she'd be cramped all up with other girls. Well, not exactly a room, the Superior interposed, but a simple cot with curtains. Everyone had the same. Too much attention to the physical made the mind sluggish. Didn't the doctor agree?

He smiled weakly. Whenever the woman spoke, the room seemed to tilt, and everything tumbled toward her. He worried again about the other one preoccupied now with her rosary beads--about her small frame. He had seen his daughter wrestle with her friends from the neighborhood. Could she handle girls like that? Well, this Reverend Mother must know if the woman was competent or not.

Goûter arrived on a silver tray. The doctor balanced the glass plate to cut into his brownie with a fork and chewed dryly. The Superior explained that cloistered nuns take food only in private. Helene refused brownie and lemonade alike for her fingernails. "Sit on your hands if you can't stop that," the father hissed out of the corner of his mouth. The daughter blew air through her nostrils and jammed her fists under her thighs.

She would make *new* friends here, Mother Adelli lunged forward.

"I have friends at home," Helene threw her shoulders about, "but I won't have any left after six months here!" She nailed her father with fierce blue eyes. The Superior tapped her fingernails on the chair arm.

"Of course you will write your friends, have your own post box," Mother Adelli burst out, then observed her Superior's countenance. Five times now.

Oh, her own post box, the father hallooed.

"What are some *Congé* activities Miss Rhenehan can write to her friends about, Mother Adelli?" Reverend Mother Gregory prompted. "*Congés* are school holidays, Dr. Rhenehan."

There was the game of Hide and Seek called *Câche-câche* where a whole team hides and the other team has to find them. Last year the Reds went undiscovered in the tool shed. The year before the Whites hid successfully in the circular fire escape. When the weather was fine, they all might go for a run in the ravines.

"And our activities are all safe, Dr. Rhenehan. We take no foolish chances," the Superior turned to the father.

"What am I supposed to do with games like that?" Helene boiled over. "I'm not wasting my time on stupid games my friends will laugh at."

"You'll watch your tongue, young lady," the father clipped her off. "And you'll do what you're told."

"I told you I didn't want to come here." The girl's lower eye lids brimmed. "You never do what you say you're going to do. And all you ever think about is sick people."

"That's my job; and I'm sure you don't mind that it pays for everything you--." The father blazed, then forced his lips closed while the cords of his neck stood out.

Reverend Mother Gregory raised her voice. "Your daughter will have a wonderful time with us." Her words were for the father, but she looked directly at the girl. "She will learn here. She will be happy. The days will pass quickly." She shifted her gaze. "There will be no problem, Doctor Rhenehan. No problem. All will be well. Mother Adelli and I will see to it."

Mother Adelli, silently saying her rosary, hoped to keep her mind from meddling in God's business here, and her lips closed. Last August she had participated in the Community's "Chapter of Faults," a spiritual discipline practiced by the nuns four times a year in which every Religious has her character defects compiled by the others. One by one, each kneels in the center of the circle to hear her faults read aloud. "Seeing too many sides of an issue," "Not able to make up her mind," "Too much of a loner," and "Failing to ask for advice" comprised the bulk of Mother Adelli's list, to which she could add a short temper, vanity over her students' affection and the temptation under pressure to lie.

Reverend Mother Gregory leaned sideways, plunged her arm into an opening in her skirt for her reading glasses. "Now," she produced a paper as well, "to our rules. I'm sure you will find them sensible."

Michael Rhenehan heard No: No improper speech; *Nolo mi tangere:* no touching of others or nuns; no leaving of the grounds; no talking except at meals, *Goûter* and special occasions; no pets. All students curtsy to priests, Religious, and visitors; are graded weekly on studies, conduct and attitude; have reports sent quarterly to parents.

The doctor set down his plate, a little sick. His fingers stole to his jacket pocket for his emergency smoke.

"Ashtray, Dr. Rhenehan?" the Reverend Mother asked in a low and private tone, as if she had caught him in an indecent act.

He shook his head, fetched his hand back. A convent bell gave out a far away ding-ding-ding. His head felt axed, nape to crown. He breathed in his own alcohol-driven sweat and eyed the barrister's bookcase at the wall where he mentally stretched himself out upon a shelf, head on arm and back to the room.

"Breeding, Doctor Rhenehan, comes not from money but from discipline. Discipline," the Superior drew out a pinch of air, "will extrude your daughter's gold for the contributions she will make to life. To discover and mine that precious ore is our task here." She handed the paper to the father who stuffed it into his inside jacket pocket. "Wouldn't you say so, Mother Adelli?"

But Mother Adelli was lost constructing an introduction of the new girl to the Third *Cours*. Of course, she stammered, everything possible would be done to make the school a home to the girl. Helene responded with a black look. But of course, Mother Adelli corrected herself, nothing could replace the home the girl knew. Acute annoyance walked across the face of her Superior who retrieved the rudder.

Dr. Rhenehan should know about the fabulous altarpiece he would see on their tour of the campus. Drawing her chair forward to close the gap between herself and the father, she exhaled something sour and old. Michael Rhenehan shrank, looked away to see his daughter's finger buried in her nose. He turned back and there was the Superior's wide mouth and a grey hair vibrating on her chin. Her voice ran over him like small rubber tires. He felt his head bob, saw his daughter at the other end of the settee, small and remote, and realized he had nothing more to say to her. The parlor floor released a waxy odor, funereal and spicy. Sweat rushed to his forehead. He couldn't seem to breathe and his hangover sawed and sawed at the split in his head.

He stretched his arm. The ruby chip at his shirt cuff flashed. His watch face emerged, arrowtips pointing to three forty-eight.

"Ten to four. I'm afraid I must be going," he heard his voice crack, saw the stiff red second hand sweep away his daughter's eyes fierce and wounded, the Superior's large opening mouth, the other one's sprung eyebrows and rising body, saw it sweep away the prancing furniture, premeditating rugs, the floor with its malevolent trickery. He saw his leg lift its trouser, saw the ox-blood shoe follow to take the long step from the settee that slowly blew its dimple out, felt his hair hoist and witnessed, as if from across the room, his hands swat his jacket into place, head swivel, his daughter collect her body,

"No, Dad--!"

felt her voice passing through his eyes, catching at his stomach, her face rising toward him, bringing the panic to a boil, making him turn to the Reverend Mother and the other one,

"I have patients at the hospital, and my plane leaves at six a.m. There is packing to do yet--."

heard the rasp of his words erase the two nuns like chalk on a blackboard,

"I'll make sure to see everything next time. Reverend Mother, Mother--Amelli, isn't it? It's been a pleasure."

heard the words scour away the daughter's bitten finger ends

"You understand, Pumpkin. You know your Dad has to--"

her lower lip, now violently alive. Oh, don't
let her face shatter--

"--see his patients. Good-bye Tootsie-pie. Write your dad now."

felt his surgeon hands grasp the square of her shoulders the fear steaming from her armpits while the kiss just over her eyes grazes the pimple coming on huge and furious,

"Don't forget me now with all your new friends."
Feels the silk of a curl spring against his lips.

She will not clear the way, her blue eyes ulcerate his cheek
"Of course, if you must, Doctor. We understand perfect--."

shakes the Reverend Mother"s pudgy hand.

"And I believe I left all the numbers with you?"
"Oh yes. We have them in case --."
the stunned nun-voices reel backwards and the deliberate floor exhales
its odor of sepulchers,
the piano gathers itself in the corner,
other furniture unsheathes its claws;
turning from the tall windows, he sees
his own long lean figure--the hound's tooth suit,
handsome polished face, darling boy curls, professional
eyes, fierce hooks yanking his lips
sideways, the broken crockery smile
ripping through the threadbare sack between his ribs--

"Mother Amelli, take care of my girl!"

the toy nun's sprung eyebrows and open mouth, one kiss more, young-skin bouquet, quick smacking sound, the low warning growl of the chairs and ringing of his steps, the bumpy ornate knob beneath his sweating palm, the foyer's cool benediction, scent of incense rivering his blazing face, his out-turned hand holding off the hurrying Portress, long shoe searching for the rubber step to fall away from the robin's egg blue eyes, from the hollow "Wait, Dad" as he lifts his thousand pound legs, the triple stitched jacket tail flap-flapping, his shoulder against the door, Mary Helen's baby's bawling sawing his bones, opening creak of the car door, shaking key searching the dark slit; Go back for God's sake; do it right, the building's hoary beard and cataracted eyes the blessed motor like a cannon; Go back before it's too late the little stones ping pinging the mouth of the front door sealing in the fury of his girl's hair and frantic awkward body his cells slamming shut the screaming tires the bull's eye of the open gate the long pluming tail of darkness

Two

The students caught sight of their favorite Religious coming along the corridor with the new girl. The light from low windows moved straight across to the wall-lockers, so that when the nun and girl entered it her hair jumped to spun copper while the nun's wimple turned to medieval parchment.

The boarders, in sports tops embroidered with double hearts, milled about the *Goûter* cart gossiping, ready for field hockey. Behind them the hallway fell off to a paneled door through which the nuns, of endless speculation to their students, daily materialized and disappeared. Next to them were the kitchen and dining hall; and beyond, the Minims' Study Hall, Third *Cours* Study Hall and Minims' Door that opened onto the convent's grounds.

"Our new girl is here at last." Mother Adelli raised her arms.

Helene Rhenehan brought the total of boarders to twenty-four with most, like her, from Chicago's Gold Coast or opulent suburbs--plus one stray from Milwaukee and three Latin Americans. Day Students--twelve of them--filled out the complement. Mother Adelli took heart at the sight of her young charges ready for action and on restless feet. She wanted their lighted eyes, their eager bodies to erase for the girl her father's fleeing back, to heal the gash it left in her.

Front porch to the basement, the girl at her side, questions had raged in the young nun's mind about how a father could cross the Atlantic without seeing where his daughter would sleep, eat, study or play. Well, she acknowledged then, parents did what they must and for reasons that could turn out to be quite right. Still, the terrible hurt! Mother Adelli had seen such grief in the faces of other boarders left flailing and falling. Sternly she ordered her mind to silence:. How was it she was qualified to judge? Never mind. She and her Third *Cours* would make it up to this Helene. They had some tricks up their sleeves guaranteed to make a sad girl laugh, for they knew well enough themselves about "first days."

"This is our new student, Helene. She is going to need you to show her where everything is, since you young ladies are experts."

The Third *Cours* boarders bunched slowly along an invisible line in front of the *Goûter* cart and stared. They had been waiting and waiting for this girl, but now something about her kept them from surging forward.

"Come, come. Have you forgotten all of your manners over the summer? Helene will think you were trained in a zoo."

Reluctant, they straightened up, brushed crumbs from their hands. "Hi," one voice folded over another; then, still balky, they peered at the shadowed ceiling, at the old tile floor with its vague smell of wet clay, at the locker doors softening with age.

Mother Adelli's eyes flashed to the cart with its few ends of brownies, then from girl to girl. "Well," she wagged her head, "I see you left a crumb or two." Orange juice gleamed near the bottom of the big-bellied pitcher; the nun's eyes prodded first one girl, then another.

"Only if she's very fast," GeeGee's Italian face relented and dissolved into dimples. She slid about, a brownie in each hand.

"Yeah, she'll starve around here." Jennifer, from under a helmet of hair, studied the disarray of the girl's outfit down to the scuffmarks on the just-bought saddle shoes.

Sylvia, taller than the others, oggled the constellations of freckles scattered over the new girl's face. "Stork" had a thin body and led with her neck when she walked. "With us she'll need long arms."

"Yeah, like some apes we know," overweight Deborah, sniggered, pointing at Stork.

"Well, she should feel right at home with the elephants we have." Stork cranked her hair over her shoulder and shot the words back without missing a beat.

In return, Deborah threw her head to haw-haw so that the rings on her neck separated and bits of brownie tumbled in her open mouth. Sandy-colored curls, a teddy bear face, Deborah walked with her feet pointing outward as if she expected someone to carry her.

Mother Adelli snapped her wooden clapper.

"That will do, young ladies. Cover your mouth, Deborah. And I don't intend to be a keeper of monkeys and hyenas, Sylvia. Show respect, please. Stand in one place when you eat, GeeGee; and it's one brownie at a time, I believe." She raised an eyebrow until GeeGee put the second brownie back.

Instead of help, her students gave out only gaping and silliness. On this very spot, only last March, new from Omaha, hadn't she, Mary Agnes Adelli, scrambled to remember the girls' names? She raised both eyebrows at them now. "I'm sure each of us remembers when she was the one to be new."

Sheepish, they shuffled back and forth, bunched their shoulders. The chitter of a squirrel near the kitchen door floated through an open window. Their job was to make this girl comfortable. They knew. They knew. But she just stood there staring like they were from Mars. So they stared back while the pain they saw behind the girl's eyes raised in their own minds dangerous questions:

Am I in here because I'm a problem or because I'm especially stupid or smart? What will I have to pay back for the 'privilege' of going to this place? When will being herded, homesick, silent and submissive make them love me enough to bring me back home? During such perilous mind wanderings, they would hear ghostly the sound of the template of the future rumbling towards them; and unable to move from its path, none could know whether it would leave behind a happy ending or not.

But Helene, moving her eyes from face to face, heard only the shriek of the car engine, the car tires slip on spraying stones. Well, and she wouldn't be caught dead crying in front of this stupid nun or these girls stuffing their faces. What did they know? Help her? She would help herself. Just because she was stuck here she didn't have to talk to them or like them--which she *definitely* did not! She turned a lazy look upon Mother Adelli.

"I'm tired. I want to lie down."

And with that, the new girl closed the ceremony of meeting, and so pilfered from her new classmates the chance to redeem themselves and retrieve their nun's beaming approval. In the wake of this betrayal, they fell silent while the new girl, without so much as a nod to anyone, started toward the staircase and took with her--as if she were a suitcase or pet dog--*their* Mother Adelli.

"Well, I guess our team is still short," Deborah pushed her voice out for the Snip to hear. "Last one on the hockey field smells like dirty socks."

Mother Adelli whirled around. The sound of her wooden clapper ricocheted off the lockers and brought all moving feet to a halt. Even at play, crude language was not permitted. "Remember where you are, Deborah. That's twice now. It's not too late to change your mark for *Primes* tomorrow."

The young Mistress of the Third *Cours* took the girl to the dormitory the long way, wanting to share with her the solace of these corridors that held like a precious ointment the intentional silence of the Community, and its doors, such as this one to the choir loft, that opened pockets of peaceful work, prayer and reflection.

"If you ever need a place for quiet or just to think, turn this knob. From here you can see the whole chapel, and perhaps have it all to yourself."

The opening door waffled out the smell of spent incense. A stained glass window gleamed darkly at the left. Below, the cross surmounting the tabernacle flared like an ancient sun. Mother Adelli gazed wistfully into the quiet.

Helene turned flat eyes upon the nun. "Is this another place a team can hide?" she asked dryly.

Baffled, Mother Adelli closed the door and plunged on to the statue of a seated *Mater Admirabilis*, it's eyes cast downward in reflection.

"Our girls put notes at Her feet or in Her lap, usually for things they are worrying about and want Her help with. They say Our Lord cannot say 'no' to His mother." She smiled.

The girl let her eyes dawdle over the near life-sized figure with its flushed cheeks, downcast eyes and sweet mouth. It reminded her of a doll Nana had given her once that she'd never taken from the box.

"Where can I lie down?"

"Just this way." Mother Adelli swallowed her disappointment.

The girl's bags stood on the window side of the dormitory, at the far left end of a long row of curtained cubicles. A matching row across broke open for the double doors to the hallway. With its pink and white striped seersucker curtains, the dormitory reminded Helene of a hospital ward her father had once shown her.

"Take a nap if you can." Mother Adelli let her eyes rest upon the mask-like face. From behind it she felt a great wrenching, as if the girl's heart were attached to the rear bumper of the father's car and was being pulled loose in stages. Again came the instinctive urge to put a hand upon the square shoulder; but *Nolo mi tangere*. Our Lady will watch over you, she wanted to say; but the father forbade religion. But if the child couldn't go to the Sacred Heart or Our Lady with her feelings, then where could she take her pain? "The time will pass quickly," Mother Adelli stumbled instead; "you'll see."

She left the new student at her alcove, her household goods at her feet.

A water cup sat on the bare dresser with a holy card of the Sacred Heart the girl swept to the floor. The alcove offered only enough space to sleep and to climb in and out of uniforms. One hook. No chair. Curtains for walls.

Six dormitory windows, their sashes open wide rattled under a businesslike wind come up and causing Helene's rear alcove curtain to swell, then climb her back as she unfolded a bed sheet.

"Get off me." She batted it down.

The air was rank with ozone. The cable on the flagpole began tapping out a wild signal. Lightning stitched the sky. Birds threw themselves into the air like handfuls of peppercorns. The dormitory filled with flapping sounds. Three alcoves down, socks beneath a bed chased round and round and a water cup and toothbrush clattered to the floor. The darkened sky threw silver coins at the windows.

From her overnight bag Helene unwrapped the flowered teacup and saucer she'd brought from home, Nana's birthday gift to her. She set them on the dresser. The wind gusted. The cup rattled in its saucer. Tucking a sheet under the mattress, she saw the rear curtain belly out again and snap its hem over the dresser's top. Cup and saucer struck the floor with a sound like bells and she stood staring while the curtain billowed again, this time to cover her head.

"No. Get off me." She thrashed free, flung the lout of a drape over the rod while thunder grumbled along the tops of the trees.

Tears spilled down her face; she squeezed her hands against the edges of the burst pieces to relish the pain.

Now she had no one--no Dad, no Nana. What was she supposed to do in this prison with its ugly cots and curtains anyone could open?

Rain was blowing across her bed. She slammed the sash behind her and lay down. Would he think of her in the morning when he snapped the latches on his suitcase and took a last look through the apartment, or when he watched the toy landscape slide away beneath places torn open in the clouds? Or Tuesday, when he woke in Rome and someone brought breakfast on a tray, would he wonder what she was doing that very moment? The questions struck a hollow place inside her and she jammed her knees over a feeling like crabs walking there. She heard rain splatter on the dormitory floor. So what. Let them shut their own precious windows. She closed her hand more tightly over the glittering shards.

She would tap, tap. The huge study door would whisper open and he would look up from his leather chair and papers to see her standing there with the housekeeper, hair still wet from her bath. His eyebrows would fly up in surprise and he would say, "Well, hi Princess," as if he'd forgotten that she lived there. Down the years she collected ways of reminding him and of holding his attention: by crying, by asking his help, and later for his opinion. Fifth grade, she would hold him with her own thoughts; they would get to "talking things over" until eventually she found she could get him to come around to whatever it was she wanted. Well, until today.

A horn with a sound flat as an ironing board began to blare. On the floor below she heard the scuffle of feet like sand shaken in a box. Was that smoke she smelled? She tried to picture the way to the front door, but corridors and stairwells tangled together. She jerked the rear curtain aside and peered out the window. There, like beads on a giant rosary, students were strung across the front lawn. Wait, shouldn't someone have come for her? She opened her hand to gaze again upon the china shards and then, in an onrush of grief, fell flat upon her bed and pulled the pillow over her head.

Maybe she was breathing smoke right now and it had already clogged tiny places in her lungs. You could die from that. Then her father would be sorry he went away. Nana would cry and wish she had been nicer to her. Mrs. Murphy would come to see her in her coffin. The horn stopped and she let the mattress take on the weight of her body. And she opened her nostrils to any death in the air that could find her.

Jazz rattles out of the radio of Mommy's convertible. "…but my baby don't love nobody but me." The dream always starts this way. Mommy has on a dress of flowers, and two tiny gold coins spin below her ears. Lake Michigan is a beautiful blue and she and Mommy buzz along toward the curve over the Chicago River. Mommy's pale hands with their pink fingernails cross over one another turning the wheel. Then the huge dull green truck looms out of nowhere. There is a terrible screeching, then a jolt and feeling of being hit hard on the side of the head as the nose of the truck pushes until the windshield breaks like ice on a puddle, and the dashboard with its dials bends like a page of her paper doll book and blood's all over Mommy's face and down her arm flung back over her head, and the steering wheel is into Mommy's chest and blood leaks out of Mommy like ink out of a huge broken fountain pen and soaks her lap; but she can't see Mommy's face because Mommy's head has fallen away towards the door and Mommy's hand on the seat doesn't move and there's a screaming sound from under the crumpled hood of the--

"Why didn't you close the windows? There's water all over the place."

The crabby voice, clomping feet, squeak and bang of one sash, then another until all remaining five were closed. The fat girl with the corkscrew hair stuck her face through the curtains.

"You let water get all over everything. Mother Adelli's going to be mad. Didn't you hear the rain?" She spoke as if to a first grader. "You have to come to dinner; Mother Adelli sent me to get you." She stood shaking her hands up and down fast. "And if we don't get downstairs right away, the best food will be gone."

Lightning lit the fat girl's face with an eerie flash. Helene felt the strike of thunder reverberate through her chest bones. She threw back the bedsheet. The fat girl's eyes opened wide, she laughed out loud. "Hey, wait'll I tell them downstairs you sleep in your shoes."

Boiling out of bed, Helene watched the fatso waddle off, curls bouncing, feet slapping the floor, backside rising and falling. That nitwit had better not say one more word to her unless she wanted a foot planted square in her giant behind. She hurried along in the fatso's wake so as not to get lost.

From the high ceiling, old-fashioned coach lamps let a yellow light fall over the room that held eight long tables and a wall of windows streaked with rain. The steaming food was carried from *Soeur* Josephine's kitchen to the tables by students who were determined to serve themselves first, if possible.

GeeGee turned to Helene, "Did you think the place was burning? Didn't that scare you?" To which Helene pulled a blank face. "I would have been scared to death," GeeGee raved on. "You would have heard me running all over like a crazy woman. But it was just a false alarm. Mother Adelli said to let you sleep."

Helene found a place at the end of the table. Mother Adelli glanced up. It was good to see her sitting with the others. Her eyes traveled from student to student picturing each one's angel, in her mind feeling the room jammed with guardian angels twelve feet tall, wings over their breasts, color moving in them like the Northern Lights.

There were mashed potatoes, celery sticks, and a bowl of beef stew with stringy somethings like whiskers in the gravy. Helene felt her throat close. There was red Jell-O with suspended furry bits. She hesitated. The air smelled of steam and vegetables. The chink of silverware and dishes. Above the tables, a scrim of low chattering broken by an occasional shriek that brought the *klat klat* of Mother Johnson's wooden clapper from the other end of the room.

Madeline tried first. Was Helene's mother a Sacred Heart graduate? A lot of their mothers, and some grandmothers, had gone to Sacred Heart.

Her mother was dead.

Silence. Rain sheeted the windows. Someone said "Sorry." Someone said, "Pass the peas."

"So, how long has your father dumped you in here for?" Deborah's voice. Sitting just catty-corner, she hung over her plate, the eyes in her porky face alive and after something.

That was all it took.

"I'm not dumped, you moron," Helene bawled back. "You poor saps may be dumped, but I'm not. I'm only here for six--"

"Well what does your father think this is," Deborah gestured about the room, "vacation time in Hawaii?"

Laughter from the others.

"You don't even know my father," Helene's face turned scarlet. "You shut up your mouth about him, you ignoramus. He's none of your business."

Illicit pleasure leapt down the table. A fight!

"Well, where is he then? Probably too busy being in the newspapers to bother with us nobodies." Hands on her hips, Deborah stretched her mouth around each word.

"And what's yours so busy about that you're stuck in here?"

A guarded kind of laughter. Everyone knew about Deborah's father.

"He doesn't have to work." Deborah showed her tiny teeth. "He has so much money he goes wherever he wants. Right now he's in India." A glint lit her eye. "But Mother Adelli says your father is a famous doctor. I collect autographs. Can you get his autograph for my hound? Pretty puh-leeze. I've never had a famous doctor sign it, even though none of us has ever heard of him. What was his name again?"

Helene saw the open mouths, fillings gleam, heard the ha-ha-has. Her eyes turned to ice. She slammed her fork down. "My father is one of the best doctors in the world." She leaned toward Deborah. "He's found new ways to fix people's hearts. He saves thousands of lives. Maybe he'll do you a favor and sew your mouth shut. Here, I've seen him operate a thousand times. I can do it myself." She grabbed her fork and reached across to ply it back and forth in the air like a surgical instrument when her shoe met something slimy so that the fork lurched and left three lines across the fat girl's cheek. They filled with red.

Deborah let out a howl, sprang from her chair and, blood seeping through her fingers, bent her other arm back and released through it all the power in her shoulder. Helene heard the girls to each side side siphon air while Deborah's fist shot forward and grazed her cheekbone.

Staggering backwards, she slipped again on the same carrot slice. Feet paddling, she banged her knee on the floor, but sprang up immediately because no fat cow was going to beat on her! In Chicago, in the alleys behind the fancy and not-so-fancy buildings, when her father was working, when the housekeeper was busy, she had learned a few things. She balled her fists.

"I'll show you who can fight."

"Mother Adelli!" someone called out.

Helene spun to come at Deborah from behind, seized a fistful of corkscrew curls and lowered her shoulder first to barrel into the backs of the fatso's legs, then to straddle her big middle as she, the Victor, demanded Cow "Say uncle" when right at her ear came a deafening sound like rocks struck together. Once, twice, three times.

She whirled to look directly into Mother Adelli's face where the skin seemed stretched as if over a board. Another nun hustled from the far end of the room, her clapper going as well.

"That's enough. Sit down both of you," Mother Adelli ordered, her voice strained and icy. Mother Johnson took a step to the side: These were Mother Adelli's students. Deborah sank into her chair, whimpering. The new girl remained on her feet, blue eyes wild.

"What on earth is going on here?" Mother Adelli tugged a handkerchief from her pocket. The sight of the blood sickened her. Some students pushed away their plates, others craned their necks to watch the nursing.

"You know better than this, Deborah, and what this will mean." She referred to marks at *Primes* the next day,.

Deborah's mouth fell open. "But it was her fault. She-_"

Mother Adelli held up her hand. "I will hear all about it." She pressed the handkerchief to the wound. "Hold that there, and go to the infirmary. Helene, I want to see you immediately in Study Hall; and then see the two of you there together; but first, you young ladies will apologize to one another." She stepped back to wait.

"She insulted my father," Helene spat, her face red. "She should apologize to him."

Mother Adelli's face remained dark and stern. The clock ticked.

But Deborah shrugged. The game was too costly already. She wished she'd known the new girl was such a hot-head. "I apologize," she mumbled while with her other hand, she snagged a scrap of meat from the serving dish when Mother Adelli turned toward the new girl.

"Apologize to Deborah, Helene."

Helene remained rigid and staring straight ahead. The table chewed in silence.

"A simple 'I apologize' is sufficient." The nun waited.

Helene flopped into her chair and crossed her arms.

"Helene?" Please, in her mind the nun begged the cold mask of a face, don't begin like this.

There was the soft sound from the kitchen of the wiping down of surfaces, and the scraping of chairs as students turned for a better view of the standoff. Beyond the windows, a blue jay called and called again. Rain tapped at the glass.

Finally, the curt nod. Mother Adelli felt relief wash through her body.

Deborah smirked up and down the table, then swaggered to the door, handkerchief at her cheek while Helene toothpasted potatoes through the tines of her fork and her pulse raced. So they wanted a fight, did they?

Mother Adelli flipped the Study Hall light switch and sat at the first desk in the middle row. She felt blurred from the sight and smell of the blood. And she might have a dreadful situation on her hands that would require a report. She shrank from the thought of Mother Crewelman, the Mistress General and her Spiritual Advisor, to whom the report would be made. Afterwards, it might go on to Reverend Mother Gregory as well. Immediately she felt shame. Her first duty was to her children, not to herself. But her Superiors might decide that she was not able to handle things. The incident had happened so fast. One minute things were fine, and then--. She massaged her temples. Mother Crewelman was often quite severe--but for good, spiritual reasons, of course. Any Religious should be grateful to have her guidance.

Silver rain continued to drape the night while its wet fragrance seeped under the sash to nose about the Study Hall. Perhaps, Mother Adelli sat back, the injury was not as serious as all that--mere scratches rather than cuts. Mother Spencer, a trained nurse, would send word promptly.

But tomorrow was *Primes*. Now she must give two *'riens'* at the girls' first *Primes* of the year. Reverend Mother Gregory would not like this. But must there be *two*? She got up to pace.

Again she watched the father bolt, heard the bang of the front door, saw the emptying of the girl's face. Who could blame the student for anything just now? Well, but it was a physical attack. Deborah was forced into self-defense. She sighed. No, there seemed no way around a *'rien'* for the Rhenehan girl. Deborah's conduct was also bad, but she was the one attacked. *Assez bien*, then, for Deborah.

She sat at Sylvia's desk and began absently to straighten the schoolbooks and papers jumbled beneath the desktop. She had never permitted herself feelings as strong as the new girl's, even as a child except for those of her parents' and brother's. She had not wanted strong feelings herself. And the priests and nuns at her school had no use for such. Besides, she'd had no time for quarrels; ballet had filled every spare second of her life. Obviously, the Rhenehan girl was not educated in managing her feelings. The school was here to teach her such things.

But what if the behavior grew worse and the girl never settled down? No, her Superiors would show her how to bring the student around. Where was that girl, anyway? She had told her to come straightaway.

Mother Adelli found Helene leaning on one elbow and making worms of her potatoes. "Miss Rhenehan, we don't play with our food. And I told you to meet me in Study Hall." She crooked a finger and frowned. "Come with me."

The other girls gaped. Mother Adelli was mad. That automatically cancelled all special favors such as shorter Study Hall or talking in the dormitory until lights out. But because it had been a real fight with real blood, name-calling, hair-pulling and punching, the Third *Cours* boarders, for the pure excitement of it, were willing to forgive the new girl the cost to them. Just this once.

Sitting at two desks, nun and girl faced one another. What happened at dinner was very serious. She, Helene, had struck another student in the face with a fork and might have blinded or disfigured her for life. But Deborah had made fun of her father. Well, Deborah certainly shouldn't have done that, but that was no reason to attack her with a fork. She didn't attack, her foot slipped and Deborah punched her right there in her face. Why was Helene waving a fork in the first place? She was just talking; and was she supposed to eat that slimy stuff with her fingers? She must watch her speech; the school could not allow vulgar language, disrespect or a lack of self-control.

Mother Adelli had learned the speaking ways of teachers she heard as a student at Sacred Heart/Sheridan Road in Chicago. The use of French was a part of it, of course.; and she had been proud to speak as her teachers had and, in the Novitiate in Omaha, to learn how language and voice could maintain respectful distances. The Superior at Omaha explained that children are tabernacles, that the Holy Spirit works in them a Divine plan, and that teachers must always remain carefully detached. This was *Nolo mi tangere (Do not touch me)* in practice. But when very happy or under stress, she forgot and spoke in a plainer and more direct way, as she did now.

"Your father will find out what's gone on from your report card, if nothing else."

"I knew you wouldn't be fair." Helene barricaded herself with her arms.

"You must be fair to us and give things a chance--not attack other students. How will you have any friends?"

"She attacked me first. Who needs friends anyway? I don't want any here."

"You are going to have a lonely time of it then. It won't be much fun."

Helene lifted her chin. "I don't see any fun. Is this supposed to be fun?"

"You don't speak that way here," Mother Adelli flared up, then dropped her eyes. This was a child. "We want you to be happy, Helene. If you'll take a little time to get to know us, I think you will like us. Will you try that?"

Helene rolled her eyes.

Deborah appeared at the Study Hall door with two band-aids on her cheek and a note from Mother Spencer. The scratches were superficial, there would be no infection or scarring. Mother Adelli felt the awful worry lift. She sent both girls to their desks to write essays on self-control, to be finished before dormitory.

The incident would run wildfire through the Community, though thank the Lord, Deborah was all right and Mother Crewelman needn't be disturbed. Reverend Mother Gregory would be at *Primes* tomorrow, however. And she, Mother Adelli, who had never in her career given a '*rien*,' was to have her record marred by an unhappy girl whose father had stepped around his responsibilities. She only hoped the cost of his failure would not continue long or be significant.

Three

The next day, Monday, and directly after Mass, Reverend Mother Gregory called Mother Adelli aside. "I understand from Mother Spencer there was a physical outbreak at dinner. One of your girls cut another with a fork. Is this correct?" She trained unwavering eyes upon the young woman.

Through the open chapel doors in two lines came an outpouring of students who glanced up, dipped fingers into the holy water fount to trace a cross forehead to belly and shoulder to shoulder as they passed the Religious.

"A minor injury, it turned out," Mother Adelli's dry tongue staggered about. "I didn't report it as Mother Spencer felt no doctor was needed."

The Superior frowned, shook her head. "But how could such a thing happen? I believe two of you were monitoring dinner. No one saw it coming? Violence is against everything we stand for. It is your job absolutely to keep the peace. We must make an example of this."

Mother Adelli swallowed. "Yes, Reverend Mother."

As Reverend Mother Gregory turned away, Mother Adelli felt the double humiliation. Called to account by her Superior with students picking up bits of dialogue, no doubt to share at breakfast. The young nun turned and walked backwards to oversee her two columns of navy jackets and checked skirts.

She had especially prided herself on peace and gracefulness. Now to see it could be up-ended so easily and quickly. At the end of the corridor, she turned to lead her girls down the stairs. If Deborah had just held her tongue, if the father had only helped his daughter. Twenty-four pairs of brown oxfords rounded the first landing. At least the Superior had not mentioned her speaking out of turn in parlor on Sunday. Clomp, clomp down the next set to the basement. She turned again and looked over her charges as GeeGee leaned sideways to whisper something to Jennifer. Klat, klat. "No talking, young ladies." The new girl was balling-up her veil to jam into her uniform pocket. "And in case anyone doesn't know, we fold our veils here."

Reverend Mother Gregory arrived exactly at nine o'clock for the weekly evaluation of studies and conduct called *Primes*. Out of deference to the Superior, Mother Adelli, sitting to one side, called out students' marks from a long record book open across her lap. Each student came forward from chairs arranged in three semi-circular rows to sink into a deep curtsy before the Superior, to hear her weekly report and the Superior's comments, then to curtsy again.

Eight such students came and went.

"Helene Rhenehan," Mother Adelli repeated.

The new girl stood before Reverend Mother Gregory, one hip out, her eyes tracing the doorjamb. She, Mother Adelli, had shown Helene the curtsy and the girl had watched eight previous students; so why didn't she make one? And her collar bow was upside-down and socks not properly turned! How had she gotten out of the dormitory looking like this? Still no curtsy. To cover the awkward pause, Mother Adelli pushed ahead to announce the dreaded mark.

"Helene Rhenehan. *'Rien.'*"

Reverend Mother Gregory, examining her fingernails, straightened up, looked at Mother Adelli, then at the girl, then at Mother Adelli again.

"Did you say '*rien*,' Mother?"

"Reverend Mother, I did."

"*Rien?*" The Superior drew back, grey fly-away eyebrows up. "I find it hard to believe, Mother Adelli, that a girl who has been with us less than twenty-four hours has managed to earn the worst mark we can give. Please look at your book again."

Mother Adelli traced across the line with her finger.

"I'm sorry Reverend Mother, '*rien.*'"

The Third *Cours*, white-gloved hands in their laps, took in the black bulk of the Superior and new girl, feet planted, chin in the air. Excitement vibrated along the rows of chairs. The Superior turned back to Helene whose eyes now followed hops and skips where the wall above the door joined the ceiling.

"You are new here, Miss Rhenehan. Look at me, please; I am speaking to you. You have not studied French. Probably you cannot translate the word '*rien.*' '*Rien,*' Miss Rhenehan, means 'nothing.' '*Rien*' means a void to recommend the student on her record of achievements. '*Rien*' means the student has not supported herself, not supported her classmates nor repaid her parents one wit for the effort and money spent to develop her. Worse, she has thrown aside her finer choices of '*trés bien*': Excellent, a credit to all; '*bien*': Yes, good effort, further to go but good effort; and '*assez bien*': No real progress, a place we don't want to remain. But from '*rien*', Miss Rhenehan, there is no place to go."

The Third *Cours* stirred.

"You may believe a '*rien*' is common here." The Superior's veil undulated as she leaned forward. "Oh, I pray you be disabused of that idea! A '*rien*' is rare, rare and regrettable. And should there be, for some unfathomable reason, a second '*rien*' in a term, we must advise the parents at once, for such a failure goes on the daughter's record, a record which precedes and describes her to everyone she meets on the path to her future." The Superior's arm swept wide to manifest the very path of which she spoke.

Helene's face darkened and jaw lengthened as if behind her clamped teeth logs were piling up.

"But it's not fair," she exploded then and turned to the Third *Cours* sitting behind her where she saw she might as well appeal to department store dummies. She turned back to her accuser. "I told Mother Adelli it was an accident. I slipped. Deborah should get as bad a mark as me; she started the whole thing. Everyone saw it."

Deborah had already received *'assez bien'* with admonitions about self-control, had padded back to her seat, baby fat jiggling, the two white band-aids gleaming on her cheek.

Helene turned furious eyes then upon Mother Adelli. "Everyone heard her insult my father. She should be--"

"That will do," the Superior's voice clapped. "Look at me, Miss Rhenehan. We know all about the fork, all about the hair pulling. The rule is *Nolo mi tangere*: Do not touch me. I read it to you in parlor. We have that rule for a good reason. If we don't touch, no one gets hurt. Simple obedience would have prevented this incident. Whatever else, the other party did *no touching*."

"She did too!" Helene burst out. "She hit me. Everyone saw."

"We have heard the last word on this affair, *mademoiselle*. You wear no bandages," Reverend Mother Gregory clipped the conversation off, her eyes two hot pokers.

And the students took it all in--the prisoner, the grave infraction, the swift unswerving judgment. And every girl knew better than to flick so much as an eyelash, although some did remember seeing Deborah strike out and connect and the new girl fall backwards. But why should they stick up for her when she wouldn't have *Goûter*, play hockey, or even speak to them except to call them poor saps? Well, who was the poor sap now? She was maybe someone to stay away from---jabbing with forks, pulling people down. You did that in public school. Still, they couldn't help but admire how she stood like a prisoner before the firing squad. And they could spare her the trouble of feeling enraged when her marks were made public; everyone knew that in this place she would get nowhere acting up; they could throw that cold water in her freckled face.

Through the partly opened window came the soft clackety-clack of the North Shore electric train tilting around the bend toward the village of Lake Forest.

Reverend Mother Gregory appraised the girl. "We have fine things to accomplish here, Miss Rhenehan. Let me show you those who have done so. Ribbons, stand please. Now turn around, Miss Rhenehan, so you can see them."

Five students rose. Each wore a wide pink ribbon looped over the right shoulder and pinned, some with a small religious medal, at the opposing hip where the ribbon's ends were left to flutter along the skirt.

"We honor girls with ribbons for exceptional conduct including self-control, superior grades and demonstrated leadership."

But ribbons came and went, the Third *Cours* knew. Every eight weeks there was a renegotiation computed from the totals in the long green book. Some girls would do anything to capture the privilege of carrying notes, leading lines, shepherding visitors; would do anything to have their parents parade them at church, their grandfathers slip a five dollar bill into their hand and give them a peck on the cheek.

"Now, there is nothing to stop *you* from becoming a ribbon," the Superior continued. "It certainly would please your father. This month is forfeit of course; but October offers a fresh start." The Superior nodded to the standing students. "*Merci madmoiselles*. And face front please, Miss Rhenehan."

Helene watched the girls sink back into the sea of heads. Her lip curled. She would never get caught with one of those things across her chest, like a prize cantaloupe at a farmers' fair. Why, her friends would laugh her out of the neighborhood.

Reverend Mother Gregory caught the belittling judgment on the girl's face as she turned. "You will straighten up that face right now, miss! Such an expression betrays ignorance and lack of proper feeling. Turn your face to me, please." To overcome the nervous racing in her chest, Helene trained her eyes on a ragged scar parting the grey hairs of Reverend Mother Gregory's left eyebrow. "And the tops of the shoes are an appropriate place for the eyes of someone still a learner."

Reverend Mother Gregory waited for the girl to drop her eyes. She would bring this upstart into line right here, right now. There would be no problem with this girl. "You will drop your eyes to your shoe tops, Miss Rhenehan, if we have to stay here all night."

Mother Adelli wet her lips. She watched as Helene forced her eyes over her jutted-out chin, over the blocks of resistance fitted together like medieval stonework. The Superior scrutinized the girl's wild hair.

"We understand you have adjustments to make; but we will not expect to hear such a report again. This will be your first and last '*rien.*' Is that clear?"

Helene raised her chin higher.

"You may sit, Miss Rhenehan. I'm sure we understand one another."

Reverend Mother Gregory wanted to move on. She had given too much time already to poor behavior. There were still the Minims' and high school *Primes* to conduct, and her bunion had already ignited in her shoe.

As Helene took her seat, she thought she detected a shift of feeling in her fellow students. Respect, she decided, because Rancid Murmur and Dilly Dally couldn't make her crumble. As the Superior looked the other way, she slid onto her tailbone and crossed her arms. But if Rancid decided to open her mouth about the fight, that might mean calling her father. That was no good. She straightened up. Dilly and Cow got her into this, so she would get them back for it, she really would. She let her eyes slip out of focus and watched the fuzzy girls curtsy, one after another, while the sweetness of her anger ate away part of that dark weighty thing that crippled her chest.

In the corridor after *Primes*, the Superior told Mother Adelli to instruct the Rhenehan girl in the curtsy. "Her posture was an outrage yesterday in the parlor, and she was slouching this morning. Her collar ribbon and socks were out of order. And do *something* about that hair."

"Yes, Reverend Mother. Reverend Mother, the girl seems so upset being here. I wonder whether--"

"Being upset is no excuse for misconduct. She must learn not to let her feelings run her life. We promised her father we would take care of her. We do not want '*riens*' chasing him all over Italy. See that she makes friends and is happy. This is to be her only *rien*. Is that clear?"

The Superior watched anxiety crowd the younger nun's eyes. "Come, come, Mother Adelli." She rocked on her heels, her chest thrown out. "Surely by now you know students are all bluff." She rummaged in her pockets, pulled out a handkerchief and honked. "We can thank the good Lord no one was blinded or scarred, and that there was no need for a telephone call." She honked again and wiped. "I do not expect to hear of any similar incidents. I have done your work for you this time, Mother Adelli. Now I leave the rest in your capable hands."

"Yes, Reverend Mother."

The Superior fumbled beneath her cape for her pocket watch. "By the way, the girl was not the only one to overstep decorum yesterday. Your efforts in the parlor to reach her were helpful; however, I'm sure you remember the rule is for you to look first to me for a nod before you speak." The woman paused, pocket watch still in her fingers. "Do not let feelings for this girl get in the way of good judgment, Mother Adelli. You must be the keeper of law and order, for everyone's sake. I'm sure you understand that."

"Yes, Reverend Mother."

Reverend Mother Gregory glanced at the timepiece. "Well, our Dr. Rhenehan is probably crossing the Atlantic by now," she exuded with satisfaction, then waded down the corridor to the Minims' Study Hall.

Even with windows open, the air was like wet flannel that night in the darkness of the dormitory. Mother Adelli could not remember such a hot September.

What had the other students made of this new girl's behavior? Might they turn on her, their Mistress, now as well? But her Third *Cours* loved her; there had been a kind of romance between them. She hiked her nightgown to her knees. And the Superior herself had spoken to the girl, so there would be no more acting up.

She pulled her nightcap from her head and ran her fingers through ginger-colored hair cut like a boy's, and for one blissful moment felt her scalp effervesce. Time would heal the father's leaving, just as it did the void inside when she left dance for the Order; just as it continued to heal the grief of her brother's death four years ago this month. She rolled onto her side.

Patience, soft ways, humor were the tools she preferred. And it might be possible to make the rules roomy for a time, but without breaking them. She always had a few tricks up her sleeve, after all. She would not let down the girl; and she would not let down Reverend Mother Gregory. With a sigh of regret, she pulled the nightcap back over her hair and closed her eyes.

On the window side of the dormitory, Helene pushed the curtain back and raised her pajama top, hoping for a breeze. If her father knew these girls were morons and snots, or that sweet-looking Dilly Dally was a witch who

THE CALLING OF MOTHER ADELLI

punished you for things that weren't even your fault, he
would send for her tomorrow. She flopped onto her back.
He seemed a tiny speck in the darkness beyond the
window, farther than the smallest star--too far to hear her
footfall or her breathing. A dangerous wall of tears pressed
at the back of her throat. She tightened her muscles against
it. No, she would get them both, Dilly and Cow. She really
would. Only she would have to be careful. Nothing that
might get back to her father.

Outside the kitchen door the next afternoon, bobbing
like men in a boat, Mother Adelli's Third *Cours* clustered
about her. The September day was deliciously warm, but
with the leaves already turning, it carried sad scents of
leaving and longing.

"Can we, PLEASE?" GeeGee hopped on one foot,
then the other.

"Yes, yes," Stork chimed in, "a run in the ravines!"

Mother Adelli, hand at her mouth, feigned
astonishment. "Why, is this a special day--a *Congé*--certainly
not a feast day I've missed?" A run in the ravines was
saved for special occasions. She looked from eager face to
eager face and couldn't help the pleasure of their hunger
for this fun that had made her famous among them.

"No-o-o, Mother." They said in one voice, argument-
poor and already resigned. Then the new girl straggled up,
squinting through her copper curls into the sun, and
Mother Adelli paused. Why, look here, she might have a
trick up her sleeve for the new girl this exact moment.

"Well," she pretended to reconsider, "perhaps just this
once--but only because it's a glorious day and we happen
to have glorious ravines. I doubt, however, that any of you
will be fast enough to keep up with me!"

Hurray, they threw their surprise into the air, dancing
and whooping. Mother Adelli reached to tie her veil back
and to hike her skirt a scant inch above her ankles.

Then they were off, plunging over the crusty lip behind the grotto and sinking into the cool shadow of the slender trees arching high above the silver cord of water.

"Too slow," Mother Adelli taunted them, skimming the slippery leaves from last winter like some exotic black animal while the laughter in her eyes reached all the way along the broken line that followed her.

And she was beautiful to behold. Never grasping for support, she would swerve without looking yet never losing sight of them, she flew along it seemed by instinct. They struggled, panting, in her wake, holding onto breaking bushes, tree branches, roots, each other, yipping and bellowing, setting the ravine ringing with their voices. Small rocks dislodged by the scrambling feet thumped to the bottom of the cleft and landed with a splash. The sun winked among the leaves and sent needles of light into the backs of their hands or necks or into their eyes. Despite the canopy of shade, their bodies streamed.

Madeline, at the rear, kept an eye on Helene. "Come on," she would call, "we'll get left." Pale, out of breath and with her gym shirt soaked, the new girl scowled and Madeline would slow down and let her catch up.

Half an hour of it was plenty and the party emerged near the hockey field. The girls dropped, prone on the grass, arms flopped out they bawled exhaustion. Mother Adelli, smiling and looking just a little self-satisfied, rearranged her habit.

"Nobody else in this whole school gets to do this but us," GeeGee scrambled to her feet, pushed her chest out and pumped her thumbs, "because we've got Mother Adelli. Hip, hip," she threw a finger high into the air.

"Hooray," came the chorus.

Leaves rustled on the branches above. Mother Adelli colored prettily and did not reach for her clapper. She shot a look at the new girl who sat with a bright pink face and soaked hairline, head hanging between her knees.

"Hip, hip——"

"Hooray."

The green and red and gold leaves danced again overhead.

With a final chorus, the Third *Cours* beat their palms together and brought a sound like rain onto the hot afternoon while squirrels jumped and scattered. Then they straggled behind their laughing Mother Adelli toward the heavy red building with its remote cupola thrown like a white ornament against the sky. They would change clothes and sit at homework and construct a dinner from the kitchen smells filtering across the transom--one of which was almost always of boiled carrots.

In the dining room, Madeline took the bit in her teeth and asked the new girl if she'd ever done anything like the ravine run before. Helene, chewing ham between sentences and with Mother Adelli listening, drawled she had done a lot of skiing with her father and it had been much harder, the inclines were steeper and snow more slippery. Skiing was not as dirty and was more fun. But she had never skied in her life.

Who did this new girl think she was anyway, and why didn't she just shut up, the Third *Cours* asked one another with their looks. This was something Mother Adelli had invented just for them, something no other nun would do. Above everything--*Goûter*, *Congés*, field hockey, sliding down the fire escape, keep-away basketball, reading after dinner, free talk before bed--they loved to run in the ravines with their Mother Adelli who had a sad and a disappointed look in her eyes now.

"But you freeze to death when you ski." GeeGee rose to her favorite nun's defense. "And you lose things." She clapped her hands to the sides of her head and looked wildly about, as if her ears were missing. Everybody laughed. Good old GeeGee.

Mother Adelli moved on, wishing she had reprimanded the girl for her thoughtless words. But really, all the girl gave was her opinion. What was wrong with that? Well, the rude way she said everything. But a reprimand might spoil the effort to bring her out of herself or drive her to an explosion like the one last night. Reverend Mother Gregory made it clear she wanted the girl happy. She, Mother Adelli, wanted the girl happy, too, but how much of an attitude should she permit? And could she always tell adjustment from poorly developed character or plain bad will?

For instance, on her desk sat a note from *Mère* Jardin, the French teacher, requesting a conference concerning Helene's butchering of pronunciation, a case so extreme as to seem premeditated. And the note from Mother Firth, the math teacher. No work completed yet. In her own English and history classes, the student came with assignments unread and answered questions with a shrug. Farther down the table now, she let her eyes drift over Helene. And the girl's hair continued to refuse the barrettes: Once latched, they immediately slid off her curls and leapt to the floor.

It was the third Thursday after "Fork Sunday," as it came to be known among the students. Only a few cookies and half a pitcher of orange juice remained on the *Goûter* cart when Deborah, now renamed "Scratch," decided to make her move with a plot she'd first developed with her confidantes, then broadcast to her teammates after they were trounced by the Whites on Wednesday, 9-1; and all because the Blues got stuck with the new girl who refused to go after a ball and picked dandelions or stared at clouds while points streaked past her for the goal. Walking back from the hockey field, "Pink ribbon Madeline" and three or four other goody-goodies had been hostile to Deborah's idea.

"Why would anyone try to get somebody in trouble?" Madline frowned, her eyebrows colliding. "Hasn't she got enough trouble?"

"Oh, I forgot a ribbon shouldn't hear things that might upset her delicate conscience." Deborah made saucers of her eyes. "But then maybe you're a friend of hers." The rest of her team, sweating and dragging hockey sticks, turned curious eyes upon Madeline who threw out her arms.

"I don't even know her. I just think it's mean, that's all." And she broke away, trotting toward the building.

"A real little librarian,' Deborah tossed her head; "always hushing somebody up. As if that stuck-up Helene didn't nearly blind me." She touched pink lines on her cheek. "And I want to get it going right now at *Goûter*."

So Deborah, Jennifer, Sylvia and GeeGee kept an eye on the new girl where she stood apart, her nose in *Tom Sawyer*, tipping the book toward the window. On the sill were three oatmeal cookies and an orange juice. Reading was not permitted at *Goûter*, a social time; but at the moment, Mother Adelli wanted the girl to read anytime she was willing.

It was exactly seven steps from the cart to "Miss Stuck-Up" and Deborah took them in an exaggerated saunter, then leaned upon the locker next to the window in a way that allowed her friends at the cart a clear view.

"I read that book," she started in.

Helene's eyes shifted over the cover, stepped neatly around Deborah's face to the Third *Cours* dopes chewing and gaping at the cart.

"It's great," Deborah pressed on. "That kid is always pulling the neatest stuff, and getting away with it." She saw one freckled hand search blindly for the juice glass. She dropped the bait. "Just like you."

The robin's-egg blue eyes swung up over the top of the book and fixed on the baby-fat face. What-are-you-pulling-now? formed in them.

"We saw you staring Reverend Mother down. And not giving a curtsy. You didn't even care if you got a *'rien'* for your first *Primes*. Well, and you sure let me have it, heh, heh." Deborah's eyes went flat with self-betrayal and she saw the barest hint of pleasure hover near the surface of Helene's scripted face, so she ran with the ball.

"We were talking on the way in from hockey yesterday. Somebody was saying they thought you might be as good as this Maggie O'Hara we used to hear about."

Jennifer, Sylvia and GeeGee strolled over as if on cue. Helene dusted her fingers against her gym shorts, her eyes still on *Tom Sawyer*.

"Once she stuffed a uniform and sat it on a toilet in the Minims' bathroom. And she stole everyone's unders from their dressers and piled them in *Mater's* lap," Jennifer invented, "and no one would take hers back."

"Once she put an egg case ready to hatch in Mother Boreman's desk," GeeGee composed, "because Mother Boreman was so boring. The next afternoon, tiny baby grasshoppers came piling out of her drawer and flying all over Study Hall." Now, there was no Maggie O'Hara, so far as any of them knew.

And ha-ha they all laughed, except for Helene; but she closed the book, her thumb in it as a marker.

"So somebody said they bet you'd be able to pull off anything Maggie O'Hara could," Deborah pressed on. "And I said I thought so, too; but then someone else said yeah okay but they bet you couldn't do the really big one, the one absolutely nobody had the nerve to try--even Maggie O'Hara. And I said I didn't know, it looked to me like you could, if you wanted to."

Helene opened her book again. Deborah waited, unsure. Then, starting to feel like a fool, she shrugged and turned just as Helene's bored-to-tears voice climbed over the book's cover. "So what is this big thing Maggie Whatshername wouldn't do?"

"Well--." Deborah picked up the cry of a doorknob from over her shoulder. Mother Adelli stood in the open door of her office. Deborah leaned forward in a hurry. "You know Mother Adelli's alcove, right next to the dormitory door? Well, there's a chair way inside at the head of the bed where she hangs her big rosary, the one she wears at her waist. Go in there and get it."

"While she's asleep?" Sylvia flung her arms around with perfectly staged hysteria.

"Yeah," GeeGee piped up on time. "Rosaries rattle you know. Why don't you just have her wear a bell?"

Deborah sucked through her teeth and patted the air for quiet. Helene returned to her book as though the idea was too insignificant to consider. Humiliation crawled up Deborah's neck. She rolled her eyes at the ceiling and played off a what-are-you-going-to-do-with-an-idiot-like-this look. Mother Adelli started toward them. Well, it would have been all over anyway.

The Religious had seen the group at the window as she opened her office door--Sylvia and Deborah, like Abbott and Costello; GeeGee always running in place, and Jennifer, a little broom sweeping in busy circles--and all knotted around the new girl. Her heart lifted and she dug for her watch to slow her pace and buy time. Her intrusion would immediately dissolve the magic. Of course. Where had her faith been? He would use the girls to bring Helene along. Had she, a Religious, strayed so far from His presence as to forget His intercession?

The drawl of Helene's voice came back from over the book.

"Well, where's the chair?"

Deborah heard it over the squeak of the *Goûter* cart as *Soeur* Josephine pushed it into the kitchen.

"Next to the dresser." She pivoted, her eye now caught on those very beads now winking in the folds of Mother Adelli's skirt.

From behind her book, Helene bit into another cookie. "Sounds pretty dumb," she drawled. The grinding of cookie bits. "And pretty easy." The robin's-egg blue eyes lazed up and past them all.

Four

It was a plain room on the second floor of the Cloister where the nuns gathered. In contrast to the elegant appointments of the first floor, this furniture was a hodge-podge donated by family, alumnae and friends of the Order. Outside of duties requiring speech, the Community, like its counterpart in monastic orders, maintained silence. However, one hour each day they came together in assigned groups. During the week, it was the hour after dinner; on Saturdays and Sundays, the hour before.

With an excuse me, thank you, excuse me, thank you, Mother Durban, Mistress of the Minims, skirted end tables and black shoes to finally sight Mother Adelli in her group with Mothers Crewelman, O'Rourke, and Byrne on the far side of the room.

"Your new girl, Mother--" Mother Durban burst upon them, took in Mother Crewelman's severe look and lowered herself into a chair, waiting for a nod from the Superior. "I . . . I'm sure it doesn't mean anything serious, Mother Adelli," Mother Durban began again, "but I thought you should know right away since it did involve fire."

"Fire?" Old Mother Byrne threw a hand to her horrified mouth. "Oh my."

"Just a little place the size of a saucer, on the tennis court. Still, where would the girls get matches, I wondered."

"Is anyone hurt?" Mother Adelli was half out of her chair. Mother Durban shook her head.

Had Mother Crewelman, Mistress General and Spiritual Advisor of younger nuns, not been present, Mother Adelli, knowing no real harm had been done, might have added, "How upsetting, for you, Mother. May I get you a cup of tea?" But Mother Crewelman would find such ministrations suggestive that the Holy Spirit, the Great Comforter, might require weak and sinful human beings to accomplish Its work. "I'm sure whatever happened can be straightened out," Mother Adelli said instead. "Please tell us."

Mother Durban nodded, ran her tongue over dry lips and began.

"I took both Minims and Third *Cours* to the tennis courts after *Goûter*. We were deep into Red Rover before I noticed your new girl, the red-headed one, and several others off by themselves. They were hunched over something in a far corner of the tennis court. Because the sun was bright and I was looking into deep shade, for a moment I didn't see the smoke--just a thin column like a thread--rising up; but then I couldn't believe they actually had something on fire! I called out, 'What are you doing girls?' And as I hurried over, I heard the new girl chant, 'Burn, burn!' She had stomped the fire out before I could reach them and everyone scattered; but I saved what was left."

From between the folds of her handkerchief, Mother Durban drew a paper doll with a penciled curly-cued bonnet, elbow-length veil and cape with small buttons down the front. The feet and bottom of the skirt were charred away. A tiny black circle rode above the end of the mouth. Mother Adelli fingered the mole on her lower cheek.

"Why, it's a paper doll of a nun," Mother O'Rourke, Reverend Mother Gregory's secretary, a heavy older woman, chirped. "Isn't that sweet? Years ago, when I was Mistress of Minims, we made paper dolls of nuns galore--

Franciscans, Dominicans, Sisters of Mercy, Benedictines. The children loved cutting out the different wimples."

"Thank you, Mother Durban. I'll take care of it." Mother Adelli drew the effigy into her own handkerchief and slipped it into her pocket. Mother Crewelman stretched her neck to peer through her glasses. As the figure changed hands, her eyes turned hard; but she said nothing. Mother Adelli prayed her Superior would not ask for the drawing. Why couldn't Mother Durban have brought it to her in her office instead? And surely she wasn't the first nun in the history of the Order to be rendered in effigy.

"I'm happy no one was hurt, Mother Durban--." Mother Adelli began, then realized there might be damage to school property--and here beside her sat her spiritual guide, the Mistress General. She felt her heart drop into her stomach.

"And the tennis court?" Mother Adelli leaned toward Mother Durban.

"Oh, I scraped what little residue there was off with my shoe, and told those girls you would hear about this. I told them," she shook her finger, "that this is not a good thing. Playing with fire was very dangerous. We could get hurt or hurt somebody else or destroy something valuable that belongs to someone else." Mother Durban sometimes forgot her audience was past fourth grade.

Old Mother Byrne tisked, loose spectacles riding her nose. "I must find some good books for those girls to read," she declared. Mother Byrne was the school librarian.

"And I would make those girls take a bucket of water and scrub that court, too; if they were mine," Mother Durban finished off, easing her round body into the chair now her duty was discharged.

"I'm going to see to this right now. Please excuse me, Mothers." Mother Adelli rose, knees trembling; and while Mother Crewelman remained silent, Mother Adelli thought she could feel the woman's eyes burrowing into her back as she crossed the room, opened and closed the frosted glass of the door and staggering under the meaning of the thing, that the Rhenehan girl had declared war on her.

The four nuns watched her leave. Mother Durban found it a shame for Mother Adelli to interrupt her social hour. Mother Byrne believed Mother Adelli should start the girl off on the Oz books because there were so many of them. Mother Crewelman's eyes glinted. She sniffed and sat back while Mother O'Rourke unlidded a cache of tales of rambunctious students from days gone by, laughing and wiping tears away while the others listened politely before they must turn to Job One, their spiritual discussion for the day.

"Please sit down, Helene." Mother Adelli motioned to the single chair near the door.

The girl sat and began trimming cuticle with her teeth while peering under the desk at Mother Adelli's pointed black shoes and the coiled jump rope not yet returned to the sports closet. She reached with one brown oxford for a strand and began to raise it onto her toe, then let it slap against the floor.

Mother Adelli had planned to bring the effigy into view, to frown and say in a severe tone, "Do you recognize this, Miss Rhenehan?" But seeing the girl, blouse escaping at the waist and toes of her new oxfords already scraped grey, she remembered the desperate eyes, the voice calling out, "Wait, Dad."

She hesitated. Clearly, everyone involved should receive a *'rien'* next *Primes.* But Superior had said no more *'riens'* for the Rhenehan girl. "I leave it in your capable hands," she had told her.

At least, Mother Adelli thought wryly, the girls were playing together. And what had been hurt anyway, except for her pride? Perhaps this was a lesson arranged by Our Lord to teach her much-needed humility and patience. Her duty was the well-being of the student; and right here was an opportunity to help the girl. Then she saw with a start that all this time Helene sat in a posture so loose, so unconcerned as to be scornful.

"Please sit up, Helene. I wanted some time with you." She groped about. "How are things here for you now?"

"I only have to be in this jail six months," the girl came back.

"It is difficult for you. You would rather be with your father in Italy."

The girl let her eyes roll away. Slap, slap the rope fell from her shoe to the floor. From the hallway came the click of a classroom door followed by a muffled chatter of rosary beads and feet padding down the old wood floor.

"You will be going to New York in November. And soon we will be having a holiday where we play--"

"Like the one where the whole team hides?" Helene mimicked Mother Adelli's voice in the parlor that first Sunday, the rage boiled up in her before she could think. Jesus, Mary and Joseph, pray for us.

Breathe. This was a child. And this was not about creating more problems. "Well," she fought to brighten and bring her eyes back to the girl, "you may feel differently after you've experienced a *Congé.*"

"I'm not experiencing it, and nobody can make me." Helene puckered her lips and, head thrown back and feet swinging, begin whistling off-key.

"That will be enough music, thank you. Well, we'll see what happens when *Congé* actually arrives." The nun brightened her voice further. "And don't forget Christmas in Rome--perhaps even an audience with the Pope!"

The girl stretched her neck as though balancing a plate on her head and, her face long and mouth down-turned, rotated a stiffened upper body to dispense blessings to the room here and there with two raised fingers.

"That will do, Miss Rhenehan."

No Religious would countenance disrespect for the Holy Father. She threw her eyes onto the bookcase to place them somewhere safe. The father didn't bring the girl up Catholic. People didn't know any better when they crucified Jesus either. Her pulse slowed.

"You referred to this school as a jail." Mother Adelli kept her voice level. "Perhaps it--."

"Bars on the windows. A rule for every time you turn your head. Pray when you get up, pray before class, pray before you eat, pray before you go to sleep. No talking anywhere, any time." She threw her head. "In my other school at least you could breathe."

Mother Adelli blinked. "We do ask somewhat more than other schools; but everything is for your good, for your future."

Slap, slap went the rope.

"Stop that sound. We are trying to talk."

The girl seemed capable of making war out of anything; but she, Mother Adelli, must not be drawn in. How could anyone go to war over a rope? She remembered the effigy below her fingertips, felt it burn through the desktop. How could she go to war over a paper doll, over the vanity of the thing, the self-importance? Were you burning me? Or, why were you burning me? How could she ask such things? But she must address the issue. Perhaps she could begin with an analogy.

"When somebody damages property, they must pay for it, one way or another. Suppose someone took your best sweater and--."

"The man who killed my mother with his truck went to jail, but he only had to stay five years because he knew somebody in City Hall. He was drunk, too." Helene's eyes deepened to hatred. "I don't think he paid very much for killing somebody."

"I'm very sorry. I didn't know how your mother died," Mother Adelli drew back respectfully. Her own father

60

staggered through her mind, whiskey slopping over the edge of the glass. But he never hurt anyone; only himself, and her brother Julian sometimes.

"Your father has had to be both parents to you then." She spread her fingers over her desk. "That must have been difficult for both of you."

"Well, he can't cook, I can tell you that," Helene brayed. A memory lighted her face. "He can cut hearts, but he can't cut vegetables worth anything." She guffawed again.

Mother Adelli couldn't make out the meaning behind the laughter. She straightened papers on her desk.

"Now, there is the matter of your classes," she made her voice serious, businesslike after a moment. "*Mère* Roussseau thinks you only pretend to have trouble with French pronunciation."

"Because I say 'asses' bean?"

"Please?" Mother Adelli searched the girl's face.

"'Asses' bean.' Helene's eyes glittered.

"I don't understand."

"Trays bean, bean, asses' bean." Helene grinned and popped a finger up for each mark of evaluation in French.

"I hope you're not saying such things in class." Mother Adelli opened her eyes wide. "Of course that would upset *Mère* Rousseau."

Helene grinned and toed the rope onto her foot.

"That is not the way to get attention, Helene. You will be very glad later that you have learned French. It is the mark of an educated person." The thrust shriveled in the dry silence. Mother Adelli went on, nonetheless. "Then there is your math. You do nothing on your tests. You do nothing in my classes either. Perhaps the work is not hard enough. Is that it?"

Helene craned her neck to examine the doorjamb behind her.

Despite herself, Mother Adelli felt for the girl--alone among strangers, filled with hateful feelings, her only parent far across the ocean.

"Let's forget these two weeks, Helene." Clemency came like a grace. "You have six weeks before first report card. That's plenty of time to earn your As and Bs."

As she spoke, the fiery mass of the girl's hair disappeared below the side of the desk. It hovered over the rope.

Say something about the effigy.

With Reverend Mother Gregory's voice coaching, Mother Adelli stared at the bookcase, at the red Thesaurus. She needed words. Her watch in the little pocket under her cape ticked away the eternal seconds and her heart speeded up as if she had begun to run. Then from the corridor came the five-thirty bell. Her lungs unlocked and took in a feast of air.

"Dinner hour now," she said in what sounded like a stranger's voice.

But she spoke to an empty chair back. The girl, still bent over, was fooling with the rope on the floor. Mother Adelli pushed away from her desk. Say something about the effigy and fire before it's too late! But ordering herself around did no good. She couldn't.

"Is there any way I can help you to be more comfortable here, Helene?" she asked instead.

The girl's flat face reappeared above the desktop, grinning. One clenched fist was raised next to her cheek; and swinging from it was the product of all her industry, a section of jump rope tied ingeniously into a hangman's noose.

Mother Adelli felt her heart give a painful knock; but then something inside sternly regained composure.

"Bring the rope with you," it ordered crisply; "I'll show you where to put it away."

At dinner Mother Adelli saw Helene pass a look of conspiracy to cohorts who knew enough to keep their eyes on their plates. All four would receive an *'assez bien'* at *Primes*, she decided, watching them cut and chew so primly. If they asked about their mark, she would tell them to speak to Mother Durban.

But it was hard to walk past them, wondering whether their snickering or an eruption of laughter was over her burned feet. Every giggle made her stomach clench. She'd had no idea any of her students disliked her. Perhaps their affection had been false all along, put on to gain favors or better marks.

And so she left them with Mother Johnson and went to sit in a corner of the chapel. With the onset of autumnal darkness, the marble figures and fixtures lengthened into grays of differing densities, and the chapel transformed into a body stretching out for sleep.

She wiped away the tears. Her Chapter of Faults was confronting her. The spirit of her vocation and of the Order counseled against getting attached to any worldly or even spiritual thing. She had become attached; her students' favor was a coat of many colors they wove with their smiles and eyes. She had worn it, thinking it impermeable; now she saw how easily it could unravel.

And if she were not vain, why didn't she take the drawing out of her desk and confront the girl, as she absolutely should have? This was moral failure. She would have to confess this sin on Tuesday. Her watery vision slid over the darkened tabernacle, over the marble Virgin to its left. This must never happen again; she, Mary Agnes Adelli, took a vow to do her duty. To the penance given her on Tuesday she would add two rosaries a day for Helene until she saw the girl's attitude improve. And she would set all of this weakness in her character right before Final Vows and Rome in June.

She mopped her eyes. She had a quiet conscience now with the *'assez biens.'* Oh, but how she staggered under the weight of being Mistress of the Third *Cours* now with Helene stirring the pot, multiplying what there was to carry. She looked at her watch, leapt to her feet. She was late for dinner!

It was old Mother Concepciòn's sixty-fifth anniversary in the Order, and the Rule of Silence during dinner was excused. Ordinarily a member of the Community read from a spiritual classic--Paul's epistles, Augustine's *City of God,* Therese of Avila's *Collected Writings.*

Twenty-two graceful black arches of nun's veils, broken by the occasional white of a Novice moved to and fro like exotic flowers under the old ceiling fan that complained as it stirred the air.

"By the way, Mother, what did you do about the paper doll?" Mother Crewelman leaned away to allow her dinner plate to be removed.

Five or six nuns turned toward Mother Adelli who dusted her fingers and swallowed the steaming center of a biscuit while tears sprang to her eyes.

"Oh, is something wrong, Mother?" asked the elderly Mother Byrne, on her right.

"No no, thank you Mother--a piece of biscuit. Too hot." She laughed and fanned her mouth.

Further down the table, tiny old Mother Concepciòn, with a large white towel over her breast, squinted through her glasses. "Of course there's cake," she was saying to everyone in a loud voice. "You don't last sixty-five years and not get cake." And, fork upright in one fist, she struck the table with the other.

"What *did* you do about the paper doll, Mother?" Mother Crewelman pressed again as three large dishes of raspberry Jell-O and slices of Mother Concepciòn's yellow anniversary cake were set along the white cloth. "The student tried to burn it on the tennis courts. Isn't that what you said, Mother Durban?" Before Mother Adelli could reply, Mother Crewelman turned to the Mistress of the Minims seated on the far edge of the conversation. As Mother Durban opened her mouth, Mother Crewelman turned back to Mother Adelli, her eyes sparkling coldly.

"Did you determine whether the drawing was of a particular nun? Was it you, Mother?"

At that, serving spoon in hand, Mother Adelli let herself be drawn into the brilliantly undulating Jell-O, its surface like a gorgeously moving ice pond shimmering with lights all the way to its center. For the smallest second, she unhooked her mind and let the colors pull her into its ruby depths and away from the white-framed faces and all their questions.

"I wondered about that too--with the little mole--was it you, Mother, do you think?" Mother O'Rourke's voice, directly at her elbow, forced her back to the room raw with light and chatter.

Then she saw it. As *Soeur* Josephine reached from behind to replenish the coffee, Mother Adelli picked up the bowl of Jell-O and there on the gleaming lake--on its back, legs askew, the wings of its plump hairy body laid out like funeral veils, huge sectioned eyes looking right and left--was a dead fly. Mother Adelli's hands began to shake. She dropped the bowl and wheeled upon *Soeur* Josephine, just withdrawing the coffee pitcher.

"A fly!" She spoke through clenched teeth in cold clipped words and a voice that rose for all to hear. "There is a dead fly on this Jell-O, *ma Soeur.*"

That was all she said and needed to say. Paling, *Soeur* Josephine, whisked the offending dish away. The other nuns stirred, not looking at one another.

To have criticized a Working Sister whom she considered to have a naturally purified vocation, was outrageous, unforgivable! But how could she have spoken so? Mother Adelli sat stunned; yet she felt repulsion and anger boiling in her yet.

"Oh, have some of this Jell-O, Mother," Mother Durban broke in, reaching to pass a different bowl.

"No, thank you, Mother. Food is not that important. I'll excuse myself. I have work in my office." Amazed, Mother Adelli watched herself push back her chair.

"But you wouldn't leave before grace, Mother?" Mother Crewelman interrupted, her fork in the air.

The question brought Mother Adelli around like a slap. She blinked twice.

"Of course not, Mother," she said, and drew herself back to the table.

Scarcely two hours later, Mother Adelli was bent over her lap at the little table outside her alcove. The short needle shot back and forth under her arched fingers, darning Madeline's sock.

The dormitory door hinges sang a half note, and Felicia Antonini, a Third Academic student and a ribbon, came in from the corridor.

"Mother Adelli?" she curtsied, hands crossed at the wrists with a textbook dangling from one of them.

"Yes, Felicia." How sweet the girl looked.

The student leaned over to whisper that Mother Crewelman asked that Mother Adelli come to her office. "I am to take your dormitory."

Mother Adelli tucked the mending into the cardboard box that was her sewing basket and arranged with the girl about baths. There was to be no general visiting, but the girls might read quietly until 8:55. Then Madeline should take the holy water font around. Lights out at 9:00. She tapped the small lamp. "You will need this," she smiled, nodding to the study text.

Felicia curtsied. She would not get much reading done in her *History of Modern Europe* tonight. As soon as these girls realized Mother Adelli had been replaced by a student, heads would poke through curtains, whispering, bumps, thumps, stifled shrieks, and bodies sliding under beds abound until Felicia called out, "All right, I'm taking names. The next sound, that name goes down on this paper." And she would have to write down at least one name--stride with grand authority across the dormitory and fling a curtain aside--before silence would start to settle in unevenly. But all the while, she knew, until sleep led them into its cave, their ears would be tuned for the rustle of long skirts and chatter of rosary beads.

"Have a seat, Mother."

Mother Crewelman had long hands, broad like paddles and, in the light from the desk lamp, the color of candle wax. She indicated the chair across from her. For a moment the only sound in the room was the nib of her pen biting paper.

Mother Adelli, armpits wet, nested open palms upon her lap, but after a moment closed her fingers over them. She wished she could see the other nun more clearly, but Mother Crewelman's face floated in gloom above the goose-necked lamp. From a darkened corner a clock notched the air.

Mother Crewelman set down her pen.

"It is unusual to ask you to come without a prior appointment, but I have done so because I have become concerned about you."

Mother Adelli's stomach fell.

"But before I go on, let me repeat the question I asked at dinner, which you managed to evade. What have you done about the incident on the tennis court?"

Where to begin? With the father's leaving? With the mother's death? With the girl grinning, the noose raised in her office?

"Of course I have spoken with her, Mother."

"Yes. Very good." Mother Crewelman's posture became tense, excited. She leaned forward. "Now, what did you say to the girl? This is very important. A great deal is at stake here."

"Well," Mother Adelli began carefully, "I spoke about her studies and encouraged her to work harder. I told her I understood times were difficult and sympathized——"

"Sympathized." Mother Crewelman bolted in her chair. "You gave sympathy to a student who desecrated the habit?"

Mother Adelli's legs began to shake. She had stumbled into disaster.

"You sympathized with a student who spit upon our holy garb, who spit," the Mistress General's lips seemed to thicken, "upon all we hold dear?" She got up to pace around the younger nun's chair--a tall, horsey woman with a nose full of blackheads. "And you did nothing. In fact, you gave it countenance? Do I hear correctly?" She cocked her head in an exaggerated gesture of listening, then bent low and turned her face up at an acute angle, a startling and ghostly apparition, the long pale angular features cut as if from stone. She drilled the downcast nun with her eyes.

Mother Adelli's own eyelids fell into a violence of fluttering.

The Mistress General stood upright again, flopped her long arms against her sides and flung herself into her chair where she sat until finally one pale hand emerged in the pool of light and slowly took up the pen.

"How long have you been with us in the Order?" she asked over the pen's scratching.

Mother Adelli searched her paralyzed throat. "Ten years since the Novitiate, Mother."

The pen and its scratching.

"Ten years," the Mistress General nodded. "Plus two years in the Novitiate. And you were a graduate of our schools, I believe?"

"I attended Sheridan Road from Third *Cours* through Fourth Academic."

"Third *Cours* through Fourth Academic," the nun repeated; "That's another eight years. Why," her voice lifted, "that's twenty years you've been with us."

Mother Adelli felt her body begin to reappear.

"Twenty years!" Mother Crewelman slapped the desk, the lampshade swayed and rattled. "That is more than half your life, Mother Adelli. Doesn't this Order mean anything to you after all this time? And with your years of training, can you not yet recognize sacrilege? Would you sit by and watch while some common criminal pilfered the tabernacle, set his dirty hands upon the holy Host to carry it off?"

Mother Adelli's horrified mouth dropped open.

Did she not see there was no difference, Mother Crewelman went on, for their Order was the Body of Christ, as the Holy Father said. She had let someone put sinful unbeliever pagan hands on that Sacred Body. Worse, she had actually given comfort to the Enemy. The Mistress General sank back in her chair. After several moments, she removed the hand covering her eyes and straightened up.

"I don't know what to make of this. What should I make of this, Mother?"

Mother Adelli sat with her hands clapped to her mouth. Mother Crewelman covered her eyes again and waited. Darkness filtered in from the corners of the room. Finally Mother Adelli wiped her face with her knuckles.

"Oh, Mother," her voice came from a caved-in place, "never would I willingly betray the love of my dear Lord. I have given my life to Him. I didn't think of the girl's behavior as so serious, in that way. I was more concerned about the—"

"Well," Mother Crewelman interrupted,, "I must gather then that you hold us quite cheaply, Mother Adelli." She sniffed long, flattening her nostrils.

"Oh, no, Mother. Never cheaply, though I did not see the deeper implications, I confess. I am devastated to think

I failed in any way to hold our Order sacred. Why, I love this Order. It is my life."

Mother Crewelman shifted in her chair, tapped the blotter with her finger. "That is reassuring, Mother Adelli," she said finally.

Mother Adelli raised reddened eyes. "What should I do now, Mother? How can I repair this?" She wiped her eyes again.

Satisfaction played at the Mistress General's lips. "Repentance is the first step. I can see you are repentant. Now," she smiled tightly, "this incident is healed in the mercy of His Heart; but you must make it clear to all your girls that sacrilege has been committed. Leave no doubt with them about those things we hold to be sacred. Do this first thing tomorrow."

"I will, Mother."

"Someone should have seen the drawing before it got to the tennis court. Look to your dikes." She drew a handkerchief from her sleeve and dabbed at tiny bubbles at the corners of her mouth. "Despite her baptism, the girl is functionally a pagan, Mother Adelli--a little pagan sunk in darkness. But Our Lord's mark is upon her. He has entrusted this girl to you, and He will hold you accountable for her." She poked her handkerchief up her sleeve. "By the way, what will you give these students?"

"'*Assez bien*,' Mother."

"'*Assez bien*'? Surely you feel they should receive a '*rien*' after the conversation we have just had."

"Reverend Mother Gregory told—instructed--me there were to be no more '*riens*' for the Rhenehan girl."

"Surely she didn't mean--. You must know she was speaking figuratively, Mother Adelli."

"I . . . she instructed me there were to be no more '*riens*' reaching Doctor Rhenehan, I believe is how she put it."

Mother Crewelman fingered the corners of her papers. When she looked up, her eyes withheld something.

"All right," she said; "I see."

Mother Adelli left the pale hands picking up the pen to write in the dish of light. All the way to dormitory, she could not stop the shaking in her legs. She found Felicia under the light leaning on her elbow underlining text, her long hair hanging over her book. Mother Adelli took out her pocket watch. It was ten-thirty.

"Dear Superior," Mother Crewelman took a clean sheet of paper. "Please schedule fifteen minutes for a conference concerning Mother Adelli. I wish to report grave doubts as to her fitness for Final Vows. As early as convenient. In Christ, L. Crewelman, R.S.C.J."

On the way to Cloister, she slid the note under Reverend Mother Gregory's door. As she continued down the corridor, the pale safety light in the ceiling cast her shadow long. She pushed the button for the elevator.

Someone must hold the line against this erosion. This Mary Agnes Adelli was a perfect example of the danger of using endowments to secure candidates who cannot pay their own way. Graduate of their schools or not, this young woman lacked sufficient depth from her family, first generation immigrants, to supply what really good background offers ready-made. Silk purses from sows' ears. This Superior herself was new money--middle class clothing stores--and her background and judgment showed in her promoting such as this Adelli girl who appeared to be something of a favorite.

She stepped into the tiny elevator.

More and more the Order suffered from Reverend Mother Gregorys. This injunction against further 'riens' for the Rhenehan girl was deeply disturbing. Small doubt the Superior wanted to make the doctor happy. She watched the mottled elevator shaft creep by. While she must hold her tongue for the moment, she could and would act within the scope of her own authority. As fourth generation Sacred Heart and old Philadelphia money, she and those like her must weed out any who weren't up to standard. They owed that much to Madeline Sophie Barat, their founder.

The ancient elevator bounced to a stop. Evil always seeps in; you must sweep and sweep. Should God one day call her to be Superior, she would restore the tarnished model to its shining original.

With a grand gesture, she flung back the folding gate, stepped out and let it bang again into place.

Five

Before Mass the next day, Sunday, Mother Adelli spoke to her Third *Cours* waiting in two lines for chapel, veils already bobby-pinned. Early morning light streamed through the dormitory windows, transforming alcove curtains to luminous bodies and outlining certain promontories of students' faces turned toward their Mistress who stood hand up and palm outward for their attention.

"This habit we Religious wear," she began, "is much the same as the tabernacle, the altar, statues and rosary beads. We call such things 'sacramentals' and, as you remember from your classes, they serve as channels for the grace of God and so should always be treated with the utmost of respect."

She looked from sleepy face to sleepy face. How many others would have burned her in effigy had they thought of it? How many who seemed so fond of her actually mocked her behind her back? Helene, standing like a dreamer at her alcove curtains, reminded Mother Adelli then that only a few girls were involved in the burning. And wasn't it just last week her girls bragged that they had the best nun in the school? And they were *children*, after all. How could they grasp objects being sacred when such a concept was hard enough for grown-ups? So how fair were her reprimands? And how could she thrust a barbed word like "sacrilege" into such vulnerable faces and minds? Nevertheless, she had been ordered to do so.

"For anyone to ridicule the habit or the Order, things blessed by the Holy Father himself to do the work of Christ on earth, would be a grave act of disrespect," she trudged on unable to name incidents or perpetrators, though she felt certain it was now general knowledge and ought to be spoken of. It was the thought of exposing herself further to ridicule, and fear of the breach such exposure might create with her students that stopped her altogether. The best she could manage was stories of where and how sacramentals played an important role in the lives of saints: St. Peter's staff, the robe of St. Francis, his waist cord with its knots. the armor of Jeanne d'Arc.

Her girls took the information in with passive curiosity. But why was Mother Adelli's face all pinched up while she told them what they already heard a million times? And weren't they going to be late for Mass?

As she turned to lead the lines to chapel, Mother Adelli heard a snicker, felt a thrust of fear and was fourteen, the brilliant *ingénue* of her dance school's winter recital at the Vickers Theater in Chicago. As her family watched from the front row, she was stepping into an *arabesque* when her toeshoe buckled forward stealing her momentum for the upcoming series of *pirouettes*. To gain stability, she anchored her eyes on her brother Julian whose mouth immediately slid into a satisfied and nasty grin. "You made a a fool of yourself, didn't you now, High Princess," it said.

The shifting of her students from foot to foot and looking at one another, brought Mother Adelli back. *Klat, klat* she used her clapper to knock her senses together pivoted, and led her girls to chapel.

That afternoon during field hockey, she carted her worries and a cup of tea to the nun's dining room. Her mind nagged at her about obedience while she scalded her tongue on the tea. How did she think she could go to confession without the priest telling her to go back and do what she had avoided--to speak to Helene and the others about the effigy and sacrilege? And what style of conscience did she think she could keep and still be able to sleep, much less make Final Vows in June?

"Well, you have a pretty conscience, Mary Agnes, I must say." In a flash, her mother's voice comes back loaded with vinegar. It is her graduation night.

"I've gotten The Call, Mama." She had blurted out the news over the fresh-cooked *tortellini* her mother carried from stove to sink. Her mother's eyes and mouth have staggered open.

"Now? You've gotten The Call *now*? We're getting suitcases down for New York and you've gotten The Call? *Dío!* You have a conscience like a perfect *tour jette*, Mary Agnes." She arches her little finger. "And may we all light candles at your shrine."

"I had to be sure before I told you. I know how hard you've worked," Mary Agnes had rushed to add. "I know it means bypassing the ballet scholarship and New York-- and how that is such a disappointment. But God has told me He wants me to give myself to Him. I wish to go to the Madams, since they have been my teachers. I will do my best to make you proud."

"And French nuns to boot," her mother spit and dumped the tortellini into the sink with the dirty pots and pans. "Ayee, look at this. Every day God mocks my life." A roar of laughter burst through the closed dining room doors and Angelica Adelli began to fork the steaming squares onto a serving platter. "I have a table full in your honor, Mary Agnes. Is it too much to ask *la Sancta Madre Adelli* to soil her hands with work right now and help me here."

Mother Adelli stirred in her chair, sighed. Well, but only eight months now and she would go to Rome and make her mother and father proud.

Helene heard a crack, then a sizzling sound in the grass, folded her arms and watched the field hockey ball shoot past her followed by Stork who threw her a searing look and clambered into the weeds. Helene gave her back a face, dropped her hockey stick and without another glance, left her gaping team to waste their Sunday afternoon on a ninny game if they wanted to.

The song of September katydids carried her down the path toward the ravine. Layer after layer of fine sepia dirt settled over her new gym shoes. She made up "-art" rhymes: dart, part, cart, heart, fart, start. She passed the rear of the gymnasium, then stopped at the kitchen stoop and scattered with a wild kick the thin blanket of golden leaves laid down by the towering elm. The road hugged the ravine before it angled toward the front of school property, and Helene let it draw her along.

Then she saw the cat.

It was a tabby, grey with a few patches of white, perched on the lawn in a disk of sunlight about ten feet from the path to the commuter train platform. The animal turned its head and trained yellow eyes on her.

"Here kitty," she called softly, holding out a hand, taking a few cautious steps. The cat's eyes widened. One cone-shaped ear scanned the air.

"Kitty-kitty-kitty-kitty."

She could see the white whiskers and the tan blotch on its pink nose, she was that close when a thick twig underfoot snapped and the cat bolted. She sped after it, trying to keep in sight the grey spike of its tail as it scrambled through underbrush, dove into a tangle of ivy and disappeared beneath the rail station platform. Helene stopped ankle-deep in the dying grasses to listen its rustling sounds fade away.

"Damn."

She said it out loud, her father's word. Climbing onto the platform two steps at a time, she sat on its edge and dangled her legs over the tracks. "Damn." She slammed a fist onto the boards.

She just wanted to see the cat--to hold it, pet it, to feel its short thick fur and look all the way into its eyes to see if they were nice or mean. They could be mean. Being locked up makes you mean. Being chased away makes you mean. Being alone makes you mean. Was it a school cat or wild?. She would watch it, then she could tell. But how could she watch it if it ran away? She stood and began to kick stray stones onto the track, clearing the platform. Now and then she peered through the planks, looking for white whiskers, for a pink nose with a tan blotch.

Did they care about this kitty, these nuns so busy praying for all the bad people? Did they even think about it being out here, needing to eat, getting cold? They were supposed to be so good at taking care of things. He, her father, paid them to take care of her so he could be Mr. Big-Shot Heart Surgeon in Italy. All they did was pick on her. They called themselves "Mother," but none would ever be a mother to her.

High overhead the sun burned down. She felt sweat at her hairline and the backs of her knees. The air was stifling. She ducked into the shelter at the end of the platform and slouched in a corner pocket of shade. She breathed deep the odor of decaying leaves. A person could come onto the platform to wait for a train and, unless she craned her neck, never see her. And so what if they did find her out here? Who gave a hot fig anyway?

So she sat. After a bit, the heat and sawing of the insects sent her into a drowsy sleep until the rumbling underfoot of the train from Fort Sheridan pulled her upright and sent her stumbling into the glaring sun to meet the scarred red and grey metal cars.

The train stood throbbing directly in front of her while her reflection, rumpled sports shirt, rumpled hair, trembled in the pocked window glass. A conductor in a threadbare navy uniform stepped from the second car.

"All aboard. Lake Forest, Waukegan, Lake Bluff. 'Boarrrdd." He gestured impatiently toward the dark opening of the door. She blinked twice in the bright sunlight and got on.

The train lurched forward and she fell against the door into the seating area. There the air smelled of stuffing and dust. In the dimmed light she saw worn green seats with aisle-side brass handles. The lone passenger, a grey-haired woman in a sleeveless dress with a black hat and big arms lowered a book to peer at her. Helene swung into a seat. The worn covering prickled against her sweating legs as she leaned at the window and watched the last planks of the Sacred Heart platform jerk away.

She couldn't think why she'd gotten on the train. She had no money. What would they do, put her off? So what, she sat on her fear; she'd walk. Besides, it felt nice to be rocking on the train. Her body yearned again toward the slippery edge of sleep. Outside her window the Lake Forest woods flickered and jumped.

The inner car door banged open.

"Tickets. Tickets please."

The movement of the train knocked the dumpy conductor against the pairs of seats until he stood opposite, a block of tickets in one hand, hole punch in the other.

"Where to, Miss?"

She felt her heart skip. But he wasn't looking at her; he was fumbling with the top ticket on the block, trying to get it out from under the rubber band. A brass button swung back and forth at his sleeve cuff. His pants bagged at the knees.

"Where to?"

She didn't know. Fear squeezed a grin onto her face. She heaved her shoulders up and down in an exaggerated shrug. The conductor returned to fumbling with the top ticket, as though he hadn't seen her response. The train clattered, then jolted him in the aisle.

"Where to!"

She held the grin in place, shrugged her shoulders again and watched the action confound him, saw anger gather in his eyes.

"Home." She said it then with grim satisfaction, and turned to the green and golden woods rampaging beyond the window.

"And where would that be? Which town?" His pale eyes sparked behind his glasses.

A knot rose in her throat. She turned back to him. "Chicago," she said, and then discovered a greasy bloom from the dusty window ledge on the underside of her arm and busied herself spit-washing it.

"Chicago. Oh?" The anger in his eyes dissolved. "Well, you're in the wrong direction, Miss. You need south. Get off this next stop, Lake Forest. You can get a southbound there." He dropped the block of tickets into his jacket pocket where they bulged. "No charge for the ride." A smile played at his lips. A weather-beaten water tower loomed and disappeared at the window. She watched his eyes follow it.

"Lake Forest, next stop," he barked down the car. "You come with me," he told her; "I'll show you where to get your ticket." He looked her over again. "The stationmaster has a telephone. Someone might be worried."

The knot came back. No one in Chicago to worry after her.

Forty-five minutes after the train departed the Sacred Heart platform, Mother Adelli, three textbooks open on her office desk, was roused from a lesson plan by the Portress' knock. The Lake Forest stationmaster was on the telephone upstairs.

The girl had no money, had told the northbound conductor she wanted to go to her family in Chicago, but the number there was disconnected. The Cathedral School, where the girl went before, directed him to the Convent. No, the girl seemed fine. Yes, he would be more than happy to put her into a taxi. And it was always a pleasure to be of service to the Sisters.

Mother Adelli stood on the bottom front step, under the portico, raking the gates and lawn with her eyes until the taxi swung up the driveway. The raw smell of gasoline burned her throat. When she asked the fare, the driver waved it off. The stationmaster had taken care of it.

She bent to peer through the passenger door, searching for the girl's eyes. They met her red-rimmed, but sparkling with a hard light. Mother Adelli held out her hand. "Helene?" She stepped back and the girl slid ever so slowly along the seat and finally stepped onto the driveway, gawking about as if she'd never seen the place before, looking everywhere except at Mother Adelli.

The taxi rumbled off.

"Are you all right? Are you hurt?" These first questions Mother Adelli wanted to ask shriveled in her throat by the girl's hard look and refusal to make eye contact. A quick inventory instead: No blood, no gauzes, no torn clothes. Thank God. Thank God.

"We'll walk," she told Helene.

She needed the help of the out-of-doors to organize her feelings. Above them a blue jay's long metallic call rode the air. Mother Adelli heard its mate answer and then a shuttering sound and a pair of blue wings blurred past her.

She turned toward the grotto. The girl did not follow.

"Helene?"

They started off in silence. It was past four-thirty and fingers of orange light tinged with rose slanted along the tree limbs, lit the veined membranes of fallen leaves and flooded the path on which their two shadows moved side by side. Mother Adelli peered around the confines of her wimple as Helene shambled along, hands clasped behind her back, and kicking rocks. Suddenly the intended grotto felt too confining and Mother Adelli turned toward the hockey field.

Where the roadway passed over the ravine, she drew a breath.

"Did you run away, Helene?"

Helene picked up a stone to pitch in a high arc into the chasm. "No," she sneered, "sissies run away."

Mother Adelli waited for more, but the girl merely found another stone, spun upon her heel and sent it high in the other direction.

"How do you explain being at the North Shore train station in Lake Forest instead of on the hockey field with the rest of the boarders?"

"That game is stupid--chasing a ball into the weeds. I went for a ride instead! Wheee." She threw her arms and began to spin, forcing Mother Adelli to step aside.

"You must have known you couldn't pay," she continued evenly. "How did you expect to buy a ticket?"

Twirling, Helene gave her a wide grin. Head thrown back, arms out like someone crucified, she spun the way babies do to become drunk. She began to stagger across the roadway in ragged loops.

"Miss Rhenehan. Stop that turning."

Helene eyed her curiously, stiffened her arms, clapped them to her sides like a soldier. then locked her legs together and lapsed into tiny, flat-footed half steps like a wind-up toy, saluting every few paces.

Despite her exasperation, the girl's theatricals tugged at the nun. Really, the child was clever, and quite funny. Something in her relaxed, let feeling into her voice.

"You aren't hurt, Helene?"

"No Sir. No broken bones, Sir. Just the bullet wound in the side, Sir." Swish, swish went the stiff arms.

But the studied distance the girl kept spoiled the moment for the nun who wanted to take her by the shoulders and shake her--for the fork fight, the burning in effigy, for slovenly performance in her classes, for unfriendliness and unreachable superiority, for this serious breach of the rules in leaving school property.

"You play a game," she stepped up next to Helene; "pretending nothing matters, making people worry over you, getting yourself in trouble. You should be attending to your studies, making friends with the other students, taking advantage of the special things we offer. The time will be over soon enough, and you will want to leave with a good record."

But Helene picked up her pace, marching onward. Mother Adelli quickened her steps too. "What would your father think if we had to call him in Europe? What if something really bad had happened? You cannot go just anywhere." The girl opened her gait to march faster.

The road crossed the ravine, sidled up to the hockey field and died there; and too soon the playing field gave itself over to prairie. Still nothing was settled. Helene continued marching, arms and legs pumping through the wild grasses, hand flashing salutes. Really, she looked like a Christmas nutcracker. Despite herself, Mother Adelli started to laugh. Well, she could play the game, too. Maybe a laugh was just what was needed.

"Halt!" she called after Helene.

The toy soldier did not stop.

"Helene," Mother Adelli called again, "that's enough now. Halt." She laughed uncertainly.

But the soldier marched on looking small and fragile in the wild growth under the great wide sky.

Mother Adelli's mind stuttered. How could she stop the girl? A fence stood at the far end of the school's property, but first the girl must pass through the long field of thorns, burrs, and stickers. Then there was the steep cleft of the far ravines.

Mother Adelli began to run. Stickers and thorns clawed at her skirts until she had gotten just beyond the girl and turned to stand directly before her, steeling herself for Helene to march into her.

But Helene, eyes staring and face wooden, merely kept time in place, tromping and saluting. An evening breeze rippled the grasses. High over the end of the hockey field, a pan-shaped formation of birds loudly sought shelter for the night. All Mother Adelli could think of was how to get the girl back into the school building.

"It's time to go in now, Helene," Mother Adelli said, panting a little from the burst of the run. "We're going in now," she repeated.

But first they must settle something. "I need your word of honor you will not leave school grounds again without permission. For that matter, I must have your word you will not leave a group activity without permission, ever again. This is a very serious matter. Reverend Mother Gregory read these rules to you and your father the day you came. Probably you were not listening. You must listen now."

Tromp, tromp, tromp, Helene's feet replied. Insects leapt and fell in the grass. Sunset glowed along the far margin of treetops. Finally, feet still moving, the girl saluted.

Oh, thank goodness, Mother Adelli gulped. "Ordinarily, everyone would lose their privilege of recreation without supervision because of your leaving the game as you did." Relief softened the nun's voice. "I know you don't want the others to suffer because of you. That would really be a shame."

To this, a grin spread slowly across the girl's face. She halted her marching to look Mother Adelli in the eye, to throw her shoulders up around her ears and open her palms toward the sky. What's it to me, her body said. They're nothing to me, it said.

Flabbergasted, Mother Adelli stumbled into silence. She searched the freckled face for anything with which to connect. "All right, I'm sure you didn't mean that," she said at last. "Go inside. Change out of your shorts into your uniform. Then go to dinner."

And the probing to reach the tender green center and there graft some mutual understanding all dissolved in the diminishing light of the failing afternoon. Helene saluted grandly and pivoted toward the building.

"I didn't run away," she threw the words over her shoulder with a dazzling smile, "but I would get away from here if I could."

Then she broke into a trot across the hockey field, loping under a sky streaked with red. Mother Adelli stood watching, the hem of her habit thick with burrs.

The tall desk lamp enveloped the Superior in light but abandoned the remainder of the room.

"You were quite right to come to me directly." Reverend Mother Gregory tilted back in her office chair while she rested her chin on finger ends and fixed the younger nun in her gaze. "Not directly enough, however." Mother Adelli's eyes widened and then dropped to anchor to the richly burled façade of the desk.

"A student should never, under any circumstances, be in a taxi alone without parental consent, Mother Adelli. Is that clear? We have legal responsibilities. Had you reported the incident first, someone would have been sent to fetch the girl."

"Yes, Reverend Mother."

"There was no physical injury? The girl had not been-- touched?" The Superior's eyes searched the younger woman.

Mother Adelli blushed and swallowed. "Thank heaven, Reverend Mother, there is not a scratch on her."

"But I don't like it, Mother Adelli, an incident like this. Send the girl to the infirmary. Let Mother Spencer look her over."

"Yes, Reverend Mother."

The Superior stood abruptly and before Mother Adelli could find her own feet, went about the room turning on table lamps. Under the warm light, the furniture gleamed forth richly while the Superior reclaimed her chair with a self-comforting groan and let her bunioned foot rest upon its heel.

"Now, did the girl explain why she got on the train?"

"No, Reverend Mother. She told me she did not run away. She seems given to pranks."

"Pranks?" The Superior fastened her eyes upon the younger nun. "We have already had the unspeakable incident in the dining hall. We can't have pranks, Mother." She shifted her weight and the chair cried out. "Pranks give students a false sense of power. This girl is testing you. Put a stop to this behavior at once."

The Superior's fingertips searched out the cool brass of the desklamp and slowly traveled its base. "This Rhenehan girl must be made to conform, Mother Adelli. Under no circumstances is she free to leave our property again. Under no circumstances--." Reverend Mother Gregory stopped. "In my nearly fourteen years as Superior here," she patted each word into the desktop, "I have never had a runaway. I have a perfect record. This will not happen again." She sat back. "Now, I see no need to inform the father as long as the girl is all right. I will consider this a prank, as you suggest; though I take it most seriously." She held the younger nun with her eyes.

"Yes, Reverend Mother." Mother Adelli ran her tongue over her lips.

"But how is it no one was supervising recreation, Mother? Is it your usual practice to leave your students without supervision?"

"Mother Boreman instructed me, when I took over last March, that weekend boarders were to have two hours of unsupervised recreation on Saturday and Sunday afternoons in place of Study Hall as a reward for good behavior. Until now, there has never been a problem."

85

"But not without *some* supervision, Mother Adelli; at least a ribbon from Third or Fourth Academic. I am surprised at you. This was a grave error."

"Yes, Reverend Mother."

Heat crawled up Mother Adelli's neck. Mother Boreman had said nothing about supervision.

The Superior drew a folder to the center of her desk, fingered the cover, opened it and glanced at the bottom line of the top sheet. She emitted a grunt of satisfaction, gazed for a moment across the gleaming furniture toward the windows, then recalled the younger nun and closed the folder.

"So, we will not see such behavior again from this girl. Is that clear?"

"It is, Reverend Mother."

"Mother Crewelman spoke to me this morning about your readiness for Final Vows." Reverend Mother Gregory paused to examine her fingernails. "I told her there is no question you will go to Rome in June, as far as I am concerned. I have been particularly satisfied with you, Mother Adelli. Without the benefit of privilege, you have advanced yourself until you are now Mistress of Third *Cours*. That is quite an achievement. But you see, don't you, that we must continue to supervise and instruct our candidates to the very end; it is necessary for everyone's sake."

"Oh, certainly, Reverend Mother." Mother Adelli forced her eyes to meet the Superior's unswerving gaze.

"Good. Now, I have other work to do."

Mother Adelli stood. The subject of what happened Sunday afternoon was closed.

In the corridor, she consulted her pocket watch. She must go directly to dormitory. After her girls were asleep, there would be time in her alcove to spend with Our Lord, to ask forgiveness because she had not been careful enough and her student had been endangered. As well, she had it on her conscience that she withheld from her

86

Superior what the Rhenehan girl had said about getting away if she could. Withheld it or forgot.

In Omaha, Brother Robert, O.P., who taught the would-be nuns liturgical music, used to say, "We come to this earth equipped with small knapsacks, and we just can't carry very much." She had thought he was talking about leaving worldly things behind, but now it seemed he was speaking about how much a person could carry in her heart and on her soul. She climbed the stairs to the third floor, feeling the straps of her knapsack cut. In the morning she must tell the Superior about what the girl had said.

In the darkness of the dormitory, it seemed to Helene that the stationmaster had closed the door to the taxi almost reluctantly, as if she was his own daughter he was caring for. It was her own father, her real father who should care for her, listen to her, search her face. Tears scalded her cheeks. She jammed her pillow into her mouth and bit down hard while the blocked cries teemed around her teeth.

But finally she forced her mind to another place, to the memory of today, to Dilly Dally peering into the cab, then chasing after her and lecturing her; and then being left standing in the field. She rolled onto her back, wet face drying. Maybe, just maybe, stealing that rosary was an idea after all.

Six

It was 4:06 a.m. on the bedside clock when Mother Adelli's eyes flew open.

In her dream the old-fashioned brass key with its long shank and cloverleaf finger-grip was floating in the pupil of the new girl's left eye. But how to get it out? When she turned to Reverend Mother for guidance, the Superior, without looking up from her work, told her, "You had the key, Mother. Search your pockets." Astonished, she saw that her entire habit was pockets, some the size of a seed, some so deep her hand became lost. And one opened hugely to the dark magnetism of the universe and wanted to draw her out among the far stars to float there forever as a pinpoint of light. "No!" She'd pulled back and woken herself into predawn, sweating. Slowly her heart's gallop subsided and she dozed off. It was the triple *grande jetté* sequence from the first act of *Swan Lake,* and as she drew herself into Fourth Positon, a matter-of-fact voice observed that actually both Superiors cared more about other things than the new girl. At that her dreaming deposited her on the Granville Beach at Sheridan Road where the grey waves of Lake Michigan reared up to knock her down, to scrub her all over before she blinked her eyes open with the sudden knowing that no one was going to help her with the Rhenehan girl.

She threw back the bedclothes. But of course her Superior would counsel her; and Mother Crewelman most assuredly would guide her spiritually. She felt the price now of this high calling, and of what she forsook for it. And she would follow their instructions to the letter, no matter what!

She swung her legs to the floor. Contain the girl before she gained influence with her classmates or hurt someone, that was the clear necessity. She dressed, buttoned her wimple, hung her rosary at her belt. That father had started things off badly. But how long could anyone put up with unreasonable behavior? And what on earth could be the meaning of all those pockets?

As soon as she could arrange for an hour that afternoon, Mother Adelli headed for the nuns' porch to develop a plan of action. She sank into a tall-backed rattan style captain's chair. Below her, the trees of the ravines billowed red and gold.

"Who's there?" A rusty-edged voice.

At mid-afternoon, Mother Adelli had counted on the nuns' porch being deserted. She peered around her chair's back. Across the way, another face, very old, mirrored the same gesture. Both froze, squinting into the bright afternoon.

"Is it Mother Durban?" the other nun croaked.

Oh dear, it was talkative old Mother Concepciòn. "If you please, Mother, it's Mother Adelli."

"Oh, Mother Adelli! I must have dozed off in this nice hot sun. I guess our Novices have gone and forgotten me. I should have been making my adoration of our dear Lord in chapel now."

The elderly Religious struggled from her chair, She stood, barely five feet, perhaps eighty pounds, and swaying dangerously. "I seem to have misplaced my cane. Can we find my cane?" Her English carried the rich overtones of Catalan, the language of Barcelona. Mother Adelli recognized it from a teacher she'd had at Sheridan Road in the first academic.

The young nun searched chairs, side tables, along wrought iron railings. No cane. She blazed through the

Community Room unseating cushions, peering under furniture and behind drapes. No cane.

"Perhaps you would be so kind as to help me to my room then, Mother Adelli. I must have left my cane at lunch."

They made their way to the ancient elevator, Mother Concepciòn not being one to hurry. For the younger nun, the elevator ride took forever, then creeping along the corridor to the tiny room with its cot, dresser, rag rug and narrow window where Mother Adelli propped the older nun against her pillow, then fled to scour the dining room. There, she and *Soeur* Josephine discovered the cane deep under a table. Up the four flights again. Perhaps some time might yet remain for Mother Adelli's own needs.

"*Gracias!* Will you have a seat, Mother?" The old nun pointed a crooked finger to the wooden chair. Here was a young woman in trouble past her knee caps; but about what Mother Concepciòn had no idea.

"Thank you, no. My Fourth Academic monitor will need to get back to her own Study Hall." Mother Adelli remained respectfully at the door.

"But in Fourth Academic it is a great treat to forego your own Study Hall, no?"

How could the younger nun refuse one who had celebrated sixty-five years in the Order? But wasn't this the one judged by some to be unstable, keeping The Silence only when *she* chose, took The Rule (with its many rules) into her own hands, repeatedly flung before the Community some bone of contention to chew?

"And close that door, will you dear?" The old woman pulled her cane onto her lap. "You know," she confided, "I was a boarding student at *Sacre Coeur de Nice* before coming to the Order."

Ten minutes and she, Mother Adelli, would politely explain she must leave. Meanwhile, she laced her fingers in her lap.

"You were from a circus family, is that right?"

"Royalty." Mother Concepciòn threw her twiggy arms. "And I was 'The Little Princess of the Big Top.'"

She, Olivita Concepciòn, had grown up with camels, horses, and elephants. At five or six, father would lead her atop *Mi Chica*. The old elephant would be all banners and feathers. Father would tap the trunk, she sank to her knees; another tap, she would roll onto her side. Then, *voila*! All done up in a sequined tutu and sparkling crown, she, Olivita, in pink satin slippers would walk across the great grey belly to a rainstorm of applause as if walking the rim of a great boat. Father had taught her that by keeping her eyes fixed on the rim of the saddle she could stave off nausea and giddiness, so that finally, standing tall and with one foot anchored under a small strap, she would unfurl like magical waters silver ribbons from around her fingers; and the audience would go wild.

The younger nun noticed the old woman's eyes sparkle like a child's. A bell in the corridor. Mother Adelli fumbled in the little pocket under her cape for her watch. Mother Concepciòn hurried on.

It had been a fairy tale life until she was fourteen. Then her mother, worried about her girl's education, put her in *Sacre Coeur* in Orleans--a small select school. Despite discipline as a circus performer, nothing had prepared her for convent-school life. Up at six, no talking, no laughing or playing, long hours in chapel, long hours in Study Hall, freezing in the winter, sweltering in the summer. The food so plain you could cry.

"I missed my circus family, and the people calling out my name." The old nun looked through the window, remembering. Mother Adelli studied the aged skin in the painterly light: like rumpled silk.

"I was a ballet dancer," Mother Adelli offered, surprised. She had never spoken of it after entering the Novitiate.

"Oh?" Mother Concepción eyed the young woman keenly. "Then you know what I mean, about missing the people!"

"Our audiences loved what we did. It took them beyond themselves, I think," Mother Adelli laughed. "It was so strange to feel some powerful kind of spirit breathe through you to lift you above anything you were before. I found it frightening, to be honest; and sometimes felt disappointed by my ordinary self afterwards. Sometimes I think it was actually the good will of all those people that bore me up on stage."

"And you had to love them back." Mother Concepción nodded, peering into her own past. She raised an eyebrow. "But what about the naughty audiences who came late or never sat still, or who waited like vultures to see you make a fatal mistake?"

The night she had bronchitis and twice fell behind the music by a beat or two and heard the disgruntled rustling, and whispering; and then saw her brother Julian's mean smile. She shook the memory away. "But worse were the audiences with no response at all. Then it would be like dragging a dead horse down the street."

The old nun clapped. "Oh terrible. We understand one another." She grew serious. "I was forced to live in the Convent until I came to love it; but you walked away from a career to be here."

Mother Adelli shook her head. "I did not have a career in ballet. I gave up a scholarship to the New York School of Ballet."

"Oh!" the older woman's eyes opened wider. "On the brink of a career and gave it up!" She released a long breath of approval. "And your family, your parents?"

"Every Italian family wants at least one priest or nun, one opera singer or the equivalent, and one doctor--in that order." The two women laughed. "I was an equivalent. My parents and I worked hard on my career. So my vocation came as a shock."

Mother Concepciòn owned that the younger nun's dear family had made many sacrifices for her. Mother Adelli 's insides puckered, her smile turned wooden. "As a student at Nice, did you know you would enter the Order?" she redirected the conversation.

That first year, her brothers were killed in Amsterdam in a freak accident from a damaged rope. Her parents made the decision never again to risk their remaining child in circus performance, and so kept her in boarding school.

"I plotted for over a year to escape that school and carry on the routines my brothers had made famous."

"I'm so sorry," Mother Adelli whispered. Then her face hardened. Who ever thought of the children, of their sufferings, of the directions of their hearts? Certainly not grown-ups. Her own mother jamming toeshoes and a tutu into the rehearsal bag, in a rage about something--always something.

"But the day my brothers died turned out to be the most blessed day of my life," the older nun took up again; "though when Reverend Mother Crechette told me of the accident--Phillip's skull crushed, Henri's neck broken--the room tilted me onto the floor. When I came to, my only wish was to find again the blessed darkness and drown in it

"But those next four years, I was carefully led as if on a silver wire across an abyss. I saw my mother and father far below, remote and dear. And step by step Our Lord brought me away from my attachments. And to what place?" She thumped her mattress. "Why to Himself, of course! Do you see? My father died of grief and drink by the time I was eighteen and Mother gave our circus to a nephew and went back to Nyons, the small town of her birth; and this Order became my chosen home."

The whiskey sloshing the rim of the glass. Mother Adelli wondered if her father too, always in grief over his life, would die of drink. She, Mary Agnes, had also made the Order her home, more than willingly.

The old nun's eyes closed on the silence that settled between them. They opened again.

"Listen to me, Mother Adelli. Those very moments I thought I was losing everything, I was gaining everything. Our dear Lord has taught me never to trust in appearances, and that He works through them--through objects, people and situations--to give us the gifts we most desire. You can rely with your life on God's will for good, Mother. Do you remember last April, my upsets in the Community Room?"

The terrible screeches that made hearts stop. The puzzle pieces erupting as the old nun, arms over her head and with the sound of agony from her ricocheting from wall to window to door as she flung the puzzle into the air.

"I never understood--."

Mother Concepciòn's face reddened. She left her puzzles unfinished on purpose. But some self-appointed do-gooder, thinking she would help the dotty old nun by finishing her work, didn't understand that she was not working on a puzzle, but on a world.

"About a year ago, as I ran my fingertips over the edges of the puzzle pieces, images sprang into my mind and made stories. I saw things as a child does, played as a child plays. Think if you were able to look down on the coast of Spain, trace and explore every nook and cranny and, as your eye passed over or around some point, exotic vegetation and remarkable creatures sprang forth with story already underway--and you a part of it." So she would leave the puzzle "as is" at night for the story ready to continue. But in the morning, when she'd find it disturbed and know the life that had burgeoned there would never came back--well, the grief and rage simply exploded out of her. On the second episode, Mother Crewelman had hurried to Reverend Mother Gregory who wrote immediately to Omaha; but there was currently no room at the residence for retired Religious, nor was any anticipated soon.

Actually, everyone wanted old Mother Concepciòn to work on her puzzles; then she didn't wander into your classroom and "assist" you with the teaching; then she didn't forget The Silence and buttonhole you in the hall with longwinded suggestions concerning methods and lesson plans.

"The third time my rage erupted was just after you came. I was at my wit's end and took the matter to Our Lord. I knelt before the tabernacle and asked, 'What is it I am doing that I lose my self-control this way?'"

At first there was only the small creakings of the pews and damp smell of minerals from the stone walls. Then, like sunlight breaking, she felt His presence and in the same instant the Lord, His sacred heart on fire, rose both from the white skirts of the tabernacle and from within her own breast to stand elevated at the altar rail, garments feathering with no perceptible movement of air, skin glowing like ripe fruit; and in each extended palm a wound glistened. And His dark eyes were lively with the recognition of her so that she felt very young in her old body.

She fell into stunned adoration. Color streamed through the west windows of the transept and over the wooden pews. Chin upon her breast, eyes closed then, there came a deep quietude. But after some long time, the old emotional pain, like a dragon curled at the back of her mind, opened one eye.

"Day in, day out I set a watch at my door to be certain that no feeling, no thought nor desire draws my heart from You. Every branch is pruned, every wild shoot pinched back. I have searched my soul regarding these outbursts and find only my puzzles, and gather that I am being punished for the pleasure I allow myself in them?"

Silently, like a Divine Blossom riding the ethers while pews creaked and votive lights sputtered, He shook his head "No". But her ancient enemies of pride and impatience had already assembled.

"I ask if it is fair, after all these years," she cried out then, forgetting to Whom she spoke, "that I am made the convent clown, flinging things like a two year-old and then crawling on all fours to pick them up? Isn't the suffering of old age sufficient?"

But she heard her own voice, sharp and driven by a child's demand for explanations. Her hands flew to cover her face. "My Lord, forgive me!" It was some long minutes before their shaking stopped, and she raised wet eyes.

But the Apparition was gone. She had disrespected the very Giver of her life. He had departed. She bent until her forehead touched her knees and sobbed her grief; but even as she did, a faint sound like the shifting of rushes started in from the four corners of the chapel and grew until His presence surrounded her again.

"My bride," she heard Him tell her from her very bones, "You have given me all except for one thing you withhold, your self-control, a thing you yourself have made. And this is not yet surrender."

She pressed wrinkled fingertips against her lips. How could she have been so brazen as to challenge the Son of God? How prideful she, the creature, was; how foolish. From everywhere then came the smell of gardenias to soothe the tempestuous spirit she had worked these long years to conquer, and whose recurring vitality she could not understand. "You see, don't you, the investment you have in it, even at this moment?" His voice was all kindness.

The old nun groaned. Yes, yes--how she clung to her ideas as if they were the very pronouncements of God Himself.

"To achieve self-control," His voice continued, "is a great accomplishment. Few climb so near the summit as you have; but to achieve My control, you must release to Me your judgments, your decisions, the rules you have laid down for yourself, accepted from your confessor, your spiritual director and, yes, even the rules of the Order, if I so desire. Yes, even the commands of the Holy Father Himself. Anything else is rehearsal."

Now bewilderment sat in her face. "But Lord, doesn't the Order stand for You in my life," she asked; "and aren't the dictates of the Holy Father and of the Church Your will?"

"My movement within you is your only dictate; otherwise, how have you totally given yourself to Me? Good is always One, is always Me. And who knows your good better than I do, or desires it more? And who will shepherd you to it with greater speed, care and faithfulness?"

Then, even as she knelt, the old nun saw herself prostrate in the main aisle, a small black arrow aimed at the tabernacle, her affections flung open. She tried to raise her eyes, to whisper her assent, but a blazing light swallowed the tabernacle and altar, swallowed her so that an erotic thrill shot through her body, striking with a charge so fierce that she felt her heart burst into flame. At the same moment she saw the light resolve into the wounded Heart of her Beloved out of which a triple tongue of fire sprang and danced.

"See." The Voice tolled through her. "We are lighted by the same Fire. Now My Love is lighted forever in your heart. All, all is My will. You have nothing to decide. You have only to say yes."

She did not see the Light fade or know from whence came once more a perfume of gardenias so penetrating it seemed to pierce her very marrow.

"I awoke to myself in the corridor, just outside the elevator, trying to get to my cell." Her face was radiant again with the memory. "And I could still feel His gaze deep upon me, within me, so fond."

Mother Adelli's eyes shone as well. She took in the old nun there like a child against her bed pillow, her ancient face and body a vessel for the sacred memory.

ZOE KEITHLEY

But human beings without help are impossibly frail, Mother Concepciòn went on, and she hadn't gone ten steps when objections started up. Surely there were some things she must bring to her confessor; this apparition, for instance; for why would the Sacred Heart appear to someone insignificant as herself?

"Immediately that thought crossed my mind, I heard His voice within me again, solemn, commanding. 'All that is, is My will.' And with that, the last question I ever had about God's will dried up and blew away."

Mother Adelli sat open-mouthed. She had never before met anyone who had seen the Sacred Heart or even a saint, though she had heard such stories. Philippine Duchesne had appeared in St. Charles, Missouri as recently as 1927, at the convent she founded there in the 1800s near the Indian Territory. Rounding the end of a corridor and shining like the moon, the smiling apparition had frightened two Religious on their way to Compline out of their wits

Perhaps they had hallucinated, the doubt picked its way through Mother Adelli's mind; perhaps Mother Concepciòn had hallucinated. But didn't the path to which the Vision pointed repeat the experience of most saints and mystics? And to live in that Divine Presence the old nun had described, wasn't that the Heaven all burned to reach?

"I think someone has hurt you, Mother Adelli."

"Please?" Mother Adelli felt her breath hitch.

"Everyone thinks I don't see very well." The tiny pleated face bore down on her. "*Au contraire*, I see quite well indeed."

Mother Adelli slid to the edge of her chair. Why would Mother Concepciòn say such a thing? With all respect, apparitions were fine; but what she needed at this moment was someone to take that Rhenehan girl by the scruff and shake her until her rebellious will rattled onto the floor. It was an uncharitable thought she could not forgo. She gathered her skirts and stood, keeping her eyes to herself. She had stayed too long, waded in too far.

"What is it, Mother Adelli?" Mother Concepciòn sat forward. She studied the young nun.

"I'm worrying about my students. I have overstayed my time. I must leave now."

Perhaps it was the compassion that pooled in the old woman that explained why Mother Adelli agreed to sit again. Perhaps it was the affection that played around the ancient eyes that made the younger nun decide to lift the lid on the cache of her troubles.

"Have you told the Superior you cannot always control the girl?"

"No, Mother. Superior let me know she expected me to handle the situation myself. Mother Crewelman has--."

"One Superior at a time please." The old nun raised a finger. "Speak to Reverend Mother Gregory. Spare yourself nothing. Do what she instructs. Now, Mother Crewelman?"

"The new student burned me in effigy--a paper doll she drew. I couldn't bring myself to name names and lay on blame in front of all the boarders, as Mother Crewelman ordered." She twisted her fingers in her lap. "I felt it would humiliate me further and perhaps entrench the situation. And I couldn't, as she instructed me, use the word 'sacrilege' to them. That felt unfair, beyond them. So I've disobeyed my Superior twice." She dropped her eyes.

Old Mother Concepciòn chuckled. "In effigy, eh? That is quite a compliment. I have never done that well, though once in Study Hall I found a highly unskilled drawing of myself on the blackboard. I made each girl in the room do a portrait of me, for which I posed. And that was the end of it." Mother Adelli could not help but smile.

"Now, for our other Superior. Mother Crewelman is keen on the rules. Myself, I would counsel you to be a bit more relaxed. At most, the things you tell me seem smaller faults. Of course, we don't encourage faults; but perhaps you will find a way to say something more to these girls in upcoming days, if you feel it is needed."

Gratitude flooded Mother Adelli.

"I see three things about you, Mother Adelli. One, someone has hurt you deeply. Two, you are very afraid for some reason or reasons I don't know and perhaps you don't know either. And three, that you love Our Lord very much."

"Oh, I do, Mother." Mother Adelli's face shone then. "I want to do everything right, everything to please Him."

"Yes. Yes, you certainly do," Mother Concepciòn nodded deeply. "I don't know what your suffering is, but you can be assured of His Presence. That is why I told you my story. You can see I did not need to know how to come to Him; He provided the way. You do not need to know the way either. Do you understand?" she shifted forward on the bed and the cane clattered to the floor. The old nun slapped the mattress. "Good. Now they can add to their senility report:. Can't manage a cane."

From the corridor the bell repeated. My students, Mother Adelli thought in a panic. Mother Concepciòn shooed her along.

"Why not see if you can find the Superior right away. Then you will have a good night's sleep."

Down the corridor, down the stairs. The Order had a rule against the forming of particular friendships, yet she had found a particular friend in Mother Concepciòn. Together they had broken the Silence; and she had left her students for two hours. Well, but Mother Concepciòn had asked her to talk; and who was she to refuse to assist, and to be assisted?

The smell of chalk, paper and healthy bodies wafted from the Study Hall doors. Her students looked up. Mother Adelli! Where had she been?

Directly her girls were at dinner, the young nun climbed the stairs to her Superior's office. As it happened, the woman was just closing her door.

"May I have a word with you, Reverend Mother?"

"Of course. But I am late for my meal. Let's talk as we walk." The Superior started off, rustling her hands through her pockets.

"I feel I did not say everything the other night," Mother Adelli fell into step, trying to see around the Superior's wimple. "It's about the Rhenehan girl. The truth is I have difficulty controlling her, am worried that--."

The older woman halted in her tracks.

"Mother Adelli, I believe we are already clear on this issue. I do not want to hear about the Rhenehan girl again. It is *your* responsibility to handle her."

And so she lumbered off, leaving the younger nun beneath the looming ceiling, next to tall windows, the dark of night crowding the glass. She watched as the older woman rocked along like a freighter, the wooden floor beneath crying out its complaints.

Grading essay exams in Study Hall after dinner, Mother Adelli felt her mother's hand grip her chin to apply the lipstick. Lately, unwelcome memories erupted into her day, shoving her nose into some awful thing. She circled a sentence for the commas-in-a-series rule. She would manage these months until the girl was gone. In June she would go to Rome, take Final Vows and fulfill the dream for which she had worked so hard. She would make her parents proud and satisfied. She scanned the desks. Always there was the ridiculous hope that the girl would not be there. But no, there she was, slouched on the end of her spine, staring at the ceiling and tapping a front incisor.

"Miss Rhenehan," Mother Adelli spoke sharply, "sit up and give your attention to your work."

Seven

It was October 4th, the Monday following the runaway episode. That left nineteen weeks until March 1st and the father's return. From her desk platform, Mother Adelli let her eyes drift over her girls with their feet in antic postures, bent to their studies before dinner. In a moment she would say, "Straighten up those feet, young ladies." In a moment. She picked up her marking pencil.

"I need to go to the bathroom."

Heads bobbed up like corks. Everyone knew you didn't call out in Study Hall. You came to the desk. You spoke in a whisper.

Mother Adelli knew who it was, of course, continued her paper work. Finally she glanced up to Helene's uniform jacket buttoned wrong and the girl's pan-shaped face all squeezed together where she clung to her desk. Whatever the issue was, it already was too late to disengage the girl. She could feel it.

"You'll be next, Helene. Sit down until then, please."

"No. I need to go *now*." Helene crossed her legs and began bouncing so that the floor under her desk creaked rhythmically.

The Study Hall prickled with excitement.

"You'll have to wait until the pass returns." Mother Adelli scanned the room. GeeGee was out.

"Pleeeze." Helene gyrated, shoes squealing against the floor. "I *have* to."

"You know the rule." Mother Adelli's hand made a lowering motion. "Sit down and wait."

Helene corkscrewed her body; stitched her face tighter. "But I *can't. I'm gonna wet my pants.*"

A gasp from the room, then a wave of tittering and outright laughs.

Stunned, Mother Adelli drew out her clapper. She would not have indecent talk in her Study Hall!

Klat. Klat.

"We keep private matters to ourselves, *mademoiselle*." This was bait. Refuse it. Stay casual. "Tell yourself you're in a movie; it hasn't finished yet and it's no trouble waiting."

A satisfied rustle came from the desks. That smart Mother Adelli.

"I'm not kidding, Mutherrr. I'm going to wet all over myself and on the floor, too--any minute! I've *reeeally* got to go."

"You are disturbing the Study Hall." Mother Adelli made another downward gesture, turned to her work.

"It'll be your fault, then. *Ooooo.*" Helene squeezed her eyes tight and twisted back and forth.

The Mistress of the Third *Cours* marked another run-on. But what if the girl had diarrhea or--oh dear--was starting her period? She herself had begun menstruation at eleven. A loud bumping sound, but Mother Adelli, eyes on the page of homework, ignored it.

Helene lay on her side between the desks, knees drawn toward her chest. "I'm gonna go-o-o, I'm gonna go-o-o," she moaned.

The Third *Cours* gawked, held their breath in gleeful horror and strained, looking for a yellow puddle.

"Miss Rhenehan's problem is none of your concern, ladies," Mother Adelli told them. "If she wants to lie there until the pass comes back, it doesn't interfere with your lives. Everyone has homework. Be about it."

Helene groaned. Her shoes clattered against the floor and the legs of the desks. Someone laughed again.

Mother Adelli responded with two raps of the clapper. "That will do. I will not hear another laugh in this Study

Hall. To your work this minute, unless everyone wishes to lose her '*trés bien*.'"

Covers flipped, pages flapped, pencils began to scratch; but the Study Hall remained galvanized. Two girls at the back stood to see more clearly. Mother Adelli slammed a palm on her desk. The girls shrank into their seats. "Sorry, Mother," they said.

"It seems the whole Study Hall wants '*bien*' or worse this week," Mother Adelli cried out, her face gone pale.

Helene scrambled up. Legs held wide apart, she danced her way to the front of the room.

"Oooo. I told you Mother, I can't wait. It's an *emergency*." She spread her legs further. A trickle of urine glistened to her sock. "Seee?" she whined. Another string of light-catching beads followed. "I need to *GO!*"

There was a shocked silence. Mother Adelli sprang from her chair, knocked it back against the wall.

"How dare you," she shouted at the girl. "How dare you do such a filthy thing? Just stand there and be wet then."

"No," Helene danced to the door and laid her hand on the knob. "I can't hold it. I need to go *now*."

"You will wait in your seat for the pass. Or, since you're wet--" a ripple of laughter eddied from desks at the back, "stand where you are. And," she turned on the roomful of gapers, "anyone who laughs is just as much in the wrong."

Helene was in the corridor before Mother Adelli finished her sentence. The Third *Cours* sucked breath while GeeGee, just returning, dodged aside to avoid collision with Helene, and then gaped over her shoulder.

They heard the steps in the corridor, on the tile floor of the lavatory, heard the tearing of paper and, nearly without a pause, the flush of the toilet; the steps coming back. Helene strode to her desk, plopped down and ruffled through her arithmetic book with a long sniff.

Mother Adelli heard the snickers. Her body shook with rage.

"Come up here, Miss Rhehehan," she said in a voice full of razor blades.

The girl lounged in her chair to farm approval from her peers. Most didn't know what they thought. It was sort of fun to see the rules upended, but why rile Mother Adelli? Mother Adelli was all right. And they had homework to do.

"I said to come up here, Miss Rhenehan. That means *now*." Mother Adelli stood, repulsed by the willful hair, the football player body, the flat face covered with freckles. She watched Helene shuffle to her feet. "*Vite*," she barked, choking on venom; "you have enough French to know what that means." But the girl sauntered, perusing her classmates on the way. Tittering took up. Mother Adelli seethed.

"You can't move quickly, is that it Miss Rhenehan?" she stepped from the platform. "You're old? You need help? I guess someone who wets herself does need help." At this remark there was an outright guffaw. Mother Adlelli whirled on the Study Hall. "All right," she cried, "that's a '*bien*' at *Primes* for everyone."

While her charges looked on in stunned silence, Mother Adelli steamed down the narrow aisle toward Helene, skirts foaming, face black. "I said 'quickly.'" She grabbed the girl's wrist, jerking her toward the front of the room. Caught off guard, Helene stumbled to her knees. Fear registered in her face for a moment before she climbed up and then made dragging sounds with her shoes as Mother Adelli, pulse pounding in her throat, pulled the girl to the blackboard. "You will apologize to me and to this Study Hall here and now."

"You pulled me," Helene jerked away. "It's against the *Nolo* rule. You broke the *Nolo* rule."

"I have never seen an act of such filth as the one you have committed here. You are to apologize immediately."

"What act?"

"You know very well. Wetting like a two year-old."

"Because you wouldn't let me go to the bathroom. I said it was an emergency."

"Then why didn't you do anything in there? You flushed the toilet right away. You didn't have time to-- sneeze."

Some students laughed outright at this and Mother Adelli whirled around. "All right. Everyone in this Study Hall has *'assez bien'* for this week."

The Third *Cours* gasped, glared, curdled. For a laugh? They weren't the one acting up. Why didn't Mother Adelli send Helene to Reverend Mother if Helene wouldn't behave?

Mother Adelli turned her face back to the girl. "I'm waiting."

Helene shrugged.

"A shrug is not an answer."

"I forgot the question."

A snicker came from a front desk. Mother Adelli stared stonily over her student body. How ridiculous she must look, shouting at a ten year-old girl, pointing from on high to issue punishments.

"You owe an apology to me and to these students," she repeated, nonetheless.

The girl looked from face to face. She saw the hunger to know what would happen next. What could Dilly do to her, anyway? The first report would not go out until nearly Thanksgiving and her father wouldn't get it until Christmas. She would see him then and fix everything. But wait, she didn't want Reverend Mother Gregory to write or call him. She tapped her thumbs against her thighs and looked at the ceiling.

"Okay," she shrugged.

"Okay what?"

"Okay, I apologize." She couldn't suppress the grin.

"Until you can be sincere, you can just stand there," Mother Adelli spat, "even if it takes all night." She returned to her desk and took up her marking pencil.

Helene rolled her head, shrugged her shoulders, crossed and uncrossed her legs and catalogued the furtive glances of her classmates until Mother Adelli ordered her to stand still. Finally the bell rang for dinner. There was the rustling of papers, the shuffling of feet.

"Just one moment." Mother Adelli held up her hand. "Someone still owes us an apology."

The last thing Helene wanted now was to be left standing alone in Study Hall while everyone else ate dinner.

"Okay, I apologize," she said.

"Apologize for what?" Mother Adelli kept her hand poised.

"For--," she looked at the ceiling and shrugged, "disturbing Study Hall."

"Is this an action you plan to repeat?"

"No."

"No what?"

"No, Mother Adelli."

Mother Adelli gestured for the others to line up, but held her palm outward in Helene's direction. As the last student left the room, she nodded sideways toward the door; unable to bring herself to look at the girl.

"You will clean up what you did in the bathroom first." She bristled as Helene ambled past. And where at this hour might Big John be found to clean up the Study Hall?

At dinner, Mother Johnson was happy to supervise the Third *Cours* along with her own students, although Mother Adelli saw her stiffen when Helene came through the door.

First, to the furnace room to find Big John; next, outdoors to clear the dreadful dark feelings from her heart.

She climbed the three steps from the Minims' door and took in with deep breaths the crisp air of evening just coming on. Rounding the front of the building, she passed the pines turning black in the faltering light and heard the twitter of small brown wrens tucked deep within their boughs.

She had felt hatred--a sin--and had broken *Nolo mi tangere* by dragging Helene to the front of the room with everyone's eyes upon her. And she had shouted--*SHOUTED*--at the whole Study Hall! When her own mother had shouted, thrown things, it had made her, Mary Agnes, want to get away from her.

Well, she scourged herself, how was her Third *Cours* feeling about having Mother Adelli for their Mistress now?

Walk. Try. The air cooled her face, and the brittle grass made comforting sounds underfoot. Daylight faded, the temperature faltered. She headed along the side of the chapel, let her eyes travel the darkened windows with their blurred and muted colors.

'Pagan' had been Mother Crewelman's word for the girl. The Mistress General's intelligence, unlike her own, never ambushed by feelings, went straight to the point. When the Romans persecuted the early Christians and desecrated holy objects, or when churches in France were bombed, or priests and nuns tortured by the Japanese in the war just ended, such acts came out of a blindness that was palpable. But Catholic Spain ravished the Indians here in America; and Irish and French Catholics in the United States bought and sold Africans. And perhaps she too, like them, had become pagan now.

A cold breeze thumbed through the grass. She rounded the east side of the building. On her right was the ravine with its watery voice and silent sentinels of trees. She tightened her shawl and buried her fingers in the warmth of her armpits. An owl hooted so near her head that she spun to scan the branches overhead before she moved on.

Weren't the atrocities of the Nazis a kind of terrible mass blindness? And doesn't blindness describe the way the Rhenehan girl acts, not seeing that she is way over here, while everyone else is over there? And wasn't she, Mary Agnes Adelli, pagan herself when she dragged Helene to the front of the room? Wasn't desecrating children more of a sacrilege than desecrating a habit? What was Helene's 'faith,' except what she can see and that moves her in her life? And isn't the one who is blind a victim as well of that blindness?

But wouldn't blindness by its nature preclude morality? A cold gust prickled through her shawl; she bundled more tightly. Then, could it be right to enforce regulations and morality beyond another's ability to understand? What about the laws of the Church or even the Ten Commandments? Was it right to enforce them on those who didn't agree with them? And what about solemn vows to obey those laws and see that those in one's charge obeyed them? The owl called again, far away now, deep in the ravines.

If she were truly so convinced, wouldn't she have to walk away from the Order rather than force obedience upon someone who didn't understand or couldn't agree? She saw the vessel of her upbringing founder in this squall. And to what shore could she swim? In a first floor window, a silhouette of Reverend Mother Gregory drew down a shade. No. Outlandish thoughts. Shake them off. The Devil had her chasing her own tail. Tomorrow she would find Mother Concepciòn and get herself straightened out.

She passed the white stone statue of the Sacred Heart on the front lawn. They felt betrayed, her girls. Angry. Of course they would get over it. Still--. This world was dark and heavy with blindness. And she felt it in herself, having punished her girls too severely. But how could she rescind without weakening her position with Helene? She moved toward the Minims' Door. If it was true that all are blind, then who could save or be saved? No, no. That road led to despair.

She grasped the icy cold door handle. Blindness could not value what it could not see. Helene could see no value but her father, and so was blind to any efforts to reach her. So she, Mary Agnes Adelli, must let the hope of that go.

She had secretly prayed that her girls would do her work for her, would turn against the new girl, or exercise moral authority over her. No more. If there was to be any chance of containing the disruptive behavior, she, the Mistress, must become something she had never wanted to be, an ungiving edge.

Talk of the '*assez biens*' foamed over in the dining hall. For most of the Third *Cours*, working for a ribbon or being under certain agreements with their parents, such a demerit was a bad blow. And not one felt it fair.

Sylvia turned to scald Helene. "Did you take your crazy pills again? You got us all in trouble. Thanks a lot." But Helene heard a thread of admiration in the voice, and smirked back, "Any time." Deborah, in an agony of jealousy, sat as far from the nutty new girl as possible; and kept her mouth filled with macaroni and cheese.

When, after twenty-four hours, Mother Adelli tried to jolly them back, her students counted their losses. But still no one would receive a ribbon next *Primes*. And there would be the parental lectures, looks and silences. Some would forfeit allowance, weekend privileges, special trips, parties or purchases. Their Mother Adelli had been acting funny for quite a while now. They didn't know if they wanted to trust her anymore.

A week later and far into the night, Mother Adelli, waking from a deep sleep thought there was a chattering sound, the squeak of a floorboard, a brush against the bedclothes and saw, through real or dream lashes, a figure angle through her alcove curtains. She sprang from bed, heart in triple time, to prowl her domain with a flashlight, but found nothing except two canker sores blooming at the base of her tongue. When she woke again at five a.m. to dress for Hours, she fumbled at her chair's spool for her rosary. It was gone.

Well, she might as well have stood naked in Study Hall that October 10th, or hung Christmas lights in the vacant folds of her habit skirt. One of her Community would certainly notice. She also saw the impossibility of letting the issue go, and that she, Mary Agnes Adelli, was cornered.

"We will begin classes late." She stood at her desk after breakfast. "I have an announcement, but first I expect to see everyone's hands folded on her desk." Helene jammed hers under her rump. Mother Adelli barked at her to put them up and the Third *Cours* grew wary. Mother Adelli was in a really bad mood again.

"Everyone in this Study Hall has an '*assez bien*' for another week," she announced, eyes red-rimmed and unfriendly. What, *again*, the Third *Cours* wanted to bellow. Mother Adelli had more.

There would be no after-school hockey, cricket or dodge ball; no ravines, no pillow fights, no *Goûter* (at this, a collective gasp), no candy purchases, no snacks from home. Mouths dropped open. She wasn't finished. There would be no library for pleasure, no phonograph, no visiting in dormitory. She paused.

"In addition, our statue of *Mater* is removed to my office until this Third *Cours* is worthy of her--until the rosary taken from my alcove last night is returned."

She didn't say how alone she felt, how violated and disillusioned. Now the canker sores throbbed whether she spoke or not. The only sounds to be heard in Study Hall were the creak of wood and clank of the radiators.

If they had any doubts before about their nun changing from nice to mean, now the Third *Cours* was certain as they hunkered down at their desks. That new girl must have fallen for Deborah's idiot challenge; and she, or whoever it was, had better put that rosary back--and fast!

They were of two minds. They didn't want punishment for a crime not theirs, but they greatly admired the exploit. Secretly everyone was dying to hear the details and where the plunder was stashed.

Deborah, sitting just to Helene's right, formed "Let me see it if you have it" from behind her hand. Filled with admiration for the girl's nerve, she didn't care anymore that Helene had taken her place as the worst headache in the Third *Cours*.

"I need help tonight," Helene whispered behind her hand; "are you in?"

Deborah, eyes huge, nodded.

Big John O'Reilly, the school's handyman and caretaker, during his early morning rounds found the near life-size Jesus facing the foot of the staircase on the second floor. Two fingers of one hand were raised in blessing. Between them hung Mother Adelli's rosary.

"Can you see whose beads these are, Muther," he held them out in the corridor after students' breakfast. "Must'uv took three of 'em to move it. Miracle they dinna' break it, though bein' hollow it ain't so heavy. But all the way from the other end of the third floor?" He shook his head and whistled. "They'd a dropt it, someone likely got a nasty cut or broke a toe. A shameful thing, this bein' Our Lord and all." He tipped his cap.

Mother Adelli reeled. Her girls had left the dormitory undetected during the night. Two religious objects were treated with disrespect; student safety and school property were compromised. She must report this now. But Reverend Mother Gregory did not want behavior problems brought to her. Mother Crewelman. she knew, would simply counsel her to pile on the punishments until the abuses stopped. Well, that was something she could do without counsel.

No one would identify the culprits, so, for irreverence to the rosary, she docked both teams all the points they'd earned since the beginning of school. For disrespect to the statue of the Sacred Heart, she revoked the privilege of speaking at meals. For leaving dormitory without permission, she extended all other punishments three weeks. "--or longer, if this behavior continues." If she must, no *would*, use her students as a battering ram against the small band of rebels and their clever leader.

Well, now the Third *Cours* was finished with Mother Adelli for good! She had turned out to be just like the others after all. They had counted on her to be fair, but she wasn't. And something else felt wrong, too. She forced them into a war they never wanted, and made them the enemy when they were on her side. Well, she could have her war, but she wouldn't be getting any help from them!

II.

Chapter of Grace

"Get thee up
and eat and drink,
for there is a
sound of
abundance of rain."

1 Kings KJV

One

Fragments of memory increasingly hold Mother Adelli captive. Waiting with her girls for chapel, Act Three of *Swan Lake* blooms suddenly and Michael lifts her into a *grand jete*. Setting her down, his hands whisper along the sides of her breasts, igniting a flame.

Her students notice Mother Adelli's face redden at times, her eyes slide into a shocked half-closed look, as if she had caught her hand in a drawer. They shrug. Who knew about her these days. And who cared?

Darning boarders' socks before bed, she is sixteen and in the yard next to the driveway with her brother's friend, Kern. Teaching her the baseball bat, he covers her hands with his. As the bat swings back, it strikes a hornet's nest plastered to a low branch, and the nest drops like a live bomb into the marigold bed. She and Kern dive for the rear seat of her father's Dodge. The mustard-colored hornets throw themselves against the glass while the two sweat and joke, watching the long vibrating stingers knock on the windows. Kern unbuttons his shirt, fans his chest. She hikes her skirt a little. Then, with an apologetic grin, Ken pushes her back and covers her mouth with his. His tongue is hot and probing; his hand finds its way under her skirt to her panties where his fingers fumble at the crotch and then breach it. In one dizzying moment, she slips like butter towards some delicious and dangerous edge.

Immediately, Sister Emerine's voice from seventh grade splits her mind like a fire alarm, screaming "Mortal sin! Mortal sin!" Frantic, she wriggles from beneath him, scrambles out the car door and into the thick and blistering summer air--but too late, for beneath the guilt she has tasted the pleasure. The wasps sting her all the way to the house.

Unexpectedly, coming and going, a longing for dance torments her. She loses the chapel, the priest, her Community and students to drown in the old sets, in the orchestra's lush sounds, in the alert and seductive quiet of the audience and an energy in her body, have it or not, that would bloom with flowers, wave with grasses, fly with birds, creep and leap with animals.

At night vivid dreams leave her exhausted. And because the magic for which the Mistress of the Third *Cours* was renowned has disappeared, the Third *Cours* withholds. They pass in minimal work, sigh, roll their eyes and constantly must be told to sit up straight.

Bound now by silence at meals, her students chew and study eyebrows, hairlines, nose shapes and emerging pimples. Twice a day, in two lines, they traverse the Convent grounds, glum beneath autumn's red and gold, honking with early colds while overhead cross-bows of geese aim at Dixie. In Study Hall, they fantasize the plainest *Goûter* of graham crackers, and each longs to be playing her hitherto most hated position on the hockey field. On the one hand they glower at "Adelli Svengali," and on the other shut out with looks of murder the small group of perpetrators while Helene and friends, feeling daring and brilliant, concoct more mischief.

Weekends students go home now whenever they can, and return at the last possible minute.

"Mother Adelli isn't any fun anymore," GeeGee tells her parents at the breakfast table that next Sunday morning.

"Hmm?" Her father shakes the *Tribune* out without raising his eyes.

"Was she fun before, dear?" Her mother slides grape jelly from the silver spoon onto a small plate. "I like it when you have fun." She gazes fondly at her daughter. "I had barrels of it when I was growing up."

"She was my favorite nun, but now we don't get to do anything good in class like we used to. We just fill out mimeographs or answer questions at the ends of chapters, or diagram sentences from our Grammar."

"Sounds like when I was in school. Served me to make a pretty good living," her father harrumphs from behind his glasses, then scans the expensive dining room appointments before he goes back to his reading.

"Oh, none of us ever paid any attention to the classes. It was the other times we had fun. Mrs. Murphy squeezed that orange juice fresh for you, Pet. You'll hurt her feelings if you don't drink it. She wants to see more growing on you."

"We used to take sides and debate about the tea tax-- you know, in Boston Harbor? Or we listened to Judith Anderson be Lady Macbeth."

"*Macbeth*? Isn't that a little old for girls, Harry?"

"Every week we'd have a spell-down. Mother Adelli would open the dictionary, close her eyes and point. Then you'd have to spell that word. And I won twice."

"Well, gooooood. Thank you, Mrs. Murphy." Her mother takes the platter. "Eggs, Harry?"

"And we'd read the editorials in the *Tribune* and write them over again, only saying what *we* thought."

"What *you* thought?" The father lowers the paper. "*Tribune* editorials?"

"But now we just sit like lumps and nobody wants to do anything because Mother Adelli is so mean. She even broke *Nolo mi tangere* and dragged the new girl."

"I'm sure she knows what she is doing, dear. She's your teacher. Are the eggs too runny, Harry? Coffee, then?"

It was Madeline who asked Mother Adelli in a whisper at the beginning of the third week how they could get things back the way they were.

"You can start by acting like sensible students," she snapped at her who had no blemish on her record. "I see the passed notes, the messy lines, the tricks." She gave several raps with her clapper. "Everyone, come and sit here on the floor."

They shuffled out in bathrobes and slippers. Now what? They sat in the midst of a current of air that played around their anklebones with icy fingers and made them stretch their bathrobes over their feet. Mother Adelli towered above with her curdled face.

"You didn't steal the rosary, move the statue or leave the dormitory without permission; but you whisper as soon as you see my head turned, you distract one another in chapel and Study Hall, you pass notes in the dormitory. I see it all--and hear from your teachers about the poor work you do. I hoped you might think how disappointing such conduct and attitudes are from you who are so privileged. I hope you will pray over these matters before confession, and ask *Mater* to guide you to a better path. Each of you knows what is right, but until I see you act on it, things will remain the same--or grow worse." Her eyes flashed. "If that's what you want. Ten minutes to lights out."

She felt so far from them now, could see only unkempt and wily youngsters who were not to be trusted. Helene smirked continually, and when she, Mother Adelli, was near the girl, there gathered within a tar-like feeling she recognized as hatred, and that covered everything so that nothing could breathe. She began to hear the voices of Reverend Mother Gregory and Mother Crewelman take over in her own voice, and this now gave her a grim anchoring and satisfaction. Perhaps this was the maturing in her the Superiors were looking for.

On Tuesdays she went to confession. These days, the required spiritual practice had become two iron blocks on her back, for she must protect herself from the threat of her own conscience as well as from penances she might feel unable to perform. She would lean at the window in the dark box, breathe the sluggish air trapped in the heavy drape and study through the latticed screen the darkened silhouette of Father Ambrose's long head and low-set ears.

"Bless me Father, for I have sinned."

How she wished she could just blurt it all out:. The hatred toward a student, the punishing of all to control one, the not knowing what else to do, her own teaching become mechanical and herself short-tempered all the time and with a desire for the approval of her Superiors overriding everything, the rationalizing of responsibility because she feared to do what duty required. And because she felt she could bear no more correction, tormented by the fear she would not, finally, be found qualified for Final Vows. Now everyday she sinned against the Order and God, and trembled to think of the punishment she ought to incur.

But in the confessional, she cloaked herself in blanket accusations of uncharitable feelings, laxity toward her Superiors, impatience with her students, each time fearing the priest's command that under pain of mortal sin she do what she found beyond her moral courage to correct these sins; and neglecting to do so, must present those same failures to this same priest again the next week. Then she would hold her breath until the priest gave the penance of a rosary or the Stations of the Cross, and she bore away within her the charge of tainting this holy Sacrament from which she should draw clarity and peace.

"I can't pray, Mother," she whispered in a hurry one evening and against the Rule of Silence to Mother Concepciòn as the Community Social Hour ended.

"So?" Mother Concepciòn nodded fondly.

"I . . .-I'm having difficulties with my students not getting along."

"A lean year," the old nun agreed.

"I count on my spiritual life to uphold me, but I am so dry." She dared not share that the Sacred Host, the very presence of her Beloved Lord, had come to feel like cardboard on her tongue. "And my meditation, Compline, adoration of the Blessed Sacrament, and even the writings of John or the Little Flower do not reach me."

"A lean year indeed," the old nun nodded as she took in the deteriorating face. She had been right to share her story with this young woman, but she hesitated to go further. "I suggest you speak to your Spiritual Advisor, Mother." She saw the fear flare in the young woman's eyes. "Remember, Mother, God is in everything. You can trust Him with your life."

Mother Adelli turned away. But she could not trust God. She could not even find Him.

Then the duck arrived.

The wooden crate, delivered on October 29th from Saks Fifth Avenue in New York, was covered with orange and black stickers that read, "Have a ducky Halloween at Saks!" Through the wood and chicken wire, Mother Ling ("Mother Mail Room") spied the tiny corpse amongst the floor straws and her heart sickened. Who would send a baby duck all the way from New York and expect it to survive? But then the fuzzy ball opened a black bead of an eye and she leapt to find water and inform Mother Adelli there was a package for the Rhenehan girl. The grandmother wrote a letter every three weeks. The father sent postcards of crumbling architecture or narrow medieval streets with a message in tiny medical-type script; but the Rhenehan girl had never gotten a package before.

It was just after lunch. Students were at their desks preparing for the afternoon. Mother Adelli stood at the Study Hall door and signaled Helene. She hoped the doctor-father had not sent something inappropriate.

In the post office, Helene turned the gift card that read, "Here's a friend to keep you company. Love, Nana." The duckling rustled about while the two nuns, one girl and three banks of partially filled letterboxes gaped at the crate on the sorting table. Helene let the card fall. Nana was always doing something nutty. What was she supposed to do with a duck? But the sight of the small creature staggering to its feet touched something in her.

She bent to look through slats and chicken wire. The duckling's body was round, feathery and lemon-colored. Two immature fan-like wings flailed at its sides. Wobbling on black stems, it plunged an orange bill into the straw and shoveled it over its head. Some straws stuck to its narrow face while it fixed a bright eye upon Helene who forgot for the moment where she was and who she was and laughed outloud. Poking a finger through the wire, she felt the blunt peck in return and laughed again. This duck was funny!

Mother Adelli was beside herself. Families often sent inappropriate things--party dresses, bubble bath, radios and certain magazines--but never a duck! Now she must take the gift away and bear the brunt of the girl's reprisals.

"Your father doesn't know the No Pets rule?"

Helene's face darkened. "It's from Nana." She crossed her arms over her chest.

"It must go back at once." Mother Adelli stiffened, ready for a fight.

"At my other school we kept a hamster in the classroom. We can't do anything in this jail." The girl's lower lip pushed out, she kicked at the leg of the sorting table. Mother Ling's narrow eyes widened, but she said nothing. This was Mother Adelli's student.

"The rule is clear about pets, Helene. We don't kick furniture here, and watch your language please." A battle with this girl was the last thing Mother Adelli wanted today.

"It's so small," Mother Ling blinked. "I don't know how it survived the trip in the first place." She backed away. She had read of certain diseases ducks carried. Still, she didn't want the little creature to die.

"I wish she hadn't sent it," Helene barked at the bank of mail slots. "She never sends me anything I can use."

The little animal, excited by the voices, wobbled about knocking at the chicken wire with its beak, falling over and paddling back to its feet.

"There's nothing to decide," Mother Adelli concluded; "it goes back."

Even if it weren't against the No Pets rule, the timing was wrong with the Third *Cours* under punishment. And Mother Crewelman would be in a rage if such a student as Helene were rewarded in any way, much less with a pet. And didn't she, Mother Adelli, agree? What kind of message would it deliver to the others, as well as to this girl, the sight of whom she could barely stand?

Through the cage wire, Helene wiggled a tentative finger toward the duckling. Mother Adelli relaxed. What harm was there in letting her have a minute before they had to take the pet away? The little duck took two wobbly steps toward the girl and then, as if distracted, stopped to dig in the straw with its bill. It was while the three of them watched it forage that Mother Adelli noticed the softness around the girl's eyes.

"See if that's something to eat," she cocked her head toward the small burlap sack wired to the side of the cage. The bit of cardboard read, "This is my favorite food. When I've eaten it up, you can get more at any grocery store."

Through the material, Helene felt the rolling of pebbly somethings. She undid the string and dug out half a dozen kernels of corn. The duckling waddled toward her, stretching its neck, its beak open. She poured the corn into a pile and watched as the little ball of yellow fluff gobbled it up. She reached into the bag for more.

Never had Mother Adelli seen this girl so focused on something outside herself, or so composed! A sour smell slipped onto the air.

"I can't have this animal in here, Mother Adelli," Mother Ling broke in, wringing her fingers. She backed further away, her eyes glued to something wet and army-green on the straw. "I can't have anything around the students' mail, the Community's mail, Mother. It's not . . . clean." She began to scrutinize the room for mite-infested bits of fluff in the air or on the floor.

"Don't give it too much, Helene," Mother Adelli heard herself tell the girl. "We don't want to make it sick." She joined Helene at the cage. "I'll send Big John to move the duck to the furnace room." She turned to Mother Ling. "It's warm there and out of the way. This crate is too small. We'll ask him to make a larger one."

Thus in one surprise move, Mother Adelli stepped over the No Pets rule and onto an unmarked path. Something in her intended that the duck should stay to help the girl, would have it no other way and cared nothing for the trouble the decision would surely bring. This was not the old Mother Adelli; neither was it the martinet of past weeks. This was a third Mother Adelli who asked no one's permission for what clearly seemed the right thing to do.

Mother Ling swallowed, batted her eyes and nodded. She raised a finger. "I'll just throw this mail sack over the cage for the time being--to make the little creature comfortable." With a delicate gesture, she plucked a musty mail sack from under the table.

"Yes, better let your duck sleep now, Helene," Mother Adelli agreed. She had noticed the little legs tremble beneath the ball of its belly.

Helene let her eyes come to rest for the smallest moment on Mother Adelli's chin. Then she nodded and tapped at the chicken wire with her finger; and Mother

Adelli watched the girl shuffle back to Study Hall in a body strangely at peace.

She helped Mother Ling with the covering and saw the duckling look up into the sudden shadow, walk a few paces, collapse its legs, dig a hollow in the straw with its rump and close its eyes.

"Oh. Oh dear." Mother Adelli's hands flew to her face. Her students were waiting unattended in Study Hall to be dismissed to their classes.

Day Students would know by lunch the next day, Tuesday, and carry the story home, she thought later as her boarders lined up for *Goûter*. Any time now, a call might come to her Superior from a fastidious mother or grandmother. But perhaps the animal would rouse no interest. Didn't most students have pets at home? But how long could it be before Reverend Mother Gregory or Mother Crewelman summoned her for a conference? Oh, let it not be until healing has taken hold, she prayed. Then, surely a Day Student or friend of the Order would take the duckling until the father's return. Helene could visit on weekends. But for now, Big John had better find a local farm, just in case.

Well, the fuzzy yellow performer ate everything from scrambled eggs to crayons, strutted and soft-shoed, fanned its tiny wings with its silky chest out full sail and shoveled straw at its visitors or onto itself until its audience collapsed in the hilarity of it all.

The Third *Cours* loved to watch the duck drink. The orange wedge with its two pinholes for nostrils would dip into the white ceramic dish and create a luminous bull's eye that sent silver ripples to its edge. Then the beak would swing up in a long arc far above the tiny shoulder and let water fly.

It took them two days to find a name. "Oooo, Popcorrrnnn," the girls would scream and wipe their hair and faces. Then the duck would race on stems narrow as pipe cleaners around its arena, head thrown back and making clipped sounds meant to be quacks, only to stop abruptly and cock its black bead of an eye on its admiring audience and begin the cycle again.

"Watch out, Mother Adelli," the Third *Cours* called to their Mistress. "Popcorn might give you a shower, too."

Within forty-eight hours, Mother Adelli saw the wall erected by her students dissolve in the aura of this one small duck. She canceled the worst of the punishments and returned *Mater* to the classroom.

As for Helene, the tricks simply stopped. Once, on an impulse during an after-dinner visit, she plopped Popcorn into Mother Adelli's hands. The duck feet, bending like thick leaves, pressed coolly against her palms and the beak went ratatattat on her fingernails. The Third *Cours* whooped. "Don't take away his '*trés bien*,' Mother; Popcorn just thinks you're *Goûter*." They rolled with the humor of it. Popcorn erupted into a mad rattling of wings. "Oh dear." Mother Adelli froze amidst her students' merriment, afraid the little creature might pitch off her open palm.

"I'll take him, Mother." With sure fingers Helene plucked the duck under its belly and returned it, black feet paddling the air, to its cage.

"Did Popcorn scare you, Mother?" Helene looked squarely at Mother Adelli, her robin's-egg blue eyes lighted with a friendliness that made the nun's breath catch.

"I . . . he--," Mother Adelli colored and laughed. "He did, Helene; he did scare me. I was afraid he might fall off. It's a good thing you know how to handle him." Then, standing on the concrete floor under the old pipes with the Best Made boiler throbbing behind them, she had to fight back the tears of something past joy so as not to shatter the moment between them. They watched as the duck rumbaed its round bottom into the straw and the black beads of its eyes disappeared into its face for the night.

Falling asleep, Helene hugged to herself images of Christmas with Dad and Popcorn in Rome. She shared her pet, raised her hand in class and passed in homework. And

127

she no longer cared to call the Mistress of the Third *Cours*,
that Unbender of Unbendable Rules, Dilly Dally.

Two

Thursday, November 5th, was the first of three Days of Recollection scheduled for the school year. Classes were canceled to hear the guest priest deliver the dreaded series of four hour-long sermons called "Conferences."

A Day of Recollection, experienced students knew, was a time to think about sin. It was a time for pinching spiritual blackheads, for solitary walks in the cold, for reading stories about saints who suffered terribly but enjoyed it. It was a time for perfect silence.

The sight of row upon row of white veils under the high chapel ceiling made Mother Adelli's heart lift. Even Reverend Mother, now in prayer, now searching her pockets, was in place for the occasion. The Retreat Master, a Dominican, phoned that he would be detained; so, following Mass, Father Ambrose, with a long chin, low-set ears and the air of someone about to ask a question, delivered the first Conference, "And Darkness Was Upon The Face Of The Deep." It floated from him like whiffs of smoke while pews creaked, feet shuffled and more than one kneeler exploded against the floor.

Anxieties about the duck distracted Mother Adelli. While she dreaded being caught in a bold-faced and deliberate violation of her Vow of Obedience, she dreaded even more a loss of the duck too soon. And Helene was not the only one affected, for Popcorn had now become the indispensable mascot of the Third *Cours*.

She led her charges to breakfast in silence. They ate in silence, in silence each chose a volume of spiritual reading, then trooped back to chapel to hear the second Conference.

A fat Dominican done up in white robes burst from the sacristy, touched down with his knee before the tabernacle, then spun to face his congregation. His bald head with its fringe of grey hair seemed set directly upon the cowl of his robe so that it appeared he had no neck. Father Benjamin raised two arms.

"God loves you, girls."

His voice rang off the walls and floor, off the stained glass windows, the wall lamps with their muted glass globes and long chains.

"God loves you more than the moon and the stars, more than the sun and the streams, more than the mountains, more than a hundred Milky Ways." He thrust his head forward. "Do you believe this?"

The near pews rustled under his gaze. Behind him the white-skirted tabernacle sat in quiet repose. It was 10:00 a.m.

"Oh, do not be like the heathens," Father Benjamin sang it out, "who have a nasty God, a God with a bad temper, a God with no sense of humor, a God Who keeps track and opens trap doors when too many points have built up against you; then 'snap'," he made alligator jaws of his hands, "and chew, chew, chew." Giggles bounced from pew to pew.

"That's right, you can laugh," he beamed like the sun itself. "We can all laugh because Jesus told us our God is a loving God, a forgiving God. Shouldn't Jesus know? Isn't He God's own Son?"

His young congregants nodded solemnly. Jesus was God's own Son.

"When Lucifer, that rebellious angel, fell to earth, his light broke into uncountable tongues of fire; and each tongue broke into uncountable other tongues, then each of those spoke itself into a particular form of evil that crawled away like a slimy beastie, looking for a soul upon which to feast."

The Dominican paused to let the girls do their picturing. Dust motes meandered in the color pouring from the leaded-glass windows.

"I want to talk to you this morning about one beastie in particular, eh? He may appear to be of no consequence, but he will destroy your peace of mind if he can, for that is his job. Oh, pray never to be without peace of mind, girls," he cried down the long chapel, "for lack of it is one of the great corroding evils in life. And should this terrible condition befall you, perhaps you will remember this talk and look for the footprints of Nolo Pacis across your soul."

The students looked at one another. Across your soul? Footprints?

I have no peace, Mother Adelli thought, her heart sinking, eyes taking in the sea of young souls. And what wouldn't she give right now to be wearing, instead, the simple small white veil, to be sitting open and listening, chin in her hands.

"Well, just how does this Nolo Pacis do his poisonous work, you ask. He does it with a special and silent killer of good people called scrup-u-los-ity." The word, like a grasshopper, erupted jointed from his lips and across the communion rail.

But wasn't a rather advanced sense of sin required for an understanding of scrupulosity, Mother Abbate, Mistress of the Upper School, frowned. Usually the topic came up around delicate sexual matters. And how many in the Third *Cours* or Minims had ever even heard the word, for heaven sake?

"Nolo Pacis, "Destroyer of Peace." Again the name slithered over the communion rail.

Reverend Mother Gregory covered her eyes with her hand. Priest of God, yes; but must there be all these theatrics?

"I saw him once, myself," the man went on, confidential, "and of all things as a slowly swirling cloud like dust." The students looked at one another: He had seen the Devil?

"But you don't need to see him to know he's there, girls. Just follow the trail of misery he leaves, for Nolo Pacis attacks only people trying hard to live good lives. Because, being a spark of Lucifer, good people make him feel the terrible loss of God, and the peace of doing God's will." Father Benjamin raised his hands. "Oh, do God's will girls if you want peace," he warbled the words out ripely. The students didn't know. Wasn't peace sort of like not having anything to do?

"You see, girls, people who are at peace enrage Nolo Pacis. He goes after them to plant that little seed of scrupulosity that grows faster than dandelions. Now peace of mind can only come from a good conscience, so Nolo Pacis is a trickster of the conscience, eh? You watch out for him!"

Belly right up against the communion rail, he leaned to his audience. "Who knows what his name means? Who takes Latin?" The students, not allowed to speak in chapel, hesitated. "'No Peace' is his name," the priest boomed. And when you have no peace, you know Nolo Pacis has unpacked his suitcase in your life. Listen closely girls and I will tell you stories of his victims, and show you just how this Nolo Pacis works, eh?"

He held up an index finger and began.

"Little Suzanne was a very good girl who one day took a stamp from her mother's desk to write to her sick Grandma. Though she meant to tell her mother and repay it, Nolo Pacis was at work there and saw to it that Susan kept forgetting. Each day the little sin became heavier but more familiar until finally the girl let it slip into the sleepy side of her soul. Suzanne grew up always feeling she had done something wrong, but couldn't remember what. Well, Nolo Pacis hopped about, happy as a puppy. You see how he does it?"

Father Benjamin held up two fingers.

"A certain Sister Alexandra of virtuous character got a new Superior, a woman with tiny eyes and a nose like a hawk. Now, Nolo Pacis was after Sister Alexandra. Her unselfish acts made her too good for her own good. One day, leaving chapel, Nolo Pacis arranged that Sister Alexandra run smack into Sister Superior, and that Superior's beak of a nose plunge right into Sister Alexandra's eye." Father Benjamin, a pudgy hand over his own right eye, staggered about.

"Superior shouted that Sister Alexandra watch where she was going. Then she straightened her veil." Third *Cours* necks craned to Mother Adelli.

"Poor Sister Alexandra. Each week she planned to tell about it in confession, but each week Nolo Pacis saw to it that her efforts failed. Soon Sister grew weary, her sunny disposition failed. And Nolo Pacis was as happy as a four year-old girl with a frog."

Father Benjamin held up three fingers. "Nolo Pacis has even gotten after me."

The students' ears grew huge. Really? A priest?

"Father Benjamin lives in a monastery; but once the Prior sent him to help out in a parish with a sick pastor. One day, Father Benjamin needed two dollars and seventy-five cents for the newsboy. Now, Father Benjamin has some trouble with being lazy, and he didn't want to go upstairs to get the money; so he borrowed from the Sodality box. Well, who do you think kept Father Benjamin feeling for months that it was too much trouble to straighten things out about that money?" He thrust an inquiring face at his audience waiting in an ecstasy of joy to hear the grisly details of his downfall.

"At the end-of-the year dinner, Father Benjamin knew the Sodality's books would be wrong by two dollars and seventy-five cents, and he determined to set things straight. But during the dinner he came to feel it would be too much trouble to stop eating and say something. Do you see how lazy Father Benjamin really is? And when the treasurer began the financial report, Father Benjamin knocked his water glass over the table and realizing he was already on his feet, he spoke up.

'Madam Treasurer, you will find you are short two dollars and seventy-five cents. I borrowed it, meaning to pay it right back; but I couldn't get myself to go upstairs to replace it. Here it is right now, and with my apologies.' And as he dug into his pocket, Father Benjamin noticed a small black cloud drift through the holes of the pepper shaker and move swiftly across the room toward the door."

A yeasty satisfaction in the pews. The Dominican let it soak in. He looked out over the young faces, over the nuns in their prie dieus along the sides. "Girls, Nolo Pacis can only really work his evil on people who can't bear to have anything, no matter how small, be wrong."

Mother Adelli leaned forward.

"They think they love God," the priest went on, " but they really are afraid of Him; and this fear comes from not being able to believe God loves them. Now, only God can be right all the time, girls--only God is perfect; the rest of us are makeshift. People Nolo Pacis picks on don't really like being human because to be human is to make mistakes. So to be comfortable they need to be Superman or Superwoman."

Reverend Mother Gregory held her head. How on earth had he derived this from her suggested topic of "Nature Redeemed?" Well, never again would she stray from the Jesuits.

The monk raised his hands. "God only asks that we be sorry and try harder next time, girls. Don't let your mistakes hound you. Don't let Nolo Pacis unpack his suitcase in your life. God made us human; He loves us human!" he pealed out until the wood of the front pews quivered, then looked them right in the eye. "And you have Father Benjamin's word on that!"

Raising the hinged seat of her prie dieu, it struck Mother Adelli she had been told her confusion, anger and bungled efforts--even broken vows--were all right because they were human. She had only to be sorry and go on trying to do better. How she hoped it was true. Kindly Mother Durban agreed to ferry the Third *Cours* back to Study Hall and secure a Fourth Academic ribbon to oversee the girls at spiritual reading so that Mother Adelli could speak with Father Benjamin before the afternoon conference.

The man was even kindlier-looking close up. Smile lines, like the edges of playing cards, fanned out from his eyes.

"Thank you for seeing me, Father."

"A pleasure, Mother."

Behind him rose a tall cabinet which held the monstrance with its flared gold rays, used to display the Host for Benediction. Mother Adelli saw also several chalices with their saucer-like gold patens which sat atop the chalice and carried the Sacred Wafer and also kept the blood of Christ free of extraneous matter. There were silver candlesticks, acorn-shaped incense burners and a hand bell to ring at the elevation of the Sacred Substances during Mass and when the congregation received the blessing of the Host at Benediction.

Next to the cabinet sat a large wardrobe within which hung the green vestments from morning Mass with crosses hand-worked front and back in gold thread. Somewhere not in view she knew were more vestments, white linen surplices for attendant priests and altar boys, boxes of unconsecrated hosts, crates of bottled wine, cartons of altar candles and votive lights, tins of dark incense, and drawers of altar linens.

"Please have a seat, Mother--"

"Adelli, Father. Thank you." She arranged her skirts, palms sweating.

He sat too, noticed the worried face, leaned toward her. "How can I help?"

Mother Adelli felt her voice flail about, cleared her throat, blushed. "I'm sorry, Father, this is more difficult--." She waved her hands, let them fall. A moment of silence.

"I've been troubled with worries about obedience, Father."

"Oh?" The priest laced his fingers, leaned forward a bit.

"Perhaps it sounds theoretical," she plunged in, "but I wonder about forcing others to do things they cannot believe in."

"Do you have an example, Mother?"

"Our students. Not all of them come from homes with the same values we have. Suppose a person is lacking in some area of moral conscience, tells lies for instance but doesn't believe lying is serious or wrong. Is it right to punish such a person for doing what isn't wrong to them?"

Father Benjamin settled back. "Say more."

"What about the laws of the Church? What if a person is not of the Church," Mother Adelli stepped gingerly, "or doesn't hold to the Ten Commandments? What if, in conscience, a person doesn't believe, for instance, that adultery is wrong, or stealing?"

"Well, but the Ten Commandments are based on Natural Law, Mother Adelli. They are based on the way our Creator made us; they are inherent to our nature. Our nature tells us it is wrong to steal, to lie and to break our contract with another human being."

"Yes, Father; but aren't there cases when a person genuinely doesn't have such feelings or believe certain things are wrong? Then what? Is it right to punish them for not obeying something to which they honestly don't relate?"

Father Benjamin looked at the young nun, so intense and earnest on her chair. He wrinkled his forehead. What was she after?

"Of course," he scratched the back of his neck, "that is sometimes the case. In fact, anthropologists show us whole nations of such people, and not just ancient peoples. Human sacrifice is still current, and multiple wives the custom for some countries--."

"So then, Father," Mother Adelli moved to the dangerous place, "'suppose a person were in charge of someone perhaps not actually bereft of a moral nature but not connecting the way others do? And what of the person who must punish her infringements of a law in which she doesn't believe? And what if that person in charge is under a Vow of Obedience and must punish against her own sense of what is right for the student? Is it moral or not for that person to be obedient under such circumstances?"

Father Benjamin studied the wimpled face with its dark earnest eyes. "You raise deep issues, Mother Adelli," he nodded. "You are a thinker. Let me say a couple of things." He sat back in his chair, raised a finger. "First, the Church teaches that a man or woman's own conscience is always his or her court of last resort. Each of us stands alone before God, eh? We do our best, eh? That's all God asks of us. Remember 'baptism of desire'? Simply the desire to do right makes one a member of the Mystical Body of Christ, as our holiness Pope Pius XII points out in *Mystici Corporus*."

A second finger. "I do not believe a person, despite the Vow of Obedience, can act against her own conscience. Either that person must come around to her Superior's point of view or be released from the vow, at least in that instance." He paused. It seemed a shame for such a gentle face to be so disturbed by worry. He thought a minute, slapped his thigh and leaned forward. A big smile. "Now you wouldn't be keeping a house guest, would you, Mother Adelli? Eh?"

"Please, Father?"

"Nolo Pacis, Mother. Don't forget the things we spoke of in chapel. God asks that we do the best we can at the moment. Don't be afraid of mistakes. Remember, God loves us human; that includes mistakes. And nothing is ever too complicated for Him. If we break it, He'll fix it, eh?"

Father Benjamin cocked his head and gave the Religious a long smile, then stood. "I'm afraid I must get ready for the next Conference. Have I been of any help?"

It did help, asking the questions aloud of a priest trained in theology. Now she could feel more certain she was doing the right thing for Helene. Perhaps some rules were larger than others. Didn't our Lord Himself say, "Render to Caesar the things that are Caesar's, and to God the things that are God's?" Her desire was to render to God the child that was His. And wasn't it just as Mother Concepciòn told her--that God would give her guidance if she trusted Him? Hadn't He sent the duck and Father Benjamin?

She wondered, walking back through the empty chapel, if this last Conference might have reached Helene, if some light might have found its way into her mind. And every moment of suffering the girl had visited upon her was forgiven as the young religious dipped her fingers into the holy water fount. Walking back to Study Hall, she realized the spring wound too tight in her chest had been transformed into a desire for a brisk walk. After lunch, she would get her girls wrapped up and out into the fresh air, get their blood moving before the next Conference.

The following day, Popcorn, denied for twenty-four hours his accustomed audience, was in an uproar. He drilled the hands of the five lucky visitors as they passed him back and forth, scavenged toast crusts and cookie bits brought up from their pockets while the black beads of his eyes snapped. His admirers danced around, warned him about Nolo Pacis and sent each other into fits of laughter which made the duck snap out the rubber band of its neck and winnow wildly while scraps of down floated in the air and the girls grabbed for them.

Klat klat klat. Too soon Mother Adelli stood at the door. They were late for cricket. Hurried hands shoveled Popcorn into his cage. Goodbye Popcorn, they kissed their fingers at him. Take a nap; you're too excited. But Popcorn ran around and around his cage raking its sides with its beak while footsteps faded and the Best Made roused itself to cough warmed air into the giant graph of pipes that ran everywhere in the building.

After dinner, Helene and four other students arrived with bits of apple dumpling to gape at the open door of the cage, the abandoned straw bed with its hair ribbons, erasers, rubber ball, tiny stuffed bear and circular imprint. Helene stared hard, as though confronted with geometry.

"Who didn't lock the door to the cage?" she finally yelled, then scoured the floor and walls of the furnace room. "He has to be here somewhere because the outside door is closed. Everybody look," she took command, "but don't step on him."

They called, crawled, bumped into one another and finally fled to the gym, to Mother Adelli who, veil tied into a knot and overskirt tucked up, was playing "Keep-away" with the rest of the boarders.

"Popcorn got out." Helene's fear filled the room.

There were screams and a stampede that Mother Adelli stemmed only with great difficulty.

"I know you want to help," she told her students, "but there is only space for a few in the furnace room. Stay here on your honor and play ball, or sit and talk while we take a look." A ribbon was in charge. Mother Adelli took Helene, Madeline and GeeGee with her to the furnace room, not daring to think.

Fifteen minutes of shifting boards, ladders and boxes, breathing old cardboard, paint solvents and boiler steam and they moved into the corridor to search behind radiators and along baseboards. From there they combed the dining hall, hesitated at the threshold of *Soeur* Josephine's kitchen, then tiptoed amongst pots and pans, looking under the stove, the huge refrigerator, in the large pantry behind sacks of grain and flour where they were sure they would discover the orange wedge of a bill at work.

"Well, it seems we have an adventurer," Mother Adelli kept her voice light, "like Columbus. Or Popcorn might be having tea right now with Reverend Mother and reporting on us." Even Helene laughed, though she was at work on her finger ends. "He will find his way back to his bed and food by morning. Meanwhile, everyone has the History Competition to study for, and then we must get on upstairs."

There still remained the Cloister, classrooms and Minims' quarters. Couldn't they just look in the classrooms? Please?

No. In the morning they would probably find Popcorn in the hall outside the classrooms reading his way through the French Revolution. For now, get those study books out.

Unsure and grumbling, to the Study Hall where each girl turned pages and made notes while in her mind searched again, room by room, for the lost duck.

The next day, standing outside Study Hall, Big John's eyes grew large and his face folded at the news.

"Lordsaveme, Muther, I dinna notice the little fella gone. I had the door open mahbe twenty minutes whilst I loaded a cabinet for Sheridan Road. Blessed Virgin Mary," he shook a bowed head, "I'll never forgive miself, the way them little ladies favored that duck--an' I come to favor it too. I'll look out fer him." He hitched his pants. "Now don't you worry none. Big John'll find that little fella."

Mother Adelli swallowed and asked Mother Durban to use her Minims' eyes around their rooms. The talk that she had fostered a pet for the Third *Cours* would spread now, and surely reach her superiors. She also sent a request through *Soeur* Josephine to the Working Sisters to watch wherever they cleaned, including in Cloister. Twenty-four hours of hope ran through her fingers. Now there would be the added charge of an emotional uproar amongst her students, whether they found the duck or not. And what if they didn't find it? Her stomach lurched.

"It's too soon to give up on Popcorn being in the building," she told her boarders after dinner, "but you should know there is a possibility he got outside."

The Third *Cours* drew a horrified breath. Helene threw her head down on her desktop. "Damn. I knew this was going to happen," she bellowed into the crook of her arm. Mother Adelli could not chastise her. From outside came the patter of rain.

It was the squishing sound of shoes against the dormitory floor that sent Mother Adelli's night cap through her alcove curtain. There Helene was, hair dripping, uniform jacket soaked, legs streaked with mud and oxfords black from that same rain pelting the dormitory windows. Too late now for wondering how the girl got out. And too late for being furious or frightened.

"Any luck?" Mother Adelli raised her eyebrows and whispered.

Helene shook her head.

"Get into something dry and get to bed as fast as you can. We'll talk in the morning." She noticed the uniform skirt soaked, its hem caked with mud. "Give me your skirt." She held out her hand. "I'll lay it across the radiator."

"I just came in for my flashlight." Helene turned toward her own alcove.

"I can't let you go back out. You know that. Even if I ignored the rules, it's not safe. And you may get sick now anyway, wet as you are."

"And what about Popcorn?" The girl spun around. "It's cold and wet out there for him, too. He's not used to it. He's from a pet store."

Mother Adelli put her finger to her lips. "Don't wake the dormitory. He's from a pet store, but he's made for this kind of weather. He knows by instinct how to find a warm dry spot. Popcorn will be fine. He will stay where he is until tomorrow. First thing in the morning we will look for him."

Helene hesitated, then gave Mother Adelli a searing look. "*I'm* responsible for him. My grandmother sent him to *me*. *I'm* supposed to take care of him. He might be in trouble or get eaten. I'm getting my flashlight."

"You absolutely cannot go out there now," Mother Adelli whispered loudly; "I will not allow you to go out there."

But Helene walked off, shoes chirping against the floor. Her bed springs squeaked. A drawer rattled. Rain beat on the windows. Mother Adelli's chest constricted. Helene reappeared with the flashlight and headed for the dormitory door.

"All right, I'm going to wake Reverend Mother Gregory." Mother Adelli snapped to life, eyes deadly serious. She stepped into the hall and started down the corridor.

In her mind Helene saw Reverend Mother Gregory lift the telephone, heard her father's voice come tiny across the ocean.

"All right," she hissed.

But Mother Adelli kept walking, Now Helene hurried after her until they stood opposite, staring each other down. It was the girl who broke the silence.

"I can find him. I know I can if I just have the chance."

Mother Adelli shook her head. "I don't have any choice about this."

At impasse, the girl lacerated the nun with her eyes, then turned on wet soles that chirped against the floor. "If Popcorn dies," she threw the words over her shoulder, "it'll be your fault, then."

"And if you wake the others," something prompted Mother Adelli to respond, "I'll go directly to Reverend Mother."

The girl made no attempt to be quiet, but finally handed out her wet things--jacket, socks, everything--to Mother Adelli waiting outside her alcove.

Three

The next morning, as promised, the Third *Cours* searched outdoors for the duck; but after an hour of squatting and squinting, Mother Adelli called her students inside. She couldn't let the whole day go. She told them they could search later in place of cricket; but by then a cold November rain ribbed the windows, and the trees and bushes roiled and thrashed with the in-coming storm.

"Popcorn won't go far," Mother Adelli assured the worried faces. "He has small legs and can't fly yet. We'll go out again when the rain stops." Helene slammed around in a temper; and no one, not even Mother Adelli, could concentrate on anything else.

Strangely, Mother Adelli's Community asked nothing about the duck. The Working Sisters and Big John were unlikely, out of the humbleness of their positions, to say anything. Among the Religious, non-essential conversation was limited to Social Groups, and then to assigned topics. Circumstances favored her for now, but she knew she rowed a leaking boat.

Something else helped to stave off the inevitable. The Vicar General of the Order's Western Province, Reverend Mother Alysse D'Gagnier, announced a visit to the two Sacred Heart convents in the Chicago area the first week of February. This news immediately became an all-consuming point of focus for the Superiors and their assistants. There would be events at Lake Forest and joint events with Sheridan Road, including a special liturgy and dinner with the Bishop. There would be the thorough scouring of the record books, the building and the grounds. To accomplish all of this meant meeting after meeting and the eclipsing of the lesser concerns of everyday affairs.

Soeur Josephine closed the great oven door. Though the seven loaves needed careful timing, her mind was occupied by her visitor. In her twenty-two years in the Order, never had a Mother asked to be served tea in the kitchen. Such a request was contrary to the Order's custom of Working Sisters and other Religious keeping themselves separate.

That morning through her kitchen window, *Soeur* Josephine had observed the Third *Cours* trooping over hoarfrost and frozen leaves, calling out like harbor horns for the lost duck. "Poor Mother Adelli must be frantic," she thought now as she hurried with the teapot to pour a steaming cup for her visitor. "A biscuit, ma Mère?" she asked.

But the Mistress of the Third *Cours* held up a hand for silence. Head cocked to one side, she followed a scratching sound from beyond the kitchen door, and in the next instance the high-pitched cry that ended on an upturned note. She crossed the corridor and had barely touched the knob when the wind hurled the door open. Dry leaves rattled along the stoop.

"R-r-r-o-o-w-w-w?"

Aross the hall, S*oeur* Josephine stood watching. Oh! That vagabond *gato*, always trying to get into the kitchen! When the cat raised its nose out of the shadows, she saw old and gold, and hair whipped into hornlike peaks; then heard Mother Adelli cry out, "No. Put it down."

Tucked deep into the cat's muzzle was Helene's duck.

Mother Adelli squatted in the doorway. The wind moaned. Leaves rattled along the stoop.

"Here kitty--." Oh, what was the animal's name?

Wariness rose in the feline face. It ceased its singing, cocked its ears backwards and dropped its head to burrow inside; but the voluminous skirts of the young nun's habit blocked its path.

"What has kitty got? Show Mother, Kitty. Nice kitty, nice--," Mother Adelli crooned.

But the cat took a step backwards, a duck wing fanning from its mouth, the decision to run glinting in its eye.

Now timing was all she had. With one precise gesture, she must reach between the cat's lips and around the duck torso, at the same moment make a vise of her other hand and lock the cat's neck.

But the animal's intuition was the quicker. Scarcely had the nun tried to force a thumb between the wing and the cat's lower lip when the animal rose on hind legs to wheel away. With a sickening turn, a valentine of pale yellow feathers and shining red beads came away in Mother Adelli's fingers. Ears laid back, the duck tucked deep in its jowls, the cat leapt away toward the ravines.

Deep within Mother Adelli's ears came a hissing sound as of many waters followed a great roaring as if portals had burst. *Soeur* Josephine caught her as the young nun tumbled sideways .The Working Sister, dreadfully worried, propped Mother Adelli against the wall, plucked the little wing from between her fingers and dropped it into her apron pocket, then dashed to the kitchen for a damp cloth. As Mother Adelli's eyelids fluttered, *Soeur* Josephine begged permission to call Mother Spencer; but Mother Adelli, deadly white and trembling violently, would hear none of it. Mother Spencer would mean people, questions.

Leaning on *Soeur* Josephine's arm, Mother Adelli crossed the hallway to a chair at the baking table. Perhaps the duck had only feigned death--she had read birds do such things--and could still escape, injured though it was, and find its way back. Or else what would become of her, her charges, of everything now?

Soeur Josephine leaned forward to set a fresh cup of tea on the baker's table, startled and dropped a deep curtsy. Mother Crewelman loomed in the doorway. The overhead light heightened the boney architecture of the forehead, temples and cheeks, the sharpness of the nose, shadowed the extremities of the lips.

Mother Adelli stood, wavering, gripping the table's edge. How would she explain tea in the kitchen? And poor *Soeur* Josephine who had helped her so much; now *her* integrity was compromised!

"Is there a problem, Mother Adelli?" Mother Crewelman asked as her eyes swept the room and its occupants.

The younger nun shook her head; then, fingertips still propped on the baker's table, took a step toward the door. The Mistress General paused, opened her mouth, closed it, nodded curtly and disappeared.

Mother Adelli breathed, turned to *Soeur* Josephine. "*Ma Soeur,* if you need me to explain--"

"There is no problem, *ma Mère.* Your tea. I light the dining room."

Mother Adelli shook her head, held up a hand. "Some months ago at dinner, I was very rude to you, *ma soeur.* I am so sorry. I was very upset and in the wrong. Please forgive me."

Then, her body still buzzing from the faint, she negotiated the problematic corridor, moving handle to handle along the locker doors.

Soeur Josephine watched her down the hall to her office, then clapped a hand to her head. The dinner rolls! She spun to the great oven, jerked open its door. Dark, but not dried out. God is good. She brushed the tops with butter and upended everything for cooling, praying that in His goodness the Sacred Heart would shower mercy down upon this Mother Adelli.

That evening during the Community Social Hour, old Mother Concepciòn shifted irritably on the couch. In February it would be the same speech the other four Vicar Generals gave. How many times could you hear it? Well, but the meals would be excellent.

She, Mother Concepciòn, had been on a run of dreams. There was one about a pig she wanted to share with Mother Adelli, but the young Religious was absent from Social Hour again. Since the apparition in chapel, Mother Concepciòn had never again worried about the Rule of Silence which allowed talking only when necessary. Well, all of *her* talking *was* necessary--for instance with this young nun who reached out to her. But now Mother Concepciòn wondered had it been a mistake not to have spoken further with her those few weeks back. First the young woman is under terrible strain and loses her temper at dinner; then she is light as a feather but doesn't look anybody in the eye. Ah, but Mother Durban would know what was going on if anybody did!

And Mother Durban, on the couch, was the sitting victim just then since all other members of her group were absent. The older nun crossed the room on her cane and eased down beside the Mistress of the Minims and went to work on her until finally the story of the lost duck popped out.

In her dream that night, Mother Concepciòn saw the duck clearly, small and fluffy with black pipe-stem legs, an orange wedge of a bill and snapping black eyes. It was trapped atop that small metal drainpipe partway down the ravine behind Our Lady's grotto with one foot wedged between the ribbed metal curve of the pipe and a rock.

Her eyes flew open. She knew what she must do.

Wishing she had worn her shawl, she hurried past gleaming bushes sleeved with ice while her breath bloomed before her and millions of stars pressed upon her. The ravine with its steep and slippery pitch seemed to help her old legs by making her knees bend and feet fly while her body bobbed and bounced until the slope itself began to rock and its frosted face tilted and sprang upward. It was while she tried desperately to right herself that her crucifix swung out and hooked over a shrub limb. Jerked from her feet, all in one instant she saw above her a gorgeous tangled canopy of dripping glass and felt the lidding of the breath in her throat as the picture book of the world snapped shut.

The Community heard of the accident the next day from Reverend Mother Gregory. The old nun had been found by Big John and rushed to Lake Forest where the doctor at the hospital estimated she had been unconscious and exposed to freezing cold for seven hours. They awaited a prognosis.

Mother Adelli's voice wobbled so that she could not say to her Third *Cours*, "Please pray for her." She could not tell them about Mother Concepción's unique and adventuresome spirit, and that her holiness could be profound and comic in the same moment. Her girls looked about helplessly while their Mistress stood before them, her mouth opening and closing while no words came out, and her face white as paper.

Thursday, the weather in hiatus before the next storm favored them for once, and the Third *Cours* again searched outdoors for Popcorn. They stumped like dwarves around the base of the building until their hamstrings caught fire and torpor began to drift over their feelings of loss. Mother Adelli said nothing about the cat. She prayed, though she knew it was now good as hopeless, that they might still find the injured pet escaped and alive.

At lunch, sensing growing disaffection with the rescue mission, Helene raked her classmates over the coals for agreeing with Mother Adelli that there were classes to attend and homework to be turned in. She declared Mother Adelli to be a coward who did what she was told whether it was right or wrong. "She doesn't care a snap about Popcorn. And," Helene sneered around, "the rest of you are just like her." A few students opened their mouths and then closed them. What were they supposed to do? How much was enough? They were tired of trying. Anyway, nothing would put Helene's fire out but the duck.

That afternoon, the dying light streamed through the ground-level windows of Study Hall and caught the room with its students at their books in a spell of peace so palpable it held Big John transfixed at the door. Oh, and wasn't it just his luck now to have to spoil it all?

Mother Adelli followed him into the corridor. He lifted the top of the handkerchief to show what looked like a discarded glove. She shut her eyes and turned away, hand over her breast. One wing was missing, and one foot gone.

"I'm sorry M'am," Big John shook his head.

She signaled him to wait, prayed she was doing the right thing, cracked the Study Hall door and drew her breath down hard to call to the girl.

Helene came, scuffing her shoes against the floor. First she saw Big John, then the white handkerchief on his open palm and how it rose along the center in a narrow lump. Her eyes, filled with one dreadful question, flew to his.

"I'm sorry, Miss," he shook his head.

"No-o-o-o-o." She hammered at the air with her clenched fists. "No-o-o-o-o." She raged in circles as if white-hot shards clung to her flesh.

Mother Adelli covered her face with her hands. "Oh please, God."

The girl beat her fists and feet against the lockers. The pounded wood echoed down the corridor. She flung herself to the floor, kicking whatever was in reach. In the diminished hallway light, Mother Adelli noticed Helene's hair appeared black, as if it had been burnt. Big John made a move to restrain her, but Mother Adelli shook a finger, no. The girl drew her body into a crouch, and with her arms covering her head like a shell, bawled untranslatable accusations into the old porous tiles. Then she heaved into a second hurricane of fists and feet, slamming at walls and doors.

Finally the storm spent itself and she lay convulsing, one hand covering her eyes. Mother Durban looked out from the Minims' Study Hall and quickly withdrew. Mother Adelli nodded then to Big John who knelt near the girl, cooing Irish things his mother had taught him until at last she let herself lean into his arms, against his wide chest. After some minutes, he helped her to her feet and Mother Adelli stuck her head into the deadly silent Study Hall and called for Madeline to take Helene to dormitory and stay with her as long as she seemed to need or want someone.

She watched the girl grip the banister up the sagging stairs, Madeline at her side, sober and straight. They disappeared around the landing and then there remained only the sound of feet striking the steps to wound the air and those held captive in it.

The following morning from her office window, Reverend Mother Gregory watched the edge of Big John's shovel flash against the dark loam, surprised. And at Mother Adelli there at Our Lady's grotto, and with a crescent of her girls.

Shifting from foot to foot under the raw November overcast, the students stood while the young nun read from a book, then they all opened their mouths. Faintly through the window glass, the Superior heard them singing "To Jesus' Heart All Burning." Next came what appeared a heated discussion between Mother Adelli and the Rhenehan girl over what looked like a cookie tin; then the student running toward the building and another girl, that Madeline from Milwaukee, hurrying after her.

What on earth were they doing out this time of day, and in such weather? Something akin to dread moved through the Superior. She picked up the house phone. It was most irritating to have to arrange another talk with Mother Adelli. What the glory had happened to that nun? She laid the receiver back in its cradle. She straightened pens and papers on her desk. Actually, wasn't Mother Crewelman, the Mistress General, the one to handle such things--rules, behavior and so forth? She picked up the receiver again.

"Come," Mother Crewelman responded to the knock on her office door. It was just past the dinner hour.

"Good evening, Mother. You wanted to see me?" Mother Adelli's pulse hammered at the base of her throat.

Mother Crewelman let her eyes traverse the young Religious from black shoes to the pin securing her veil. With an index finger she indicated the chair in front of her desk.

"Reverend Mother Gregory tells me you had your students out in the foulest of weather this morning, instead of in classes where they belonged, and that you appeared to be burying something, with the help of Big John, near the grotto."

"We were having a funeral, Mother." The young Religious swung from word to word, so high and alone, along the dreaded sentence that stretched out like taffy.

The Mistress General threw herself backwards in her chair, pressed the long pale paddle of her hand to her heart.

"Not anyone we know, I hope."

"A duck, Mother." Mother Adelli swallowed, let the words out carefully, explosives that they were.

"*Duck?*" Mother Crewelman's face went blank. She batted her eyes. "What do you mean, 'duck'?"

"One we were keeping for the Rhenehan girl. The grandmother sent it. We had it in a cage in the furnace room until--." She stopped herself. She had not yet tried to find a farm. "--until it got out and was killed. We--the girls and I--created a liturgy for it."

"*Liturgy? You* created one? And which was your class at Quigley Seminary, pray, Mother? When were you ordained?"

Blushing furiously, Mother Adelli dropped the lead weights of her eyes while the Mistress General flopped back in her chair.

"And how is it you assume the authority to conduct a liturgy? *A liturgy!* I'm fascinated, truly." She leaned forward. "Tell me."

"If you please Mother, in *Mediator Dei*, the Holy Father says he wishes lay people to become familiar with the Roman missal. I thought, rather than to simply say some prayers, we might read from the Mass for the Dead."

"*But following the priest*, Mother Adelli. *Mediator Dei* says nothing about nuns and children making things up as they go along. We have many beautiful ceremonials, but evidently none to please you." She wet her lips and sat staring at the younger woman, then let her eyes drop and fingered the corners of the papers on her desk. She raised her eyes.

"The rule concerning pets--. You know it, I believe?"

"I do, yes, Mother."

The Mistress General waited, tapping her desktop with her finger. Mother Adelli struggled around the boulder in her throat and took the deeper step. "I excused myself from that rule for a short time, Mother, because the duck was the first thing that seemed to help the girl." Even as she spoke them, she could hear how feeble and condemning her words sounded.

Mother Crewelman's eyebrows flew high; she straightened. "Oh," she responded, nodding like a horse pawing, "*I* see. You *excused* yourself. The rule didn't suit *your* needs, so you set it aside--but to help the girl, of course. I remember very well our conversation about this little pagan. I doubt you recall it however, since your behavior has not improved but worsened." She let seconds pass, her refolded hands illuminated in the pool of lamplight. From the hallway, the library cart with its squeaky wheel came and went. "Tell me, if you were in my position, what would you recommend for a nun who ignores her Superiors and takes the rules and Sacred Liturgy into her own hands--concerning Final Vows, I mean?"

Mother Adelli bowed her head.

Mother Crewelman stared into the gloom of the ceiling. Either the woman was a fool or an insurgent. In hiring her, Reverend Mother Gregory had, as usual, lacked acuity. She drew her eyes back to the bent figure. "Should we now expect you to break your vows whenever you see fit, Mother Adelli?

"No, Mother."

"Well, I have seen your tears before, Mother." She curled her lip. "I no longer have faith in them." The desk lamp began to buzz. The pale fingers moved back and forth over the papers, then stopped. "Or perhaps you have been inspired to found a new Order. Are you here to file for a release from your vows?"

Mother Adelli shook her head.

Mother Crewelman dabbed at the tiny clusters of bubbles building at the corners of her mouth.

"Your lack of judgment boggles me, Mother Adelli. You should never have told the girl about the duck. You should have simply sent it back and written a clarification to the grandmother. Certainly there should never have been a funeral. Nature took care of the problem for you, had you left well enough alone. Can you see now the pain and disruption your disobedience and wrong-headedness have caused?"

Head bent low and blotting her face with the back of her hands, Mother Adelli nodded. Yes, yes, she could see it. "I want to explain about *Soeur* Josephine, Mother," she stumbled forward. "I asked for the tea. The cat came to the door. It had the--"

"Not in the kitchen. She didn't give you tea in the kitchen?"

"I asked for it, Mother. I didn't want to be alone."

"You have twenty-four students, Mother Adelli. How can you be alone? Do you see how corrupting it all becomes? You have no judgment. I can only wonder how you got this far with us." She drew out a large appointment book. "You must be watched. I will meet with you every Thursday evening from now on. Eight o'clock. Have someone take Study Hall and dormitory."

"Yes, Mother Crewelman."

"You will not--I repeat, *not*--make decisions of any kind that depart from the ordinary without first passing them through me. Is that clear?"

Mother Adelli nodded.

"What did you say, Mother?"

"It is clear, Mother Crewelman."

"You will use only established ceremonials when one is called for. Is that clear?"

"Yes, Mother."

They sat then in silence, except for the tapping of the Mistress General's finger upon her writing paper.

"Well," Mother Crewelman looked around, lightening her voice as if a cloud overshadowing them had passed, "*Congé* tomorrow." She pulled her handkerchief from her sleeve and dabbed her mouth. "Everyone needs a holiday. Give your students that, Mother Adelli, but re-establish your authority *immediately*. You may go now."

The wax-colored hand picked up the pen and Mother Adelli rose. "By the way," the Mistress General looked out through her silver-rimmed glasses, "we will announce in chapel in the morning that Mother Concepciòn passed quietly into the arms of Our Lord about four o'clock this afternoon. Of pneumonia."

Should someone have kicked away the center post inside her; Mother Adelli couldn't have felt more vacant and falling. She crept the mile to the door and, forgetting altogether to close it behind her, felt her way along the hall to the stairs, carefully, slowly, like someone newly blinded.

Having heard such news, how was it then she sat up straight in the chair in the dormitory only minutes later with darning egg and needle, cross-hatching a hole in a white uniform sock? And how was it she responded so evenly to students with bath towels and toothbrushes when her only confidante had gone forever? But then into what other arms could she now throw herself except those of her duty?

She gave permission for visiting before lights out as a step into tomorrow's *Congé*. The holiday meant late Mass, no classes, no homework, no Rule of Silence for students. Her girls sat cross-legged in twos and threes on beds or sprawled on cotton rugs to talk about the duck, the funeral, their own lost pets and lost people, trying to wrangle meaning from mysteries that balanced people's lives on such prongs of pain.

"Take Deborah and see how Helene's doing." As she passed, Mother Adelli caught at Jennifer's sleeve. "Tell her I want to know if she's had her bath before we close the tub room."

Parting the curtains, the two girls found Helene fully clothed and face down in bed, her oxfords visible under the sheet. On the dresser a postcard picturing a crumbling temple was propped against her water cup.

Deborah, baffled blinking eyes, and Jennifer, face pinched and worried under her helmet of hair, hesitated.

"Helene," they called then. No response. Deborah threw her shoulders up and turned to leave, but Jennifer hooked a staying arm through the crook of her elbow. "Come on, Helene. Hey, we're really sorry about Popcorn. We feel awful, too. Mother Adelli wants to know if you had your bath before they close the tub room."

No reply from the bed.

"Yeah," Deborah took it up, "you never hear her ask one of us if *we* want a bath. 'Get in the tub or fifteen demerits' is all we ever hear." It was as close to comforting as Deborah could come. Hanging at the opening in the curtain, the sight of Helene, so remote--as if she were dead--raised goose bumps along the backs of her legs.

Then, with a sudden thrust Helene sat straight up and swung her legs over the side of her cot. "She doesn't care about me or Popcorn. I know I could have found him, but she wouldn't let me go out again. Then it was too late." She dug her fists into her waist and stuck her chin out. "I *told* her if Popcorn died it would be *her fault.* Now it's *her fault!*"

Deborah and Jennifer looked at one another. Anything they could say would only make the girl madder.

Helene stood. Her rumpled skirt fell about her knees. "And she turned out to be just like I always said. All she cares about is *the rules, the rules*--just like the others." She peeled away her uniform jacket and threw it to the floor. "I'll take my stupid bath." She unbuttoned her skirt; a wicked light lit her eyes. She dropped her voice. "I'll take my bath, and I'll do everything just right, to fool her; but *I'm going to get back at her for Popcorn.* You'll see. She won't know when, but I already know how." She grinned a satisfied and evil grin at them, and Deborah and Jennifer escaped through the curtains.

Mother Adelli looked up from her sewing as Jennifer approached. She had been thinking about Julian's death four years ago. Surely Helene, a child, would heal faster than she had. And how long would it take to heal from Mother Concepciòn?

"How did you do?"

Jennifer glued her eyes to the darning egg; she would not betray her classmate.

"She's going to take a bath."

Then, after some minutes came the slap of slippers. Mother Adelli felt the breeze from Helene's body cross her face, but kept her eyes to her sewing. She had heard all the girl's loud words, was sure she was meant to hear them. Still, the girl had gotten up to take a bath. And tomorrow was *Congé*.

Inside Mother Adelli, the place Mother Concepcion had filled with her words, voice, gestures began to ache. From the hall came the heady sound of water rushing into a tub.

Four

"Donnez, donnez nous un bon jour,
donnez, donnez nous un bon jour,
donnez, donnez nous un bon jour."

In and out of the alcoves and carrying the holy water, Mother Adelli sang the *Congé* song, "Give us a good day." Tired and pale, still she nodded and smiled into their eyes as her boarders dipped and blessed themselves down the front, then shoulder to shoulder.

At Mass, they would see one large satin cross gleam on the back of the priest's vestments while a second glanced off the front when he turned to display the Host, small and white, and to intone the *Agnus Dei*; after which he would carry to them where they knelt at the communion rail and press against their tongues with fingers that smelled faintly of oranges the very God and Author of their lives.

French toast piled into pyramids waited in the dining room. *Soeur* Josephine filled silver syrup boats and handed over dishes of hot pared apples dotted with cinnamon and melting butter, while steaming jugs of cocoa stood about on the tables.

Next came Red Rover, then drama. GeeGee, notebook paper fluted about her face, played Mother Adelli, and Sylvia the fictionally slow student who conjugated *oublíér*, to forget, backwards. Helene sat to the side of all this, quiet, but not, Mother Adelli noticed, staring from a black hole as she had every hour since Popcorn's death. Memories of the duck moved among them all, probing with electric fingers, shocking first one then another in the necessary and age-old choreography of grief. Outside, the blue of the sky began to withdraw behind a tall army of clouds marching down from Minnesota.

Well, it was *Câche-câche,* everyone waited out the clock as they jammed down a *Goûter* of devil's food cake and milk. Finally Mother Adelli called them to divide into teams. "We'll stay inside. Cloister and chapel are off limits. Mother Ling is on her way." Mother Ling--Mother Mailroom to the students--was always late.

"Aw Mother, can't we go out?" They slumped, flapping their arms and turkey-bobbing their heads. "We won't get wet. We'll wear our jackets. Can't we, please?" All day they'd fantasized squatting under shrubbery at the hockey field or flat on their stomachs beneath the North Shore train platform, or clinging to the backside of the grotto.

No. The weather was raw; the sky could open any minute.

One, two, one, the students divided into teams. Mother Mailroom, who never said much, arrived finally. Since Mother Adelli was feeling strong about rules again, everyone prayed to be on Mother Mailroom's team. And Mother Adelli had reasons of her own for the decision she would make dividing the girls into teams. Passing behind Jennifer's chair at lunch, her eyes were drawn up to find Helene's locked upon her in a stare of total abhorrence. So, with the need to manufacture distance between herself and the girl, Mother Ling was appointed to the team of fifteen near the desk platform, at whose edge Helene hung. The remaining sixteen girls at the blackboard she would take for herself.

When the nuns turned away, Helene, leaning at the window sill with a scrap of chalk in her hand, slid into a pocket of shadow on the far side of Mother Adelli's desk and waited during the eraser toss to decide which team would hide first. It hit the floor face down and a cheer went up from Mother Adelli's team who knotted together whispering, then banged out the Study Hall doors as they bolted the stairs to the second floor and down the hall. Just opposite *Mater*, Mother Adelli held up a hand, then led them on tiptoe down the wide center staircase to the foyer where the girls tapped fingers at their lips as they passed the smiling Portress, then threaded their way to the basement, to the laundry room where, sweating heavily and breathing only sips of air, they would huddle behind laundry carts of soiled sheets.

"Three hundred!"

The searching team rushed through the Study Hall doors and up the stairs to gain the second floor corridor, then stopped, ready to run in all directions, while Mother Ling, spinning in their midst, made a count of fourteen heads.

It was no problem for Helene to slip out the Minims' Door. Turn, pull and her breath bloomed in the cold air. She crouched to give her classmates a moment to pass beyond the lower stairs' landing with its view of the door's window, then sprinted up the two cement steps.

She ran toward the ravine. Once over its lip, she could travel the incline out of sight of the school. She had not counted on the rising wind and freezing mist, now almost rain, that turned her wrists red and socks to ice. She buttoned her jacket, visualizing the large concrete drainage pipe just beyond the old fence that she saw weeks past when they all snaked and slid, keeping up behind Mother Adelli.

It was the night before Popcorn's funeral when she had decided to hide in the old pipe the first chance she got, and to stay there until Dilly, Rancid, all the Holy-holys--maybe even her father--gave up looking for her. Let them feel bad for a change, be scared until their stomachs hurt like hers had. Then they'd see. The ravine hung rapt and silent in silver mist. Spent leaves sank and split under foot and released a perfume of decay.

Now her soles burned with the cold; silver beads stood all over her uniform jacket. A shiver of loneliness slipped through her. She searched over her shoulder for the cupola, small and fairy-like, aloft above the trees, nuns, classrooms and dormitories, above the Third *Cours* hiding and searching. Oh ha ha, soon they would be searching for her, and Rancid's knees would be shaking under her big belly telling the Famous Heart Surgeon over the telephone they had lost his little girl. And before that, Dilly would read "bye bye" chalked onto the floor next to her desk. Clutching at limbs to keep her shoes from skating out from under her, she turned it all again, relishing it in her mind.

Now the incoming storm brought rain.

Wet hair in her eyes, she came upon the sagging old fence, bent rusty wires down enough to climb over to the pipe whose curved bottom lip, about two feet off the ground, jutted from the side of the ravine. Quickly as the rain began, it ceased; but now the wind turned manic, quiet one minute, shrieking and thrashing the next. She fought the tearing at her skirt and the slope's downward pull while she broke away small branches to make a screen at the pipe's opening, beneath which she uncovered layers of leaves dry enough to put inside for a mattress.

But she could sit up in the pipe only with a bent head and hunched shoulders; and then her breath would be cut short. Lying on her side was better, but the slope in the pipe forced her feet and knees toward her waist. So what. It was fun, like sleeping in a cave. The dry leaves smelled nice. She would get more. She grabbed the pipe's upper lip to hoist herself out and heard a light cracking sound and concrete bits rained over her knees. Gingerly she tested with her fingers around the thin jig-sawed separation just above her. Well, nothing moved, and she wouldn't be getting out again until they found her.

She bent her arm under her head, lay back and pulled up her knees. Cold air through the thread of fissure waffled down her neck. She raised her collar. She could stay here for as long as it took; she had cake from *Goûter* in her uniform pocket. She peered through the twiggy screen she'd raised. Why, this was like being a fox or mole watching the bushes bow and dance before the fury of the weather, smelling the wetness and seeing everything shine. She remembered how she and Gimme her cat used to hide under the dining room table and watch the housekeeper's thick ankles go back and forth below the hem of the cloth. A moment of longing pierced her.

Then the rain came on again in earnest, straight down, tramping. But good, the rain would make Dilly even more worried; and when she came out to search, her candy wrapper ruffle would melt onto her face and her feet would be soaked and freezing, just like the duck's had been and like hers, Helene's, were now. She had thought Dilly was going to be her friend, but then she let Popcorn die. She gritted her teeth and hatred of all that had happened surged in her chest.

Rainwater ribboned along the crack, began to slip inside. The one trouble, she thought inching back to let it fall clear of her body, was that she couldn't watch the fear jump into the grownups' eyes when they found her gone. No, her job now was just to keep quiet until she heard voices or footsteps, and then pull her navy jacket over her head so her hair wouldn't show through the branches as they walked past the pipe. Oh, they would be missing her a long time, maybe even think she was dead, before she walked into Study Hall and flopped down at her desk to stun them out of their wits. THEN she would laugh. The light of day lost its hold on the sky while she fed upon such scenes.

Muddy water began to trickle along the bottom of the pipe. A large clump of earth loosened and fell over her feet, cold and slimey. The weight of it, like a dead thing, gave her a sick feeling and she kicked it off. Maybe she should find some other place. No, this was the best. They would never find her in this old pipe. And next *Congé*, the whole Third *Cours* would want to hide where she did; but she would be a long way away by then, at home in Chicago with her dad.

The threadlike stream along the floor of the pipe widened until she could inch away no further and it began to soak her skirt, to edge up her thigh. And with every inhalation she tasted the vapor of wet clay; with every exhalation a spidery ghost from her nose and mouth hung before her.

Now her small white bed at home with its bulky comforter filled her mind; and with it the piquant smell of her father's cigar, then the feeling of his arm pulling her against his chest so vividly that everything in her, soaked and freezing, wanted to bolt to him. Lightning winked a giant eye; thunder boomed. She shut down hard against the tears clawing her throat. No. It would all be worth it in the end. It would all be worth it.

The hail started in.

Ice bigger than mothballs bounced and rolled toward the floor of the ravine. Through a curtain of white pellets, trees, bushes and rocks turned dreamy-looking, like those paintings at the Art Institute. Above her on the pipe was a sound as if many people were running, say, a block away, while two hairline cracks sprinted out of the fissure and down the sides of the pipe.

Thick mud oozed now where her soaked skirt had bunched beneath her into a hard knot that hurt her thigh. She raised onto an elbow to smooth it but her fingers stumbled in the soaked cloth. To straighten it, she jacked herself up to higher and rammed her head and shoulder with a searing pain against the top of the pipe. A large piece of concrete broke free, riding her, laying her low against the pipe's bottom. It was as if a giant had stepped on her. Stars exploded behind her eyes and out of the crown of her head while the left side of her face was pinned now against the pipe's bottom with its thick muck and moving water.

She'd had no time even to cry out. Her first breath drew the thick sludge into her submerged nostril so that her mouth popped open and the mud with its thick taste of iron oozed over her lower lip. Pain split her head and something warm ran down her neck. One arm was pinned beneath her and the other twisted behind her back. She tried not to swallow. Mud and water inched up her legs to her stomach. She heard the hail falter and cease; and then no sound except of random drips.

The sight of Mother Adelli and Big John reeling through the trees grew in her mind. They should be coming any time now, calling her name. She longed to see her father, to feel his arms lift her from under this slab, out of this muddy place. Tears burned her throat, but she dared not cry and draw in more mud.

The pitty, pitty, pitty of fresh rain, and then the downpour began once more. Maybe Mother Adelli would wait until the rain stopped. Oh, how could they ever find her in this old pipe? Why had she hidden so far away? Between breath-catching flashes of pain, she tried to think what to do. More than half of her mouth now was under water. She tried not to swallow, listened far along the ravine for footsteps and voices. Then, as if someone had opened a faucet, water began to course in the pipe. A blanket of mud toppled over her legs. The worst of possibilities filled her mind while her stomach clenched in terror and she wished with all her heart there was a God Who would help her, a Sacred Heart burning with love for her, a Blessed Mother or Guardian Angel to carry her from this place.

Steadily, the grim wet line gained her chest, her neck, her chin. She closed her free eye to shut out the writhing black water. Finally a line like the edge of a sheet eased over her second nostril and her mouth yanked itself hard to the side and up. She listened for footsteps, for voices, while through the small opening at one corner of her lips she felt her lungs pull in a ribbon of air. The icy edge crawled to her eye. Her lungs clung to their store. Her body seemed a separate person now, and she watched it flail and fight though it could not move. She thought she heard the faint crackle of twigs under foot. She held on, she held on. Then, trembling violently, her lungs seemed to burst apart with a brilliant flash of pain.

The pounding rain mellowed into notes like flower petals, and a spring-like breeze took up and buffeted her cheeks. She saw that an astonishing light poured from her body to wrap itself around her and cradle her as a mother might. And a brilliant disk of that same light also appeared at the end of a sort of tunnel above her; and she wanted more than anything to go to it, but she was so afraid. And then she heard a clear sweet voice, a voice from very long ago, one she recognized at once. And it called to her. "Come on, Helene," it said. "Here I am. Come on my baby. Come on."

Back in Study Hall, Mother Adelli wheeled from the laughing triumph of her team to scan the room. Where was Helene? She caught Mother Ling's eye. "Is the Rhenehan girl in the bathroom?" she mouthed. Mother Ling leaned on one foot and put a hand to her ear. Mother Adelli mouthed the question again. Lightning, like an enormous flashbulb, lit the bushes outside the windows; thunder cracked behind it. Mother Ling smiled and nodded as her team bunched, buzzed, then flew away for their turn to hide.

Hail began to ricochet off the windows, and by the time Team Two had squeezed into a broom closet on the third floor, a downpour of rain had taken up. Crouching behind a wall of toilet paper and cleaning supply boxes with fourteen girls, Mother Ling's feminine mustache glistened, everyone's hamstrings burned, and the air became thick as uncombed cotton.

One hour later, having seen her own victors tie the game and crowd exulting into the dining hall, Mother Ling stepped toward Cloister when Mother Adelli called after her.

"The Rhenehan girl, Mother; I didn't see her go into dinner."

"Rhenehan girl?" Mother Ling's forehead wrinkled.

"Yes, Helene Rhenehan. She was on your team."

Mother Ling thought, shook her head. "No, she was on your team, Mother. She was never on my team."

"But you told me she was in the bathroom after the first round." Mother Adelli's eyes searched the nun's face.

"Did I say she was in the bathroom?" Mother Ling's brow crinkled again. She rattled her rosary in the folds of her skirt.

"The first time I asked you didn't understand, but the second time you nodded yes."

"Oh," Mother Ling laughed, her very white teeth gleaming. "I thought you said 'laundry room' or 'broom.' It gave me the idea of the broom closet on the third floor. *Merci*," she bowed and started down the hall again.

"But she was never on my team, Mother. I deliberately didn't put her on my team." Mother Adelli followed after her.

Mother Ling stopped. Her eyes shifted back and forth. Fourteen at the top of the stairs, fourteen to hide, fourteen back. And never once was one the Rhenehan girl.

"I'm sorry Mother Adelli if she was supposed to be on my team. I didn't understand or take any notice of her. I don't know what to say." She scanned the corridor as if for a clue. Pebbles of hail clattered down the window. She bowed, then started again toward Cloister, searching under her cape as if she might find the missing girl there.

Mother Adelli called Madeline from her dinner to look in the dormitory. Helene's alcove was empty. She was not in the library, not in any classroom, not in chapel nor in the choir loft. She was not in the infirmary, not in the

Visitor's Parlor, not on the telephone, not in the furnace room, not in the gym.

Perhaps Helene was having her own game of *Câche-câche*, Mother Adelli suggested after dinner. The Third *Cours* fanned out for one hundred team points and a small gold medal of the Sacred Heart Mother Adelli had been saving; but after an hour and no luck, everyone grew tired of Helene's bad joke. They watched Mother Adelli's face turn sick-looking, saw her eyes grow wild as the clock crept toward dormitory time. Rain pounded the darkened windows. They trooped upstairs to end *Congé* feeling cheated in some way, uneasy at the sight of Helene's alcove curtains. A fourth academic ribbon took them into lights out.

Mother Adelli threw her shawl over her head and ducked into the wet freezing night. No Helene at the railway platform, not hiding at the grotto, not in the fire escape.

She knocked on Mother Crewelman's door.

"Why do you always wait and wait before you act?" Mother Crewelman pounded her desk with the flat of her hand. Then, her knees buckling, Mother Adelli stood outside Reverend Mother Gregory's office with the Spiritual Director who burst in the moment the Superior called, "Come." Every inch of Reverend Mother Gregory came alert at the sight of the two nuns descending upon her desk.

"That Rhenehan girl is missing. This one--" Mother Crewelman pointed a long finger at Mother Adelli, "has managed to let the girl slip through her fingers again. The child has been gone since three-thirty and this one has just now comes to report it."

Dumbly, the Superior indicated two chairs. The nuns sat. Reverend Mother Gregory folded her hands on her desk and squeezed her pudgy fingers together.

"Where is the Rhenehan girl, Mother Adelli?"

Mother Adelli felt the chair under her dissolve. There was a mix-up during *Câche-câche* and--

"This woman is not competent to keep track of chalk," Mother Crewelman blazed.

Reverend Mother Gregory bestowed a hard look upon her colleague, then nodded to Mother Adelli to continue.

The younger nun told about the teams, the noise, the mouthing across the room. "--and so I thought she was in the bathroom."

"You *thought*," Mother Crewelman burst out again. "Did you ever *think* had those girls maintained their usual silence you might have been able to hear Mother Ling?"

"We have quite enough going on here," Reverend Mother Gregory's jowls trembled. She raised a hand to the Mistress General. "Please save your evaluations for a more appropriate time."

"Thank you, Superior, I will do that. In fact I will put them in writing tonight."

"Fine, but as I am in charge here just now, I will ask the questions."

Across the desk, the older nuns traded a moment of intense dislike; then Mother Crewelman closed herself into her horse face and yielded the floor.

"Now," Reverend Mother Gregory returned to Mother Adelli, "I take it you have done some looking?"

"The boarders searched inside after dinner. I searched the grotto, train platform and fire escape." Her face collapsed. "This is my fault, Reverend Mother. The girl was angry with me. She may have run away."

"The girl has been angry with everyone since the day she arrived; and we had an agreement that you would handle that." The Superior looked closely at Mother Adelli. "I must tell you that to see this circumstance come before me is most irritating--and a great disappointment."

Mother Crewelman sniffed with satisfaction and re-folded her arms. The Superior looked at the young nun another moment and then cleared her face. "But you think this to be something other than a prank?"

Mother Adelli nodded and while the story of the duck spilled out, Reverend Mother Gregory puzzled over this young nun she had liked so well and who had become such a hazard.

"Probably," the Superior suggested, "she took the train again--to Chicago: or she is trying to get to New York to her grandmother, or rambling to give us a good scare until someone finds her."

"Superior, about two months ago--." Oh how Mother Adelli wished she could withhold the truth now! "When Helene got on the train, I failed to inform you that she told me afterwards she would get away from the school if she could."

Mother Crewelman drew a loud breath.

Reverend Mother Gregory lifted the telephone. Now was not the time for blame. Young Mother Adelli looked pale enough to faint. The operator connected her directly to the North Shore stationmaster in Chicago. It was an emergency. She let her eyes drift to Mother Crewelman balanced on the Louis XV like a dangerous collection of rocks. This was precisely the kind of drama the woman loved.

The stationmaster assured the Superior they would alert all train conductors to look for the ten year-old red-headed girl, about five foot--

"One," Mother Adelli supplied, leaning forward.

"weighing--?"

"Eighty-five to ninety pounds?" She saw the square frame.

"And wearing--?"

But now it became too real; her mind turned arthritic. Well it would be the uniform, and perhaps her outdoors jacket--. Reverend Mother Gregory turned toward Mother Adelli.

"--Quilted. Green, buttons--no, a zipper up the front--grey fur around the hood."

A square-built girl, perhaps looking rumpled, the Superior added, with red hair and freckles on her face and hands. She would have little or no money. The school would send a car wherever she was found.

Call the police, the stationmaster suggested. A runaway might be hitchhiking. This the Superior did, then telephoned her Superior, the Vicar General of the Western province, in San Francisco.

"That girl was your responsibility, Mother Adelli," Mother Crewelman exploded when the Superior returned the phone to its cradle. "You, with your starry-eyed disregard for all rules designed to keep students safe, let her slip through your fingers. Now we all must all be taken for idiots and incompetents."

Mother Adelli shrank. Mother Crewelman was right. She had handled everything wrong, *and* disobeyed The Rule. Oh Helene, where was she in the darkness with no money and no one to help her? Oh, please God, help her, she prayed and waited for a verbal beating from her Superior.

But Reverend Mother Gregory had nothing more to say to either nun. A strange calm filled her face. She made Mother Crewelman busy digging out the Rhenehan girl's papers. With that nun firing off at her every thirty seconds, Mother Adelli would be catatonic by the time the police arrived.

Together then, the two nuns picked over the details of the just-finished day. The wind, having spent its rage, whined softly past the windows, a dark river lit with flakes. Reverend Mother Gregory's house phone rang. "Show the officers to the Parlor," she told the Portress. "We'll be right down."

They jumped to their feet as the Superior entered, good Irish boys awkward on the settee, their big shoes polished, hats in their hands and snowflakes melting on their leather jackets. The heavy-set one, a Sergeant Mooney, produced a yellow tablet as they sat again, Reverend Mother Gregory to their left, Mother Adelli, white as a sheet, to the right. It was 9:45 p.m.

"We have a student missing," the Superior told him.

"Yes M'am." The Sergeant wrote on his tablet.

"The father is in Italy. The girl has been, let us say, disturbed at being separated from him. She's run off once before several months ago--a jaunt on the North Shore train to Lake Forest--a prank, nothing we needed to report. This evening, Mother Adelli," the Superior nodded to the younger nun, "in charge of the girl, searched the school with her students, and the grounds as best she could in this weather. I called the North Shore Authority; they will watch for her."

Sergeant Mooney nodded again, his face carefully blank. "Do you have a picture of the girl?"

Reverend Mother Gregory sent for Mother Crewelman whose tall figure at the door caused the officers to leap again.

"This is our Mistress General; she will be available later if you need her." Reverend Mother took the folders and nodded dismissal. Mother Crewelman punctuated her departure by closing the door loudly.

Young officer Halloran saw in the photograph a girl with a pan-shaped face and hair with a mind of its own, staring out from over a school uniform collar.

"The picture was taken last year," the Superior explained, "at the Cathedral School in Chicago."

"Well, Sergeant Mooney stood up, his jacket creaking, "we'll start with a look around. Is there a telephone? I'll call in some extra men, if you don't mind, M'am, for fresh eyes. Could be the girl's playing games and is right here on the premises. Then there'd be no need to disturb the doctor in Europe. And if she's hiding outside, the weather's been bad."

Four additional officers arrived. The white beams of their flashlights glanced off of every surface, even in the Cloister where the Religious, roused from bed, hustled down to the Community Room in bathrobes and nightcaps. There they huddled together, obedient and silent, while male hands and feet explored their sacred and committed space. The officers felt compelled to speak in whispers as they wove through lavatory and tubs, small cots and dressers, the tiny infirmary, private chapel and the Community Room itself.

Officer Halloran asked Mother Adelli for an article of Helene's clothing. She led him to the girl's locker and there discovered the jacket she had described, hanging by its hood. The officer folded it under his arm.

"We brought two dogs, though with this snow I'm not sure what they can get. We'll stay on it all night since the temperature is dropping. If we have no luck, we'll be back tomorrow when the light is better, and bring fresh dogs." Mother Adelli saw him out the Minims' Door into the dark. It was 1:30 in the morning.

Helene had no protection but her uniform. It was snowing now. She could go out to look again with the men, but had a dormitory for which she was responsible. A longing to help the girl passed through her so fierce she thought it would cleave her in two. She let her body collapse onto the lowest step of the staircase. She didn't know how long it was before she could draw together the pieces of herself and lug them up the interminable stairs to the third floor.

Five

The next morning, the manager of the *Hotel Roma*
informed Reverend Mother Gregory over transcontinental
telephone that Dr. Rhenehan was en route by limousine to
Sorrento, on the coast, and could not be reached for six
hours. The Superior called the grandmother. The
housekeeper took the message; Mrs. Rhenehan was at the
doctor.

Just after breakfast, additional officers and fresh dogs
arrived as the Third *Cours* began Study Hall, hands folded
and eyes shut tight to pray for the lost or strayed Helene.
But she pulls this stuff all the time, they looked at one
another; and she always shows up eventually looking so
superior. Experts now on their classmate, most were not,
like Mother Adelli, haunted by endless specters and
versions of horrible possibilities.

The long loose muzzle came snuffling at the windows,
blowing up snow while the stiff cordlike tail knocked at
snow-laden bushes making clouds of snow rise outside the
Study Hall windows. Some students stifled a laugh, and
most found it a little creepy, the dog smelling everything
that way. They looked at one another, wrapped ankles
around the legs of their chairs, fingered their hair. Mother
Adelli, grading history exams, saw the wariness taking hold
in their bodies.

But it was not the dog that found the girl.

Big John, in search along with everyone else, noticed
the collapsed pipe just beyond the school's property line.
Those blasted Lake County people, he thought, with a
busted-up pipe and fence ready to fall down--and right in
the lap of the Mothers' school! And the devil if he

wouldn't report it, too. As he stepped across the fence for a closer look, he saw there the twisted tongue of navy uniform skirt sticking through a bad crack in the side of the pipe.

Oh, holy Mary. He clambered up the slope calling for help. A police officer just beyond the grotto came on the run to where the big Irishman stood pointing his quavering finger.

Then indeed it was a matter for the law.

Sergeant Mooney presented himself at Reverend Mother Gregory's office, hat in hand. Everything about the man announced disaster. The Superior held off the toppling walls, and while Sergeant Mooney phoned the coroner, she placed the second call in as many days to her Superior on the West Coast. Next were calls to Bishop McCaw and the school's legal counsel. Finally, she sent for Mother Crewelman while the snow continued its work of laying a muffling cape over everything.

At 11:05 a.m., Mother Adelli copied onto the board a gargantuan sentence from Winston and Windsor, *A Basic Grammar:*

"Many florid and flabby gentlemen gobble flounder and gulp grape wine at the annual St. Whitcomb's Day formal dinner before the long-awaited recitation of sentimental poetry and finally the highly competitive song contest after which occurs the issuing of prizes large and small, and finally the long-winded speech of the incoming president filled with high humor and a bouquet of promises."

A groan went up.

"You have fifteen minutes to punctuate and diagram."

Yoked to the break-neck engine of her anxiety, the simplest everyday activity became monumental. She leaned back in her chair, let go of her mind. The tap of chalk sticks against the classroom blackboard. Eighth grade voices reciting next door. Her eyes drifted to the window, to the snow descending peaceful and innocent through the barren honeysuckle, and building upon every branch and twig a gorgeous coxcomb.

Then, crossing behind the branches as as if into a picture frame, appeared first one dark figure, then a second and carrying a stretcher covered by an olive-green army blanket and walking gingerly, as if careful that nothing should cause their burden to topple. Mother Adelli's eyes flew to the oxford caked with mud emerged from the hem of the covering and threw herself to her feet with a cry.

Blindly, she tore open her classroom door, the Minims' Door. *Oh, my dear God.* Up the stone steps, her narrow black shoes cutting into the fresh snow, *Oh, dear God, please!* She streaked through the curtain of white. Where did they go, where were they now, those men? They would go toward a car, an ambulance, wouldn't they? Frantically she searched among the dark verticals of the trees for anything that moved.

Then she saw them as they trod carefully past the shrubbery near the train platform. Already their burden wore a veil of white. A third man walked many paces behind, dark business hat pulled low, hands sunk into overcoat pockets. All moved toward a white police wagon with its darkened alarm globe parked near the entrance gate.

Mother Adelli lifted her skirts to free her ankles and ran. "Oh, gentleman, if you please--gentlemen!" she cried out.

They answered with a look but did not stop. She saw pity at work in their eyes, took in the oxford sticking out and wobbling a horrible little wobble. She hurried along behind, feeling as if she were shouting at them. "Please, who are you carrying? Please, I need to know!"

The officer at the rear turned his head. "Police business, Sister." They speeded their pace. She had to trot to catch up.

"But who can I ask? Please!"

"The Coroner. Right there behind you, M'am," the officer threw the words over his shoulder.

She turned to look, the word "coroner" tolling through her body.

The head of his lighted cigarette brightened under the shadow of his hat; he exhaled and she saw deep brown eyes look evenly at her through silver eyeglasses. He was a short heavy man with a maroon scarf filling the neck of his overcoat. She waited, breath wavering and white upon the air, until he drew alongside her.

"Please, may I ask who you've found?"

"A red-headed girl, Sister, in a navy jacket and plaid skirt; dead, I'm afraid, back there a-ways in an old drainage pipe in the ravine."

His words might as well have been snow touching but the most superficial surface of her mind, then melting as if they had never been. She was that far from any part of herself that could take them in.

"Are you a teacher here, Sister?"

She nodded.

"Perhaps you could make an identification?"

Make an identification. Her head and mind locked up in ice. She nodded again.

"Yo." The Coroner waved his arm. The bearers stopped a dozen paces from the wagon to turn the dusted bills of their caps toward the squat man and slender Religious angling toward them.

She wasn't prepared for it when he grasped the blanket and pulled it back. One side of Helene's face was under frozen mud and leaves; dark runs of dried blood angled from her matted hair. Her face was swollen and blue, freckles faded, mouth on one side jerked into an idiot's grin. The sight made two giant blocks of wood clap deafeningly inside Mother Adelli's head. She staggered backwards. Then, "Oh, Helene," she cried out, but instead an only animal sound, horrible and high-pitched, was wrung onto the air; and, as it twisted through her body, brought her to her knees and elbows in the snow.

She inched this way across the ground, habit and veil gathering twigs while grief leaked out her mouth, over her knotted hands in an uncanny cry. It poured from her very cells, her bones, her baffled broken mind stiffening everything through which it passed.

Several policemen leapt toward the dreadful keening where the dark lump of veil and woolen skirts moved like a monstrous snail over the snowy ground, and the sounding out of grief raised hackles along the backs of their necks. They took another step and stopped. This was a nun, a woman dedicated to God. They moved aside, watching where they stood, until finally, slowly, she gathered herself onto her feet. Then, head thrown back, arms out, she staggered, keening, in a circle, like someone drunk. A young officer caught her before she fell and supported her through the kitchen door.

Sleep evaded Mother Adelli in the infirmary. When she heard the door latch and Mother Spencer's steps fade in the direction of the stairs, she got up and dressed. A terrible energy dragged her up and down corridors and finally through the kitchen door and onto the snow-drifted path to the ravine. She slipped over its snowy lip and, walking like a skier with the sides of her shoes biting into the snow, headed for the drainage pipe where she found the old wire fence cut open and bent back.

She took in the preen of white over the pipe's lower half, the odor of old cement and stale air that hung about it. A broken-off arc lay on its back, snow-covered; and a small brown wren settled upon it to ruffle its feathers and pick for mites. "Ny-ahh!" She charged the air with her rage that the bird--that anything or anyone--should dare touch the place Helene had been, should dare even to be alive. "Ny-ah!" The bird leapt away on a blur of wings.

She ducked under the police wire with its red signs strung tree to tree, then to the broken pipe to run her hand under the thickness of its cement. For a split second she felt the crushing weight fall upon her own body, closed her eyes, drew a breath laced with fear, took in the deep meringue of new snow that covered what of the top remained intact. Peering directly through the damaged opening, she saw sheets of dark silt mixed with leaves and pressed into the shape of a torso. Her midriff buckled. *This was where Helene was when*--she sank to her knees--*where she--*.

She retched until her stomach ached, then wiped her mouth on her sleeve and rested her head against the cold concrete with its hoarfrost. She would if she could stop this breath, this heart beating in her chest, though the desire to do so was a sin. Sin or no, she longed to be, too, in that deep featureless peace she realized now had drifted up from the girl on the pallet.

"Why didn't you tell me where you were going?" She spoke to the departed Helene, already at her Last Judgment, and to the body in the refrigerator drawer in Lake Forest. "I would have gone there with you. I would have carried you to your mother, to your Maker in my own arms."

She lay down beside the pipe and turned her face from the falling flakes. She did not feel the freezing ground beneath her nor notice the snow begin to turn her habit white. Her mind could do nothing but witness the great curved knife that continually curled its searing blade through her with excruciating and rhythmic grace. It was then that she made her confession to the frozen brambles, the trees, the notch of the ravine with its motionless silver cord.

"I was to be her protector and helper, and could not even keep her alive."

Then she lurched to her feet and the blanket of snow fell from her habit in clumps. She unbuttoned her wimple and ripped it with the veil from her head to fling high, away, for they could no longer belong to her. The weaknesses in her had cost a child her life. The headdress flew upward to hang above her like a great white-faced black bird, then to fall, fanning out black wings that caught on the lower branch of a tree. "She paid the price for my sins," she cried to the snow-sifting sky. "*She* paid."

How could she continue now in this world, face any person after she had opened the door to death for another? She would go to the North Shore platform and stand on the near end and throw herself beneath the wheels before the train could stop. No, first she must go to confession. She could not die with the child's death on her conscience. She scrambled up the slope, panting from tree to tree.

Once inside the building, she sought Reverend Mother Gregory, but came instead upon Mother Crewelman leaving the library with several large volumes of law against her chest.

"Mother," the Mistress General rose like a wall. "Where is your wimple? And look at your habit. Where on earth have you been?"

"I need a confessor, Mother."

"Tuesday, Mother Adelli, is our day for--."

"It is urgent, Mother. I cannot wait until Tuesday."

The Mistress General took in the frantic eyes, the tear-streaked face, the soaked habit, the dirt and clinging leaves. For the space of a moment she thought she saw the student's open grave inside the young woman and a chill ran through her; but she collected herself. She would indulge none of this.

"It is improper to disturb the chaplain when he is not on duty. I see that you are ill again. Wait in the infirmary. I will inform Reverend Mother Gregory of your state; at present she is with the police. Clean yourself up. And what have you done with your wimple and veil? Have *Soeur* Elisabeta get another. Go up the back and stay out of sight. What if a student should see you?"

She watched the muddy shoes spoil the waxed floor that took *Soeur* Fiona three hours to bring to a proper shine. What terrible grief this woman had brought upon herself and everyone else! This death would discolor everything for everyone, and who knew for how long. All because of disobedience.

In the infirmary, Mother Adelli fell into agitated sleep and did not wake as the door was opened by Mother Superior

Reverend Mother Gregory, hands locked across her girth, stood at the foot of the infirmary cot. She saw a woman not yet thirty, and victim of these circumstances. What of that was hers? And what of the rest of them? She had come to the Order, her life in her hands, and they had taken it. Now here she was with a scar too deep for any but God's grace to reach.

Mother Adelli's eye lids fluttered.

"How are you, Mother?" the wide mouth asked.

But Mother Adelli was forced to wait upon her body. It came slowly from a far tangled place and dragged her tattered mind behind it.

"I want to go to confession, Reverend Mother," she finally managed.

The two Religious had not spoken since the girl's body was discovered. Reverend Mother Gregory had directed a physician be called when an officer had commented on the young nun's state after viewing the corpse. The Superior also made an identification for the Coroner--a quick look, then turn away. Horrible. Horrible.

"I'll call a priest immediately." The Superior kept her eyes on the face and away from the exposed head with its shorn hair. *Like a lamb to slaughter.* She could not stay the image and how it moved her to pity. The thought that perhaps she had asked too much of this nun moved along a back corridor of her mind. Right now she must focus on present realities. Could the young woman sustain herself through the ordeal pressing upon them?

"Why did you go out, Mother? The doctor told you to rest in the infirmary. You need your strength. We all will need it."

"My body couldn't be still, Reverend Mother. I had to see where--. She was all alone and--." The words crawled from a terrible pit. "I don't know how to go on living. I wish God had--. How could He take her? She hadn't even lived yet."

Reverend Mother Gregory raised her palm, made her voice stern. "Listen to me, Mother. You tried. The girl was difficult." She felt her logic stagger. "God gives each of us free will--."

Mother Adelli began to rock like a child on her cot. The Superior could not go on, looked away. Each must deal with personal responsibility as best she could. Still, here was this burst pot, and her Vicar General today reminding her at whose door the work of mending lay as well.

The Superior noticed the soiled habit on the chair, the black shoes caked with mud and rotting leaves. All, all carried the death site. And young Mother Adelli had sustained the blow of that place, would carry that mark forever.

She leaned at the window and began sorting. Reverend Mother d'Gagnier would listen to anyone who offered an opinion, but the Order was beholden neither to bishops nor cardinals, and answered only to the Pope, an agreement secured by their foundress Madeleine Sophie Barat, a woman ahead of her time. All convents were under obedience to their Motherhouse in Rome, *Via Nomentana.* Even so, immediately Bishop McCaw heard of the tragedy from the father, he was on the telephone to the Vicar General, adding fuel to the fire and running everyone's nerves ragged. If the bishop didn't have some drama of his own going on, he would elbow his way into yours. Thank God the grave financial crisis at Lone Mountain had stayed her Superior's coming by a few days. She would arrive late on Monday and be spared the requiem Mass. Keep the Vicar General away from Mother Crewelman if possible, and keep everything well-choreographed. She must sit with her schedule book right away. She turned from the window. Mother Adelli's eyes were open.

"I will need a great deal of information tomorrow, Mother Adelli. The girl's records, schoolwork, *Primes* marks, your comments and notes; but try to sleep again now." She patted the thin mattress near the pillow and started for the door. Mother Adelli's voice came before she could open it.

"If you please, Reverend Mother, yesterday, at the pipe, I realized something about all that behavior, that it was really just about trying to get away from the pain. She had so much pain."

The Superior's eyes rested for a moment on the young nun's face.

"I suppose," she said and closed the door softly behind her.

Mother Adelli slipped back into sleep again. In a dream without pictures, the bony hand of old Mother Concepción slipped into hers and a profound peace settled into her body. It lasted until an hour later when *Soeur* Elisabeta called to her softly.

"Mother, a Father has come, from Lake Forest. He is waiting for you."

She helped Mother Adelli into a habit one size too big and arranged the fresh wimple and veil. A dark calm prevailed in Mother Adelli now as she went to meet her judgment from God.

"Bless me Father, for I have sinned." Wimple to the screen, Mother Adelli whispered the story.

Father Hilary, an older man who had put off his dinner to attend the urgent need, blinked. A death! He was not expecting such a thing and did not know what to say. And the woman was in enough pain to have murdered the girl. He swore he could smell her tears through the screen. But from the jumbled story, it sounded as though it was the student who got herself into trouble.

"Let's not hear any more about deserving to be dead," he told her firmly. No, she should not have broken the Rule, but the girl certainly had played some part in her own death. She was to treat thoughts of suicide as a direct temptation from the Devil. Most people did the best they could, even when they made bad mistakes. They confess and go on, asking God to take care of things. Did she understand? He could tell she did not. "To take the whole blame, Mother, is to call God's will and mercy into question. This is an act of great arrogance."

She was not to think of leaving the Order. She was to stay put and do what her Superiors directed. Right now, her students had lost a classmate. She must care for them. For penance, she was to offer Mass and Communion for the next month for the girl and the family.

"I do not feel I can go to Communion, Father."

"Are you greater than God?" he exploded finally. "I order you to go to Communion. And I give you absolution. It comes from God. Accept it."

He dismissed her before he said more. Leave the Order! Where on earth would she go, having burnt her bridges, as all priests and nuns must?

Reverend Mother Gregory came to Study Hall after dinner to tell the Third *Cours* about Helene. There was a shocked silence and then spatters of sniffling and crying.

They were glad the next day when they got their Mother Adelli back, comforted by the familiarity of her figure, by her quiet walking, soft looks and ordering of their hours. They went on under the unwieldy burden of these shocking happenings, encouraged at the sight of their Mother Adelli going on also, and through a maze of unpredictable shocks and blows dealt back from the most innocent of spaces and unassuming of objects.

In the gym after dinner and waiting for their Mistress to come, they tried to understand their classmate's death by putting themselves in her last moments. They blew their cheeks into balloons, stuck thumbs into their mouths, held their noses and turned red until the noisy air burst out. They laughed and then hushed, uncomfortable and worried.

Mother Adelli came cradling two basketballs. She smiled at them.

GeeGee raised her hand. "Did Helene suffer a lot?"

The blue face, the idiot grin, the dried blood. Day and night she saw these and more.

"Do you remember that Shakespeare calls sleep 'a little death'? Well, I like to think she just fell asleep, and then her Guardian Angel carried her to God."

"But wasn't it like someone holding her head under water?" Jennifer picked at her shoe and looked like she might cry. Once her brother did that to her, and she remembered the panic, the fighting in her body.

"We don't know about the last moments, do we? No one has come back to tell us." Standing before them in her habit, she felt her poverty--real poverty--in the face of their need.

"Why would God want Helene to suffer and die? Because she did bad things and didn't go to Confession or Communion?" GeeGee tore at her fingernails while others sucked the ends of braids or picked at scabs on their knees.

"Helene had trouble inside, like we all do sometimes; and her father had his own reasons for not wanting her to receive the Sacraments. Neither Helene nor her father seem to have been given the gift of Faith."

"Why wouldn't God give them Faith? How can they go to Heaven?" Jennifer pleaded.

Mother Adelli shook her head. "I don't know why." She had to be truthful, she was their teacher. "I know He does not punish you for not having something He does not give you. There is Baptism of Desire. Remember your Catechism? It says to do the best you know and you go to Heaven."

Madeline held up her hand. "Did we make her die?"

"Of course you didn't. How could you? Don't ever think that!"

They glanced at one another. They hadn't really liked Helene, except when she got Popcorn. They didn't talk to her much, weren't that nice to her, didn't really want to make friends.

"Come on." Mother Adelli started bouncing a basketball. The hollow sound reverberated around the room. "Keep-away from Mother Adelli." She didn't know where the strength came from. She fought for her girls, fought the poisonous lethargy of death invading their bodies. What more could she say when she herself didn't know the truth about Helene's death.

"On your feet," she challenged them and bounced the echoing ball to Madeline who backed away and then chased it down. "Keep-away from Mother Adelli. Come on, Madeline," she called. "Two hundred points if you can keep the ball away from Mother Adelli for five minutes." She pointed to the clock.

Madeline bounced the ball to Jennifer, sitting and wiping her eyes. Jennifer swatted it to Sylvia, then got to her feet. They struggled up like bodies rising from under water. The room began to ring with the squeaking of shoes and the thump of the ball, and with Mother Adelli calling out, "Too easy. You're too easy." A few voices began calling back, "Here. Over here. Keep-away. Keep away from Mother Adelli."

Six

Two altar boys lit the tall candles on either side of the tabernacle, then waited in their black cassocks and white surplices at the foot of the altar as the choir released the mournful *Dies irae, dies illa* exactly at 9:00 a.m. as Father Ambrose swept through the vestry door, shoes clicking lightly against the marble flooring of the sacred space. Two deacons in dalmatics followed.

Everyone rose except the dead girl's father who sat alone on the left in the first pew.

Father Ambrose spooned a dark powder into the censor, secured the perforated hat-shaped lid that began to smoke sparsely with, the Third *Cours* thought, a smell between baking spice and bath salt as the deacons held outward the edges of his chasuble wide like wings and Father Ambrose strode back and forth swinging the censor and blessed the sacred space and its congregation.

Next he descended to the foot of the altar. *"Confetior Dei omnipotenti,"* he bowed, and began a dialogue with the choir that dragged along maddeningly for students' complaining stomachs and burning knees. *"Mea culpa,* he beat his breast, *"mea maxima culpa."*

Oughtn't they, the Third *Cours*, beat theirs as well for mean thoughts, cutting looks, snide remarks about Helene that haunted their minds now since such things did not waft away like the incense, but piled up inside.

The Introit. The Espistle. Then the Gospel, *"Laus tibi Christi,"* the deacons intoned in plainsong after the reading while organ and choir wove a spectacular wreath of voices and students stood shifting from leg to leg.

Now the priest stepped to the lectern, arranged written notes then looked up.

"My dear friends," he began. "We celebrate a *requiem* today for a beloved daughter, treasured student, dear friend." His disengaged voice spread a lost feeling over the pews. "Yet how do we celebrate when the one loved is taken from us so suddenly?" He drew a breath, looked over the pews. "Our beloved departed ate of this very Bread; and so we can celebrate--Yes, I say 'celebrate,' for we know," his voice rose, "she lives forever, even as Our Lord Himself has promised!"

The Third *Cours* gaped at one another. Mother Adelli's eyes widened. Reverend Mother Gregory clapped her hand over her mouth. She had forgotten to remind Father Ambrose of Dr. Rhenehan's orders that his daughter was not to practice the Faith. Surely the cleric remembered he had never once seen the girl at the communion rail!

Father Ambrose tromped on. "Raised by careful parents in the religion of her baptism, none need worry nor even question her death." The clap of a kneeler. "It is for us now to, follow her in faithfulness to the safety and embrace of our Creator."

GeeGee didn't know about that, but being freed from homework, tests and endless silence would be worth quite a lot.

The doctor father sat bolt upright, gripped, Father Ambrose humbly assumed, by the moving ideas in his homily. "So this beloved daughter thanks her father for raising her in the Church, and for bringing her to this most excellent of schools from which He has now called her home."

A loud bang from the front pew and the father on his feet, face dark as an iron fry pan and looking around as if for someone to kill; then slowly reclaiming his place while Father Ambrose, like cleaning a window with the side of his hand, blessed the congregation in the name of the Father, Son and Holy Ghost.

Reverend Mother Gregory shook her head. How could it have been worse? And there was Mother Crewelman's face in a grimace of satisfaction: Father Ambrose had never been her choice as chaplain. Thank heaven Reverend Mother D'Gagnier was not due until dinner time.

The Offertory. The Consecration and elevation of Sacred Substances. Then the students crept along to the Communion rail, eyes sliding sideways snatching a glimpse of the father, of Mother Adelli and each other, looking for clues about how to feel. To die without being old was a thing they wouldn't wish on anyone. *Mea culpa*. Each reached into her sack of guilt for some token for the father, for Helene. And when Father Ambrose turned later for the final benediction, the Third *Cours* found, mysteriously, even as they closed ranks without her, a place for Helene in their midst.

Then down the worn accepting stairs behind Mother Adelli, folding veils into pockets, vowing to be kinder to those they liked and, when they could remember, not be so mean to those they didn't. And because they couldn't help it, they stretched their necks toward the kitchen, searching the air for the fragrant profiles of breakfast.

In the Visitor's Parlor, Michael Rhenehan took in the sallow Superiors on the walls, strode to the window to fling aside the long lace drape which flared and settled around his back. Another trapping he and other poor fools had paid for in this goddamned school, along with the grand piano and the matchstick chairs. His white convertible, parked at the front door, called to him. Just find her things and get the hell out of here. At the thought of his dead girl, he gripped the window sill to lean a sweating forehead against the cold of the window pane.

The parlor door swung open. Mother Adelli peered into the room, saw the man-sized bulge behind the drape, the backs of polished shoes.

"Doctor Rhenehan?" she asked carefully.

He hurled the drape aside, set for a fight; but it was the small perky one that he'd worried about from the beginning. She moved toward him now, head bent a little to one side and eyes upon his face greatly careful, as if they touched a burn victim. This one had been close to his Helene, had everyday seen her robin's-egg blue eyes, copper hair, heard her voice. But wait, wasn't she the one responsible? Yes. She was the one!

"These were overlooked among your daughter's things, Doctor." She held out the little stack of postcards, her legs trembling violently under her habit. "She carried each one as it came in her uniform pocket."

Dumbly he gestured her to a chair across from the settee. He sat as well, the coffee table between them. He held the cards gingerly, as if they smoldered. After a moment, he searched for his voice.

"Is this all of them?"

She recognized his pain. "There may be more among her things, Dr. Rhenehan." It could be true.

An awkward silence. "We are all stunned and grief-stricken."

Well, she might as well have struck him in the face.

"Grief-stricken!" His voice came loud. "Oh, let me show you 'grief-stricken,' Mother."

He grabbed up the antique magnifying glass from the coffee table--it sent a crazed spear of light about the room--jammed his face against the glass, stood, and pressed toward her until the frame was all but upon her wimple. "Have you seen a father who would like to tear his own flesh from his bones? Take a look at him, Mother." Red snaked across the jelly of his eyes; the corollas, a deeper hue than his daughter's, shuddered and jumped.

Mother Adelli pulled her face away.

"No, look at him, Mother," he hissed; "a man driven near madness, who thought his daughter was safe and comes back to find her dead." She felt the pellets of his breath strike her chin. "While the holy nuns were praying, a ten year-old girl was left to drown in a pipe. No one was watching her." His face pursued her further, into the chair back. "No one was watching her, Mother. No one was watching her."

"Please, Doctor Rhenehan," she begged, crawling her back up the chair to lift her head away from him.

He clattered the glass back onto the table, took a few steps away, then wheeled. "Where is that Reverend Mother of yours? What on earth takes you women so long?" Before she could respond, he lapsed into an affected stroll toward the portraits. "Well, they won't be hanging *her* up there with the others. She can get that glory out of her head." He turned, pointed at Mother Adelli still plastered against the chair's back. "We are getting rid of you incompetents. You won't be losing anyone's daughter again. At least I can protect someone else's child. Wasn't that your job--to protect her? Isn't that why I left her with you?"

"I would give my life to undo what has happened," Mother Adelli whispered.

He opened two fingers, looked through them like the sighter on a gun. "And I would gladly take it, Mother, believe me."

He watched her wipe her eyes, and for a split second knew there was a way in which this woman was not fully at fault; but quickly as the perception came, it died under the memory of the Coroner's report: fractured skull, broken shoulder, death by drowning. He thought for a moment he might vomit. He collapsed onto the couch, and let his head drop between his knees. "My God, what am I going to do?"

"Oh, Doctor Rhenehan, we will pray for you."

"*Pray!*" he roared. "And were you praying while she was in the pipe?" He ran his hand through his hair. "My God, do you have any idea what it's like to be crushed under concrete, to have your skull fractured? Get out." He threw himself onto his feet, took a step around the table. "Get out, get out before I murder you."

Reverend Mother Gregory stood in the parlor door, eyes jumping from father to nun; but then fixed them on Mother Adelli's face, her hand making a low urgent fanning movement toward the foyer. Michael Rhenehan watched the young nun's shadow weep over the rugs. *May she rot in Hell.* He turned, and the Superior's wimple and wide mouth set him off afresh.

"You." He pulled his lips back coming to meet her. "How do you explain the idiot at the altar? Is this how you honor the dead; or did you, against my express wishes, indoctrinate my daughter into your spooky rituals? Perhaps you were so busy listening to your cash register, you didn't hear me forbid that?"

Reverend Mother Gregory held herself with dignified reserve. She had expected this.

"Father Ambrose made an unfortunate mistake. We have observed your wishes to the letter; but I'm afraid he sees so many students, he sometimes--."

"Something else you've muffed, is it? This time it didn't cost a life, it only tore someone's innards to shreds. You're the one I want," his voice rose. "Let the little murderess go."

"Mother Adelli is no murderess. Of course you are distraught. We understand. Please take a seat. We are--."

"Oh no? Who killed my daughter, then?" Fury boiled into his face. "If it wasn't that one, it must be you, the Big Cheese. I'll take this seat," he planted himself upon the settee. "I've undoubtedly paid for it and for who knows what else in this mirage from Hell."

The Superior heard the Portress buzz someone in. A man in a business suit slowed to glance into the parlor, to nod to Reverend Mother Gregory still just inside the door, then to move on.

"No, come in," Michael Rhenehan called after him. "Let me tell you how they let my daughter die here, how they lost track of her and let her die!"

Reverend Mother Gregory heard the footsteps hurry down the corridor. Keith Christopher. On the Executive Board. Not good.

"We will need the parlor for a time. You'll be outside?" The Superior eyed the Portress meaningfully, then closed the door and crossed the room to stand beside the chair at the coffee table.

"That priest never once said her name. Not once. Perhaps no one here learned her name. It was Helene. Helene Rose Rhenehan, August 8, 1938 to November 11, 1948." He drew a great rattling breath.

The Superior sat. Of course the grief was terrible.

"You know something funny? On my dresser is a red and yellow yo-yo I bought the day before she--. Now what am I going to do with that?" A mean light lit in his eyes. "Oh. Why you can keep it for your desk. And I'll make sure you get it."

The Superior held her peace, eyes on his distracted face. Let him run on, run down.

"Another funny thing." He fished for his wallet. "I have a card--here--that lets me into the Vatican ,night or day." He held it up, white, trimmed in red, embossed with a gold seal. "I don't even believe all this," he waved abstractly; "yet I can walk right into the office of the Papal Secretary. If I want to see the Pope, I can do it like this," he snapped his fingers. He leaned across the coffee table. "But I can't see my daughter when I want to, can I? No. Not anymore."

He was on his feet again. "I noticed this commendation from Pius XII about the wonderful schools you people have. What would they call what you do--*really* do--in the world out there you so abhor--grand larceny?

Well, I'm going to see that the public knows all about this place." He strode back to the settee. "And you will not need to revise your brochure because you won't need one anymore."

The Superior straightened her skirts. These were things this man would have said to the press had Bishop McCaw not intervened the day before the funeral. Understandable, of course. And, like many fathers, he was so little aware of how things actually were with his daughter.

"Doctor Rhenehan, please, our hearts go out to you. Your daughter's death was an unfortunate accident that--."

"Oh, well, an accident." He threw up a hand, gave an exaggerated shrug and leaned back. "That makes all the difference in the world. An accident isn't anybody's fault."

"And the accident was doubly unfortunate because it was brought on by the unhappy girl herself."

His stunned silence told her immediately her words were a mistake.

"You listen to me," he leaned forward then, "if she was unhappy, what were those in charge of her doing about it? I recall you told me she would be happy, that there would be no problem. Didn't you tell me that?"

"Most students are happy here."

The girl and father on the settee. Mother Adelli across. The *Goûter* tray. The drape billowing. She hadn't paid much attention to the girl, really. Angry. A sloucher. It was longevity with the father she'd been after. She felt her face heat. "We expected as much with your daughter."

"And?" His eyes gleamed.

"Mother Adelli tried--."

"That woman is not big enough to manage a mattress let alone girls that age." He pushed his face forward. "You should have gotten rid of her long ago."

"Mother Adelli does her job extremely well, and she received what should have been adequate guidance from both of her Superiors."

"Back in your lap, I see; where it belongs."

"Your daughter had a personality that did not integrate well here, Dr. Rhenehan. I'm sorry to say it. And she did not seem to recover from her separation from you, as most students do from their parents--and as we expected she would."

The father opened his mouth, closed it.

"Your daughter was a behavior problem. She was determined. We did our best."

"Determined? Yes, to get some attention, for God's sake. If she got some attention she would still be alive, wouldn't she?" His eyes blazed.

"Perhaps," she brought her voice up, "the loss of her mother--."

His body went limp. He let his face fall into his hands. "Oh God, I've lost them. I've lost them both." His voice came muffled through his fingers.

The Superior dropped her eyes and waited. The rumble of a truck through the gate. A bell called someone to Cloister. Dust settling on the magnifying glass.

The father sat up again. "My mother will die from this, mark my words." He jabbed toward her a finger timed to each word. "And her death will also be at your door." He turned to stare out the window, turned back. "I've decided to take this to the press, despite what I told McCaw. What does he care about one girl?" He put out a bitter laugh. "You people look after your own, like we do in Medicine. I know how the game goes."

"We care very--."

"'Criminal negligence,' that's what it is. 'Wrongful death.'" He reared back, dusted across his trousers, head held high. "People will be more than interested, Reverend Mother, believe me."

The newspaper headlines. The public scrutiny. A circus to embroil them. This was very bad. Very bad.

"Your daughter was off of school property. We have reason to believe, from her classmates, that she planned to hide as a retribution. The law calls for 'reasonable precaution.' Mother Adelli certainly took that; she is as conscientious as they come. Helene ran away, she stole, she damaged school prop--."

"Ran away?" He shook his head as if to bring his eyes into focus. "What do you mean? Why wasn't I informed?"

"A poor choice of words," the Superior batted the air, quieted her voice "A prank. She was new. We understood. You were busy and far away."

"That is negligence, pure and simple. What else should I have heard about, her brain surgeries?"

Reverend Mother Gregoroy gave him a narrow look. "Had we called over such an incident, would you have sent her to her grandmother in New York or brought her to Rome? Would you have cancelled your contracts and come home?"

"I should have had the option. Oh," he shook a fist, "this will go hard with you, very hard."

The Superior starched herself up. "We did what we thought you would have wanted."

"Well, don't think for other people. You're not qualified."

He stood; but then sat again and slumped forward with a moan.

"I wish--we can't always work miracles," the Superior told him, moved by his despair. "In the end we must leave results to God."

His head snapped up.

"Oh, that's right. Now God is responsible. That's what you people do when you've gotten yourselves into some mess. Well, that won't serve here. I have spoken with your Reverend Mother D'Gagnier. And we are not finished either, you and I. We will see each other tomorrow at the Bishop's place. I will not let my daughter's death go by. The world must know what happened to her, how you treated her. You'll see it in all the papers. And you will find your students will not be back after Christmas. I have an appointment with the State Board of--. "But hey," he shrugged large, "why spoil the fun?"

Then, as if off to the side, a part of him watched himself angling like some tall winged Mercury, hair curling and wild, rising out of Hades with the fire of Holy Vengence, legs long and fluid, striding over scattered Persian islands while the rubies at his cuffs flashed power, himself the destroyer of all he left in his wake warrior's face cutting through the stifling room with its multiplication of idols crossing on giant legs the clip-clip on the marble of the foyer and heaving down its steps to open the forbidding door his girl's cache safe at his bosom long trousered legs bounding free from the confines of Hell to his white magical machine the low door the slot the key the roar and jump forward the ping ping ping of little stones the great arched gate falling away.

Seven

A young cleric showed the three Religious into a Victorian parlor groaning under bowlegged side tables, animal-footed chairs, straining bookshelves, and ponderously-framed portraits. He offered refreshments; the nuns shook their heads. Light from ornate wall fixtures and Tiffany tablelamps cast vague shadows over everything.

Reverend Mother Gregory had seen the room before. The man could not throw anything away. She glanced at Reverend Mother D'Gagnier, arrived from the West Coast the previous night and now removing her gloves finger by finger as she read the gold-imprinted titles of ecclesiastical tomes. The door opened. Bishop McCaw entered on short legs.

This was a man of rosette cheeks, quick blue eyes and very fine white hair. He wore a black cassock trimmed with magenta piping and magenta skullcap to match. Reverend Mother D'Gagnier, followed by the others, creaked to her knees to kiss his ring of office. He invited the Religious to sit, then pulled a chair forward for himself. After a few moments of courtesy chat, he leaned back and made a steeple of his fingers.

"I thought we might take a few minutes before the doctor arrives. I hate to see him, in his grief, damage your educational institution and our best-educated Catholic women graduates who will partner with our young Catholic men destined to be local, national and world leaders."

Always a sideways compliment. Never a word about the nuns' own graduates, successful in their own right, Reverend Mother Gregory simmered. Her experience was that most priests saw women as a specialized and exotic life-form endowed with limited but dangerous magical powers. And the Order's Superior from the West Coast seemed to soak up every word the man said while Mother Adelli, facing another day of inquisition, and with what well might be strep throat, looked washed out altogether.

"Should the aftermath of this death damage you, it will hurt us here as well." Bishop McCaw patted his breast. "My reading is that right now Dr. Rhenehan thinks he is the only father who has ever lost a child to an accident. And since the girl was in your keeping, he wants you to pay for it."

Reverend Mother Gregory stiffened. "This is but one instance, Excellency. And sad as it is, would not be the first time a student has died at a school, even one of our schools. Our parents live in the world, they understand such things."

"But not at the school *their* child attends," the Bishop raised a softening chin and narrowed his eyes. "The laity is a fickle lover, if you will excuse me, Mothers, and hops easily from bed to bed."

"During my novitiate at Nice," Reverend Mother D'Gagnier raised a light melodious voice, "a student hanged herself. Nothing at all to do with us, but we took the blame. It was ten years before our enrollments recovered. Tragedies cast long shadows."

"Exactly," Bishop McCaw brought his hands together. "Of course, the whole thing might blow over and your enrollments drop but a year or two. On the other hand, popular feeling might turn families to, say, the Benedictines, the Sisters of St. Joseph, the Dominicans. And where parental interest goes, money goes; and where money goes, money goes. I could show you statistics. I'm afraid I sense a prairie fire here I just hope we can put out."

An uneasy silence. The shadows of tree branches flickered over the book spines. A telephone rang in another room. Bishop McCaw, hoisting his small frame, was not finished

"I'm sorry to say there is a hunger for stories like yours." His voice thickened. "For shock, for--I hate to bring it up--another Suzanne Degnan." Reverend Mother Gregory swallowed.

Hearing that name, a chill ran through Mother Adelli. Though a full two generations apart, she and the murdered Suzanne had for a time walked the same neighborhood streets--Granville, Hood, Glenlake. The five year-old sister of a Sheridan Road student, little Suzanne Degnan vanished. Ten days later, her body parts turned up one after another in Chicago sewers. Mother Adelli saw again the small white casket at the girl's funeral mass, heard the singing of the children's choir, excruciating and tender. The broken pipe. Helene's mud-packed face. She gripped the chair, again fought her body's will to escape into a dark tunnel.

"...and you can imagine the circus the press made of everything until that demented University of Chicago student was caught six months later." The bishop dry-washed his hands, then let them lie loose and comfortable at the base of his belly.

Reverend Mother Gregory bristled. Really, the man's theatrics were maddening. "Our case is not the same at all, not at all. Ours was an accident brought on by the girl herself and--."

"I'm afraid the public does not make nice distinctions, Reverend Mother Gregory. The girl was under your care. They will think, 'Can't those nuns even keep their students alive?'" The pink tip of his tongue slipped across the Bishop's lips.

They had gone nose to nose before, he and this daughter of a chain store magnate. Now here was a sticky wicket in her front yard. And it had taken some fancy talking to get the doctor to agree to a conference. If it weren't for his ecclesiastical position, for his acumen and cleverness, by now the death would have been bawled from every street corner in Chicago. These women would thank him one day.

Silence.

The doorbell.

The bishop raised his eyebrows all around.

"May I take your coat?"

"I know where it is."

The doorknob.

Michael Rhenehan stepped into the room.

He saw fluted ellipses, pale female faces, the small cassocked bishop with his stomach resting in his hands like a beach ball.

"Dr. Rhenehan. Please come in." Bishop McCaw bounded from his chair smiling, but not broadly under the circumstances. "Dr. Rhenehan is our neighbor, Mothers. He lives right down the street." He gestured toward apartment buildings out the window. "Please take a chair, doctor."

Mother Adelli noticed the father wore the same suit as the day before. A long thread from one trouser leg dragged across the rug. His hair was ruffled, his face a storm-wrecked beach.

"I don't plan to take more than a few minutes. I have already decided to go to the press and State of Illinois. It's the least I can do--for justice, for everyone." His voice was harsh, hurried.

"I understand." The bishop gave a deep fatherly nod. "But here is Reverend Mother D'Gagnier, the Vicar General of the Western Province. You asked to see her. She flew in last night from San Francisco just for this meeting," he soothed, motioned to the cleric at the door to bring a chair behind the doctor. "I know she wants to hear what you have to say, no matter what you decide."

"We have already conveyed to Dr. Rhenehan how deeply grieved we are for him, and that we pray for his daughter and family each day in our schools," the Vicar General inclined her head toward the father. "And it is a pleasure to meet him, despite the great sadness of these circumstances."

Michael Rhenehan felt the chair behind his knees and sat. He had thought it would be impossible to be rude to a woman his mother's age, but the sight of the repulsive Reverend Mother Gregory and the weak-chinned other one who let his girl die overwhelmed him with rage all over again.

"Nothing is a pleasure now." He curled his lip. "And all this will soon become public knowledge. I have people begging me for the details." He pulled his jacket into place, swatted at his trousers.

The doorbell again. The cleric brought in a tall man with a briefcase. Michael Rhenehan, his back to the parlor door, turned and, looking over his shoulder, waved largely.

"Come in, come in, Phil. Join the party." He turned to the group. "This is Philip Martin, my attorney. Sit here, Phil," he patted an empty space next to him which the cleric hastily filled with a chair upon which Philip Martin sat carefully, letting his briefcase down to rest againt a leg of his chair. This was a man narrow of face, small ears, glasses and tight blond curls going grey. His eyes scampered over everything .

Bishop McCaw introduced the Religious. He noticed that behind her careful exterior, the Vicar General stiffened as if her bare feet had been forced into boiling water. And didn't that just describe her predicament, for no mention had ever been made by any party of the inclusion of a lawyer at what was to be a simple conversation among mutually interested parties.

Martin stood, acknowledged the nuns with a chopped-off bow, sat again.

"Some coffee or scotch, gentlemen?" the young cleric, waiting through the courtesies, asked from the door.

Bishop McCaw swung his head to look at the clock. "Eleven-thirty. Why it's nearly noon. I believe I'll have a scotch, if the Mothers will excuse me."

The nuns murmured in the affirmative and withdrew into their habits. Michael Rhenehan pulled his mouth down, shook his head no. Philip Martin raised a finger.

"Well, it's always good to have acess to a mind trained in the law at a time like this," Bishop McCaw put a firm hand to the tiller. "Of course, if you have read the police and coroner's reports, Mr. Martin, you know the girl was off school property at the time of this tragic incident. There was no foul play nor other legal matter."

"No legal matter except 'criminal negligence,' except 'wrongful death by criminal negligence,'" Michael Rhenehan bellowed and pounded his fist on the chair arm.

Reverend Mother D'Gagnier's eyes grew large.

"The matter of criminal negligence remains." Philip Martin leaned back in his chair, his hand at his pocket. "May I trouble you for an ashtray?" Cellophane crisped on the air. "With your permission," he addressed the nuns, slipping the cigar from its wrapper. "Well, the girl was not carefully watched. That much is clear. And there is the question of the pipe being an--'attractive nuisance' is the legal term. We are drafting a statement to that effect right now. The State will want to look into--."

"Excuse me, the girl WAS carefully watched," Reverend Mother Gregory's veil flared. "We do not neglect our students."

"Pfffffffh," the doctor flicked his fingers at her. It was exactly a week since the call had come at the *Bella Vita* in Sorrento.

"There is the question of your knowledge of the risk of the pipe being so close to your property; and of disregard of that risk. And we plan to interview the girl's classmates, have already arranged for some casual telephoning."

"There is a fence between our property and the pipe," Reverend Mother Gregory spoke up, but not strongly.

"Evidently it was not a sufficient deterrent." Philip Martin lit his cigar; the smoke carried onto the air an odor of spices dark and piquant. "The Mistress of the Third Course--that would be you, Mother--?" He raised his eyes to Mother Adelli.

Mother Adelli swallowed, nodded.

"'C<u>oor</u>'," Reverend Mother Gregory stepped in. She couldn't bear the garbling of French words. "Third C<u>oor</u>, Mr. Martin; from the French. Our order was founded in France."

The cleric arrived with a tray, served the drinks and, walking backwards, disappeared through the doorway.

Phillip Martin could see what Michael Rhenehan meant. The woman must be smaller than some of the girls she supervised, and sat there like a shadow. He trimmed his cigar ash carefully against the glass dish. "You left your students alone at times?" he continued without looking up.

Everyone turned to Mother Adelli. The white skin of her neck emerged from the shadow of her chin. Her eyes were freighted with fear

"Not after--. I was given to understand from my predecessor that on weekends boarding students could play sports together without supervision," she forced the clouded sounds from the crypt of her throat while the canker sores at the base of her tongue caught fire. "Reverend Mother Gregory informed me that was not right, so I did not permit it again."

"After what, Mother?" Philip Martin sat forward, his cigar hung from his fingers. "You said 'after' something."

"After my Superior told me."

"No, the first 'after.' You said, 'Not after--. Then you stopped."

205

She hesitated. "After Helene ran off on the train."

"And they say they were watching my girl." Michael Rhenehan, jacket flapping, sprang to his feet and stood swaying. Philip Martin patted the air.

Reverend Mother D'Gagnier pressed a small hand delicate as bone china to her breast, then entered the fray, "Our Lake Forest Superior tells me, Dr. Rhenehan, that your daughter had some unfortunate difficulties with--."

"Is that the way you watch your students all over the world?" the doctor swallowed the Superior's sentence then punched his face toward her. "Well your death toll must be quite high."

"Dr. Rhenehan," Revernd Mother D'Gangier starched herself up, "and with the deepest respect for your grief, we will never get anywhere if you will not let us speak."

"Oh, you'll have plenty of time to speak--to the State and to reporters from every paper in the country." He threw his head and sat down.

A bus rumbled past and the fringe beneath the chairs, small glass balls on the table lamps trembled.

"And from what my nuns report, your daughter had unusual difficulty with adjustment to--" Reverend Mother D'Gagnier trebeled on.

"Dr. Rhenehan tells me you never informed him that his daughter was having trouble," Philip Martin came right back. "In *loco parentis* does not mean you do not consult the parent." He raised his tumbler. "If the girl was having trouble, the father should have known about it."

"We spoke of this yesterday, Dr. Rhenehan and myself." Reverend Mother Gregory's eyes snapped. "His daughter was with us only ten weeks. The girl was playing a prank when she got on the train. If we disturbed parents with every prank rebellious students think up, we would be out of business overnight."

"When I remember some of the stunts my chums and I pulled," the bishop rolled his eyes, threw his hands with a laugh, "I have to--."

Michael Rhenehan thrust himself forward in his chair, bawling at Reverend Mother D'Gangier out of a red face. "You people should be out of business. What good are these institutions if parents can't keep their children safe in them? What is this, some kind of scam and educational black market you people run?" He slammed the arm of his chair. "Your doings have to be exposed. Parents need to know their good money--and that's *plenty* of money--lines somebody's coffers, buys antique furniture and tapestries while the children die." He choked down the last words, then turned with a black look upon Reverend Mother Gregory. "From now on, I will advise all parents that if they must leave their children, to put them in jail. They will be safer there."

Bishhop McCaw turned his drink in his hands. Not good so far; and he hoped these women knew better than to brawl in quicksand. His eyes shifted from speaker to speaker.

"Certainly, if you feel you must go to the State," Reverend Mother D'Gagnier intervened, 'you must do whatever your conscience dictates. We do not fear the scrutiny of the State." She hoped it was true. How lax had the Superior become? "But tell me, Dr. Rhenehan, why did you place your daughter with us?"

"You know very well why--or your Reverend Mother here does. I had an engagement in Europe. I could not take my daughter with me."

"Because--?" Reverend Mother D'Gagnier nodded.

"It would have been impossible. I would be lecturing, traveling, meeting people, demonstrating surgeries in hospitals." He gestured impatiently as if everything was clear and standing right in front of the woman.

"And to have your daughter with you would have--." She led him on to fill in the blank, an old teacher's trick.

"It would have been too incon--." He swatted at his trousers. "These people were paying me a great deal of money, a great deal. And a lot was riding on this tour.

There wouldn't have been the time. She needed a lot of looking after." He felt his pocket for a cigar. "She needed to be in school, not running around Europe." He stripped away the cellophane, lit it and puffed the red ember grey. The smoke gave off a mild odor like stale bread. Reverend Mother D'Gagnier waited. He swatted at his trousers again. "Lots of people put their children in boarding school." He waved his hand.

"Yes. Yes, they do," Reverend Mother D'Gagnier agreed.

"They want them to get a good education."

"And we try to provide one." She leaned toward him. "Did you have a choice about the length of your tour?"

Michael Rhenehan wagged his head back, forced a plume of smoke through his lips. "Carte blanche. Rome, Milan, Florence, Venice, Sorrento." He reached for Philip Martin's scotch, took a swig and clattered the glass back into place to let his eyes laze from face to face; then he began to shake his head. "Oh no. You're not doing this to me." He pointed his cigar at the old Superior, then turned to his lawyer. "Oh no. Do you get it, Phil, what she's after, trying to make *me* look bad when it's my daughter who died because *they* neglected her?"

"We had no way of knowing your daughter was so unprepared for being separated from you," Reverend Mother Gregory swung in, jowls trembling. "It surely is the parent's responsibility to gauge the fitness of the child for the experience."

Bishop McCaw took a sip of scotch; it clawed its way down his esophagus. He shot a look at Michael Rhenehan. Did he catch that soft spot, the side-stepping?

"Oh no you don't," Michael Rhenehan raised half out of his chair. "How could I know she couldn't take it?"

"We assumed you knew from her behavior at home and in her previous school if she was ready. And I read the rules to you both in the parlor. You had every--."

Reverend Mother D'Gagnier stared hard at Reverend Mother Gregory and snapped her fingers. The Superior closed her mouth abruptly.

"A case can be made for the academy's responsibility to manage any behavior not classified as 'disturbed,'" Philip Martin hefted his briefcase onto his lap and began to unbuckle it. "If you had signs the girl was out of hand or doubted your ability to manage her, you should have contacted the parent. I have something here--."

"We never doubted our--." Reverend Mother Gregory began, than caught a second look from her Superior.

Michael Rhenehan set his cigar down. "And that's what I'll tell them in any article I can bring out--that if she was so bad, why wasn't I contacted?" He waffled his chin and crossed his arms, his eyes chips of stone.

"Of course, the press will ask for the Order's side of the story as well," Bishop McCaw maneuvered an opening. "And they will want everything." He ran his forefinger around the rim of his glass. "Everything."

"Good. Yes. Let them hear everything. Let these women put themselves out of business. That's all I ask."

"Well, and the story is bound to concern itself with your daughter--her feelings, behavior, being left behind--." The bishop spoke slowly, the smallest smile on his lips. His forefinger traced around the rim of his drink. His skullcap gleamed.

"Let them say whatever they want, it doesn't change 'criminal negligence,'" Michael Rhenehan flung himself back in his chair.

"The press will tell about how unhappy your daughter was. They will root out every detail," Bishop McCaw ground on, "such things as how often you wrote her. How many letters were there to the girl, Mother Adelli?"

"I remember two letters, your Excellency."

"She's lying. I wrote more than that," Michael Rhenehan swept his arm around and Philip Martin's tumbler went flying. Scotch and ice cubes fanned into the air, then rained to the floor.

"Were there letters you might have forgotten, Mother?" the bishop pressed while out of the corner of his eye he watched the tumbler roll to Reverend Mother D'Gagnier's pointed black toes which she lifted daintily and settled to one side.

"Dr. Rhenehan did send a postcard about every two weeks. Helene carried the one current in her uniform pocket."

"Was there other correspondence?"

"The grandmother wrote nearly every three weeks." Mother Adelli hesitated. "And she sent a duck for a pet."

The bishop raised his eyebrows. "I didn't know students could have pets. Nice," he nodded to the nuns.

Mother Adelli looked in alarm at her Superiors; she had broken their dictum not to volunteer information.

Philip Martin caught the look.

"Are students allowed to have pets, Mother Adelli?"

Mother Adelli shook her head. "No, they're not."

"Did you send the duck back, then?"

"No, I didn't."

"You didn't send it back? Did your Superiors know?"

"No."

"Right there. The woman doesn't even keep the rules of the place herself." Michael Rhenehan thrust in. "And her own Superiors don't even know what's going on."

"What other rules did you break, Mother Adelli?"

"I had not seen Helene so happy or relaxed since she came." She said it to the father, to her Superiors. "I felt she needed the duck. I had a cage made in the furnace room. I intended to send the duck to a farm when--later on."

"Oh, when you got caught?" Michael Rhenehan gloated.

"Where is the duck now?" Philip Martin pressed.

"Dead. Mauled by a cat."

"See that. She couldn't even keep a duck in a cage alive," Michael Rhenehan brayed and turned an ugly face on Mother Adelli. "And how did Helene feel about her dead duck, Mother? Was she happy then?"

"How *did* the girl feel?" Philip Martin asked evenly, and wished for the third or fourth time that, friend or not, Michael Rhenehan would stay out of what was not his work.

"She felt it was my fault." Mother Adelli's hoarse whisper filled up. "I couldn't let her search during the night, of course, and in the rain." She remembered the dictum, did not say the girl had already been out of the building, swallowed painfully around blazing canker sores. "She was very angry with me and may have been trying to retaliate. She told her friends as much."

Bishop McCaw pressed a buzzer under the rug at his feet. Interrupt this damaging mood. "We have a spill here,' he told the cleric who returned with a rag and dust pan. Whisk, whisk with everyone watching and he backed out the door.

"Your daughter was so unhappy this religious felt she had to break the rules to try to help her." Bishop McCaw leaned toward the father. "That is what the press will say." He let the words sink in. "You should know that."

"Mother Adelli was wrong to break the rule about pets, even temporarily," Reverend Mother D'Gagnier hurried in; "but she was trying to help."

"--a student so unhappy she stole, lied, dishonored sacred objects and fought with and injured other students. The press will say all that. Is this correct Reverend Mother?" Bishop McCaw turned to Reverend Mother Gregory, who nodded. Against her will she had to feel gratitude to the man.

"I have seen it too often," the bishop shook his head. "When the press gets its teeth into a story, everything comes out--family and professional life, intimate relationships, finances--. It's a struck match to gasoline."

He drank off his scotch. "Can I replace that drink, Mr. Martin?" He leaned back, eyes upon the father.

Outside, shush, shush. One car after another heading for the Outer Drive.

Michael Rhenehan turned a pitiful face to his lawyer. "It's not just for me, Phil. The State should close that place. And both these women should be locked up like common criminals *where they can't hurt anybody else*," he hammered the words in.

"We are drafting a letter to the State of Illinois now," Philip Martin reset the argument. "There is no give here. Let's not forget we're talking about a girl in your care who drowned in a drainpipe. We have 'attractive nuisance', we have 'criminal negligence'--."

"And you don't even know what your own people are doing. What kind of leader are you?" Michael Rhenehan wheeled upon Reverend Mother D'Gagnier, "In the medical profession, your 'staff' here," he flung his hand, "would have been dismissed long ago. And you would be sued."

Bishop McCaw cleared his throat. "I believe we are hearing the same things over and over now."

"Yes. That's what I want. Over and over until--."

"It seems to me," the bishop stepped across the remark, "publicity, in the long run, will serve no one. That is, it will hurt as many as it will help. Despite this tragedy, the fact remains this Order has a long and nearly perfect record. Everyone knows the Madams of the Sacred Heart. This is the first incident at Lake Forest of its kind since the building went up. 1904 was it? My belief is that you will have difficulty making a case for mismanagement sufficient to close the school."

Michael Rhenehan spun to his lawyer "Is that right, Phillip? Do you agree with that?"

Martin sighed, pruned his cigar ash, tapped his fingers on the chair arm, leaned to his friend. "This could be a weak spot," he nodded in a near-whisper, then turned to the bishop and the nuns. "If you will excuse us a moment." He took Michael Rhenehan by the elbow to the front corner of the room where the bookcases met.

Bishop McCaw started up a chatty conversation while the two men conferred in muffled tones.

"But what about criminal negligence? That should hang them. I want these damned women punished."

"Oh, I think we can get a judgment; but I'm not sure about a judgment to satisfy you."

"Why not? It's all there--the nuisance thing and--."

"I believe you can win a suit against the Order and come away with decent damages; but even if they were convicted of a felony, no judge I know would put nuns in jail, if that's what you want."

"We'll find one. There are plenty of them out there with an appetite." He rubbed thumb and forefinger together as if counting off dollar bills.

"Then there's the nuns' record, their graduates married to so many people in high places in this state." Phillip Martin shook his head. "I believe we will have a hard time making a case sufficient to close the school. I have to be honest here. We can try; Michael; but any case against nuns will bring in the press. There's always that again."

As if a vacuum had begun to suck everything out from under him, Michael Rhenehan turned to stare at the pudgy bishop, the crafty old women, the young nun whose bumbling cost him the most precious thing he had in life.

"Well, these two can never be in charge of children again," he announced loudly then, turned and strode to his chair brandishing an unopened cigar. "I will talk to the parents myself. I will call the State Board of Education and every appropriate agency until the Order removes them." He flung himself back into his chair. "They are a disgrace to the profession." His eyes raked Mother Adelli, chin on her breast, hands hidden in her sleeves. "You and that goddamned duck."

Bishop McCaw's gaze sidled across to Reverend Mother D'Gagnier. Get him while he's weak, it said. Reverend Mother D'Gagnier studied the shriveled tips of her fingers. She let the clock tick, let the doctor drink from the lawyer's scotch and light a cigar; then she looked up.

"If that will satisfy you, we shall remove them."

It was with regret that she took the action; but they must finish this thing. She and Bishop McCaw had arrived at this solution over the telephone days before. The Order could show they had replaced those in authority. It was the vote of no confidence in her nuns she fought, even after the telephone poll of the vicariates and the consensus that this would be the most prudent action.

Philip Martin leaned across his chair arm and motioned Michael Rhenehan closer. "Won't this do? These are the ones you want."

'I want them in jail and the goddamned placed closed." Michael Rhenehan pushed the words through his teeth.

"I know you do. If I felt certain you could get that, I'd tell you. What I think you can get is a good judgment, though it will take time. Civil law is arthritic."

"I'll go to the Pope. I'll go to Life magazine. We'll bankrupt the place." His eyes were wild again.

"And all that would bring in the press, Michael. Do you want Helene's name dragged through the mud, your private affairs examined in every alley? I speak as a friend; it could take years to undo. And there's your mother and the papers in New York--and your own reputation. Of course, do what you think right. I'll stand by you all the way."

Well, and Michael Rhenehan had begun to see how people could make things look, could make Helene look. He thought of his colleagues, of his mother, of his friends at his club. He threw the unopened cigar into the ashtray and stood, turned toward Reverend Mother D'Gagnier to thrash his finger.

"You see that those women are gone before the students come back from Thanksgiving. And I'm not finished, so don't get your hopes up. You will be hearing from Philip Martin. And you can be sure whatever I decide will cost you the prettiest penny ever found in your till."

He stalked from the room. Philip Martin grabbed up his briefcase and followed while at the back of his suit jacket the horizontal wrinkles fell out.

Bishop McCaw raised his eyebrows high, held them there until the sound of the front door closing. "Well," he breathed, "hopefully you are out of the worst of it. I'd advise you to have your own counsel offer a private settlement as quickly as you can. It will cost you. You may have to dig into your resources." He craned his neck. "One-thirty. Can I offer something to eat? We can make a cloister in my dining room."

No one had an appetite. Mother Adelli was positively white. The old Superior felt weak herself. They ducked into the limousine.

"We will speak more of these matters when we reach Lake Forest," Reverend Mother D'Gagnier told her nuns as the automobile carried them past the lake on one side and a mixture of old Victorian houses and modern apartment buildings on the other. "Who is your legal counsel, Reverend Mother Gregory?"

"Ian Christopher, husband of the Secretary of the Alumni Association, Superior."

Reverend Mother D'Gagnier nodded. The tires thrummed.

"Did you ever contact the county about the fence?"

"They put it up at our request ten years ago."

"When was it last checked for flaws?"

"Two years ago."

The Vicar General let her eyes drift to the window, to the endless body of Lake Michigan, listless and grey today. Two years. Not good enough.

ZOE KEITHLEY

III.

Chapter of Bliss

"I am the joining and the dissolving.
I am what lasts, and what goes.
I am the one going down,
and the one toward whom they ascend.
I am the condemnation and the acquittal.
For myself, I am sinless.
The roots of sin grow in my being.
I am the desire of the outer, and the control of the inner.
I am the hearing in everyone's ears,
I am the mute who is speechless,
great are the multitudes of my words.
Hear me in softness. Learn me in roughness.
I am she who cries out,
and I am cast forth upon the face of the earth.
I prepare the bread and my mind within.
I am called truth."

From The Thunder: Perfect Mind

Gnostic Gospel

ZOE KEITHLEY

One

Soeur Katherina, a new kitchen assistant with great dark eyes and all concentration and hesitation, served the nuns a late lunch of vegetable soup, French bread and *gouda* cheese. Outside, the sky was dense with clouds.

"How are your students, Mother Adelli?" Reverend Mother D'Gagnier dipped bread into her soup.

The Mistress of the Third *Cours*, who had barely touched her meal, poured more water, then set the glass down without drinking. Her students' faces, grown strangely patient under the tutelage of grief, crowded her mind. "If you please, Reverend Mother, they feel that in some way they might be responsible for Helene's death."

The Mistress General nodded. "Death forces an examination of conscience even upon children." She let her gaze rest at the window where grey rain outside turned the tree trunks black. "The girl has walked into a new level of life," she mused after a moment. "She has been saved from many mistakes."

She turned the conversation then toward Reverend Mother Gregory, but her eyes passed from time to time over young Mother Adelli, still dogged at her meal. Here was a good mind, an unusual depth of feeling, and wisdom however embryonic; but for now, and until recovered from the trauma, she was a weak link. Where to put her?

They finished their meal. The Mistress General bid Mother Adelli good-bye. "Very soon you will receive instructions about your future. And you are always our daughter, Mother," she told her. "We will help you through your troubles. Meanwhile, place all in Mater's lap."

The three stepped into the corridor. The Vicar General and Superior, heads bent in conversation, moved toward the elevator while Mother Adelli stood watching the large and the small, between them carrying her life.

Once alone, Reverend Mother D'Gagnier was direct with Reverend Mother Gregory. "You are to be gone by Sunday. I am sending you to my own convent, the one that nurtured me. Do not believe your service will be of any less value in Montreal. Of course, there may be legal reasons for us to meet again in Chicago; but we'll hope not." Then she wiped her spectacles and set them back over small eyes, light grey and shot with brown. "God will be with you, Mother."

Then, portmanteau in the trunk, she was in the limousine and on her way to the Dearborn Street rail station. The first airplane ride of her life would also be her last if she had anything to say about it.

Reverend Mother Gregory returned to her office but could not make herself sit down. Ridiculously, she wanted chocolate milk, and then to clear her desktop with one swipe of her arm. She looked about at the tall windows, the shining floor, richly textured rugs, cherry-wood desk with its neatly organized folders. So this was to be the end of it all.

She fled to chapel, to her prie dieu, to fix her eyes upon the tabernacle. Dinner hour came and went. At 9:30 p.m. the Community assembled for Compline. When they had gone, she sank again to her knees. At 1 a.m., her eyes were still upon the tabernacle. At 5:00 a.m., *Soeur* Elisabeta came, dusting tool for the altar, steps and communion rail under her arm, to find the lone figure seated, her chin resting upon her breast and snoring lightly. At 6:00 a.m., Reverend Mother Gregory woke with a start to the sound of kneelers knocking against the floor. Looking about, she dropped her own kneeler for Mass.

At noon, the Third *Cours* boarders trooped to the dormitory to pack. At morning Mass, in the refectory, in

Study Hall they had cast looks at one another: Helene's death had made their Mother Adelli shrunken, pale and silent.

Still, today, the day before Thanksgiving was a half day. Then home, home, they were going home! Engulfed in winter coats, out the Minims' Door they streamed. Careful, Mother Adelli. Don't eat too much turkey, don't eat too much pie. And not knowing what more to say, they threw back to her over their shoulders in glad goodbyes the joy of their escape.

At 1:30 p.m., it was not Reverend Mother Gregory's "Come" that answered Mother Adelli's knock. Behind the burled façade of the Superior's desk and writing in her careful hand sat Reverend Mother Crewelman. She glanced up. How faded the young woman looked, so shrunken in her habit--like a child.

"No," she answered the unasked question, "you have not made a mistake. Your appointment is with me." Her eyes gleamed. "It is not yet announced, but I have, by order of our Vicar General, taken the Superior's position here." With a slow luxurious movement, she sat back in her chair and watched surprise, fear and an emotion she could not name pass across the younger nun's eyes. The expected "God be with you, Reverend Mother" followed; and Reverend Mother Crewelman felt her blood tingle. She pointed Mother Adelli to a chair.

"Reverend Mother D'Gagnier has ordered you be relieved of the Third *Cours* immediately."

It was a knife-blade to her windpipe. Mother Adelli's hands flew to her collapsing chest.

"Come, come, Mother. You knew this was to be. The girl's obituary is published in the Tribune, the Sun Times. Parents will expect a change."

The younger nun straightened, pulled her rosary beads into her lap.

"Disobedience, Mother Adelli," the new Superior gave the young woman a long look, "has its price, as you see."

The oval face before her now had been the source of infinite frustration; to watch every approach at development die under the woman's deep-seated ambivalence had been maddening. Well, the Novitiate was full of new faces.

"Reverend Mother D'Gagnier offers you three alternatives; all very generous, I think," she went on. "You may remain at Lake Forest in a capacity to be determined, you may accept a non-teaching position at our new Day School in Santa Fe; or you may move to Lone Mountain in San Francisco, attend the Jesuit's university there and complete a degree program."

"But not to be with the children, Mother--Reverend Mother--."

"Let me remind you that a child died under your care." She tapped her papers to even the edges. "The father and our Mistress General have rightly laid the price of it upon you. And to the family, I'm sure this is no price at all, for they must go on now without her."

A muffled groan. Mother Adelli bent into her lap.

"You are the cause of your own suffering, Mother Adelli. As your Spiritual Director I must say it." With long fingers, the new Superior pulled a handkerchief from her sleeve. "You have a wild and confused will. Just see where it has led you. Obedience is your only salvation." She dabbed at the corners of her mouth. "I must have your answer by Friday evening. The new woman will be here Saturday from New York. You are excused."

She returned to her papers, heard the chair cushion sigh, the light steps upon the wood, the squeak of the knob, the door close.

Mother Adelli found no comfort in her office. Half-way through the third essay on "From The First Thanksgiving To Our Own," she realized she would never again correct such papers, be here when her girls returned, and had no way to tell them she had not left them of her own will. Oh, had she known at noon, she would surely have given them a different good-bye. The thought came then to phone her parents. She pushed it aside, pushed the papers aside, threw her shawl about her shoulders. In the next two days her battered mind must find an answer for Mother--Reverend Mother Crewelman.

Under a brilliant sky, her blue shadow sprinted ahead or trailed behind while, fingers tucked deep into her armpits, she exhaled specters and the silver Jesus crucified at the end of her rosary twirled and scattered light. Submerged in Nature's quiet, her heart, as if under some mysterious hand, let go its latch and fell open; and matriculating as she had in the School of Death, she found the willingness to read whatever text chose to stand before her.

But it was Julian, her dead brother, who filled her mind then, vivid as if he stood before her--Julian, who would always listen when she was little and, despite all that had passed between them, was the one family member who knew her most deeply.

"I wanted to give her something bigger to hold onto, Julian, since her father couldn't pay attention. In Omaha, we novices would sit in a circle by the kitchen door and listen to the letters of Philippine Duchene, our first missionary to America--written from her first convent near St. Louis where she taught the Indians. Splitting peapods with our thumbs, we too dreamed of carrying the vision of the Order to someone. But now I don't know if our teachings and practices help children or harm them.

"My stomach hurts all the time. I'm out walking the grounds, ordered to make a decision about my future, and I can't think.

"What does God say to a murderer, Julian? And why didn't He protect her from me?

"It's you who should have been the pride of the family, Julian. Remember at home, the piano top covered with pictures of me? And only two of you. No wonder you left. If it weren't for me, you might not have gone to Oregon and died cutting trees.

"There's something I never told you. When I was nine, in a recital at the Schubert Theater, I came off stage doing pirouettes. The applause was huge. Mama was in the wings, and she gave me a look that told me too much-- how she needed--NEEDED--me to succeed; and the way she hugged me, I knew she hated it--hated me--that I was so good. I turned to ice seeing that in her face, feeling it in her body. Then she gave me a good shove and sent me out for an encore. Julian, I could never try my hardest after that. Dance became a bitter thing. I knew the better I got, the more Mama would hate me. Something in me wouldn't do it after that-- improve or reach farther. To me then, dance ruined everything for all of us.

"And I couldn't ever tell them--spending money on me they didn't have. And I couldn't let myself improve. Every year I saw Mama's face grow harder in those cold theaters. Once she said, 'I'm going to get you to New York if I have to break both your legs.' I was thirteen. And Pop, how he'd raise his glass. 'Here's to you, Pretty Feet!'--I'd just feel sick because the harder he'd work, to bring home more money, the more he'd drink and the more Mama would fight him. At least my vocation put an end to his extra jobs.

"It was an icy day in January my senior year when God said inside me, 'Give me your life.' Oh, I thought my heart would burst with happiness--God wanted me, was paying attention. A month later I heard Him call again and I told Mother Clare. I remember, packing for the Novitiate, how you said, 'What do you think you're going to do, hide under God's skirts?' I wish you could help me now, Julian, to think straight.

"Did I ever tell you I was angry with you? Because you stopped being close. I didn't have anyone but you, and still don't. Did you know I used to sneak into your room and hide your empty beer bottles? I couldn't bear to hear Pop slap you around. And I was angry that you weren't strong enough to take charge of the family, Julian. How could you? I wasn't strong enough either."

She crossed over the ravine and stepped along the narrow path that ran beside the chapel. The flakes were larger now, the outdoors become a fairyland. And it was then the questions finally came. Had she entered the Order to get away from her family and dance? And didn't that invalidate her vows? Heart pounding, a new horror drove her around the school. Had she ever had a real vocation?

The following day at Mass, she kept her eyes from the tabernacle, choked down the Host to avoid scandal to other Religious, and lived eaten alive by fear. The monster Guilt looked out through her eyes, joined her at toilet, moved in the very folds of her habit, rode the fork to her mouth, swelled in every thought in her mind until she felt she must drown.

The exception was one moment after breakfast, on Friday when, at work on notes for the new woman, a voice like her own but not her own commented dryly that her Superiors had had time enough to notice things deteriorating with Helene. So hadn't it been their duty as well to protect the girl? The sense of a shared guilt immediately made her want to pile everything onto them; but that didn't work either: Hadn't she covered over her problems with the girl so as to protect herself, her trip to Rome and the taking of Final Vows?

Now her stomach relaxed a little. Well, and that was the truth. She straightened textbooks on their shelves. If she stayed at Lake Forest, could she bear to see and hear her students in chapel, in the corridors, on the hockey field? Of course, that would be the most painful and therefore the most fitting punishment. And what good would it do to go to Lone Mountain and the Jesuit's university when she couldn't even think? So that left Santa Fe and the wilderness of the Southwest.

Closing her office door, her conscience searching further, the full consequence of her mother's look and words that time in the wings flooded out. She, Mary Agnes, had put a brake on how far she would let herself grow as a dancer so as to hold her family to her when she'd known even then she could become better than they ever imagined. To control her mother's ambition, she had let them pay and pay for something she would never allow herself to become. Well, they were all of them finished with dance now.

Two

For an instant, answering a call to parlor, Mother Adelli, saw an immigrant man and woman in tired clothing peering into the polish and gilt of the room. The familiar landmarks emerged: The woman's small bones, roman head, darting eyes; the man's square-cut peasant body, open face, thick hands. There was a painful knock in her chest as she quickened her step to her parents. It was 2:00 p.m. on Friday.

"But you told me you wouldn't be coming. Oh, this *is* a surprise."

When the first mention of her student's death appeared in the Chicago Tribune, Reverend Mother Gregory told Mother Adelli to phone her parents. It was wise counsel, for their friends had already seen the story. And a second article had appeared in the Daily Herald, a third in the Sun-Times. Alarmed, the parents took the North Shore train up from the city.

At the sight of her haunted eyes, Lorenzo and Angelica Adelli felt the bridge of dutiful letters to their daughter collapse. She had been ten years away, and then back in Illinois since March; why hadn't they been to see her? Well, it was nearly two hours on the train--and she hadn't asked them, really. Now they visited the chapel, Mater, the high school library; but the worried parents took in little besides their Mary Agnes. In Third *Cours* Study Hall, they wandered down the narrow aisles, touching the worn, stained and abandoned inkwells, the pen cradles.

"Everything looks just like Sheridan Road," the mother sniffed. "The same statues, Study Halls, desks." She hitched her handbag.

"Schools are schools," the father waved his wife off. "In Chicago, the Archdiocese orders all of its stuff from A. A. McNeilly--warehouses of you-name-it, floor to ceiling." The rumble of a cough started in his chest before it exploded and bent him double. Mother Adelli's eyes widened; the mother looked away.

"Sit down Pop, both of you. I'll get some water." To say "Pop" in his presence after so long--. The father slumped onto a small chair that forced his knees high.

In the kitchen, she filled the tumblers too full and dribbled down the corridor. Crossing the threshold, the slanting afternoon light made luminous the multiple folds of her parents' faces and hands, and she realized with a jolt that they had entered the last long phase of their lives.

"Here we are now. Salud." She pressed the wet glasses into their hands.

They turned eyes of dreamers upon her, their daughter whose bare bottom they saw disappear around doors when she was two; whose perfect arabesque stunned them when she was nine, was twelve, was sixteen; here now dressed in a veil, cape and long skirt, a teacher of children of the rich, studying to be a saint. In these ten years they had never gotten used to it.

"That cough, Pop. How is your health?"

"*You* look worn out and half starved," the mother elbowed in. "Their idea of cooking here is probably boil, boil, boil, and then a teaspoon of everything."

"Dio mio, she's been through a nightmare, Angelica." The father grabbed his head and coughed some more. "Salud." He raised his glass.

Father and mother glanced about as if they were in a museum, careful to keep the wet tumblers off the wood. Above the door, a carved Jesus stretched His crucifixion over the family.

The parents began with neighborhood news. Mrs. Corelli's son finally went into the seminary. Old Arturo Vincente got a heart attack lugging too much potting soil. Their new dog Arabella caught a nasty piece of glass in her paw.

Mother Adelli clenched and unclenched knotted hands.

"I must tell you both something. Since we talked on the phone, our Vicar General has ordered some changes here. Reverend Mother Gregory has already been replaced."

"Oh?" the mother nodded; the names meant nothing.

The father's eyes narrowed. "Because of--?" They all knew he meant the girl's death. "I phoned a lawyer, Mary Agnes." He never could, like some parents, call his own daughter 'Mother.' "He says the school could be held responsible for her--for the--." He didn't want to say the word. "And he asked about charges against--anyone."

Mother Adelli shook her head. "So far, Dr. Rhenehan has not filed any charges."

Cautiously, father and mother let out their over-held breath. Thank God. They stood and stripped away their winter coats and laid them aside.

"I am also to be replaced."

"Oh." The mother sat down hard. "Oh." She turned her back to her daughter and floundered in her purse until she found a handkerchief to press against her mouth.

"Then he--they--blame *you*!" the father boiled. "But wasn't there another nun? Gesu, Giuseppe, e Maria, the girl snuck off on you--." Beneath skin softened by drink, he drew his face up tight and hard.

"I was in charge of her, Pop."

"She climbed in that pipe herself. And you're the one to blame?"

"Lorenzo!"

"I've heard people say worse, Angelica. And they want you to be a mind reader, too? Who can know what comes into someone's head! What about the doctor? He left her here."

"He expected we would take care of her!"

The father closed his mouth. Mother Adelli was immediately sorry; he was just trying to help.

"My replacement, along with Reverend Mother Gregory's, was one of Dr. Rhenehan's conditions in exchange for not going to the press and the State."

"Well, it's been in the papers. He scammed you on that one. And what was she doing off of school property in the first place?" The father looked as if he wanted to take a swing at someone.

The girl's face half under the mud. Breathe. Breathe.

"I am supposed to be a mind reader; and it was my responsibility. She was off school property, and probably trying to punish me." She saw the pain leap in his eyes, standing as she did against his defense of her; but she had no energy now to stay any blow, to herself or them.

The father batted the air. "You're too hard on yourself. You couldn't harm anyone, Pretty Feet."

"I could and have, Pop. You just don't know. I've done a lot of thinking lately, and remembering."

Angelica Adelli turned at her daughter's reply. This was the one whose dance shoes, tights and tutu she had packed away, bowing to the will of Heaven that their Mary Agnes pour her mortal life into a cloister--but a cloister of the most prestigious religious order in the world. They'd had that cold comfort these ten years. Now this horror.

Mother Adelli stepped to the window to escape into the puzzle of the lilac branches. She must put herself on trial with her parents; she owed them the story.

"Why didn't you go to your Superiors immediately when the girl became a problem, Mary Agnes?" The mother zeroed in as soon as her daughter finished speaking and Mother Adelli felt the honed appraisal pierce the familiar place high on the left of her rib cage.

"I did." She turned from the window. "Several times. Reverend Mother Gregory told me to handle things on my own. I tried. And if I had followed all of Mother Crewelman's instructions, I risked making matters worse for the girl, she so hated being here."

"That's where you made your mistake, Mary Agnes, following your feelings instead of your Superiors." The mother shut the mouth of her purse with a snap. "And the duck thing. Going against the rule when--."

"And turn my back on a way that might make things better for her? And with everything slipping away so fast? I might as well have told myself to breathe under water."

"When you were a child, you did as I said and I--."

"Dio mio. Everything looks so easy from the kitchen sink, Angelica," the father burst in. "Those higher-ups make bad mistakes and then lay it on the guy under their thumb. I've had students like this girl who walk the thin edge just for fun, to get your goat, too slippery to grab hold of and too smart for their own good."

"If you want my opinion, you should have done exactly as your superiors told you. The Rule would have protected--."

"Sono tutti diavoli--devils, students like that. There are a few necks I would still enjoy giving a twist." The father wrung the air between his hands.

"Oh, you always were happy bringing your petty schoolroom violence home to the dinner table," Angelica Adelli turned on him. "You always loved that kind of--."

And so it always began. A dagger, an ax in return, then a shovel. Mother Adelli propped her elbows on the windowsill and let her head down into her hands to cover her ears and screen out their voices. She felt the clumsiness of the wimple she had ten years ago so longed to wear. What did life in this Order mean with its filigree of tightly intertwined rules? It seemed such a vanity now, a bauble set next to the uncut stone of the life of a child.

The mother carried on, but the father watched his daughter turn from the window, sensed the terrible gulch yawning before her.

"No one is safe from trouble, *figlia mia.*" He said it softly, sadly to his girl. "Trouble climbs the highest walls." He shook his head.

From down the corridor came a muffled clatter of pots and pans. *Soeur* Josephine was in her kitchen.

"But this thing won't affect your progress in the Order." The mother straightened up.

The daughter raised her head, surprised. "Oh, I'm sure everything is in question now; probably beyond question."

The mother's face collapsed. She dug into her purse. "We tried to do the right things. First Julian, now this for my Mary Agnes?" She bawled the words into her handkerchief.

"Per Bacco, as usual you're the only one who's suffered." The father's hand came down hard on the desktop. "You just never got over wanting a diva."

"And you didn't? Or were those extra classes you took on only an excuse to sit up late and get sloppy drunk?"

It was at night the knives of words would fly back and forth until the shouting rattled the demitasse cups above the piano. She, Mary Agnes, the usual trophy in their wars, would creep with her schoolbooks to sit behind her bedroom door. She was the reason they fought, the reason her brother left, the reason there was never enough money. Her dancing ruined everything.

"Stop it." She spun from the window, hands over her ears like a child. "You always do this, and it never solves anything. Don't you realize you took it all away from me, that I came to hate having to dance?"

It was as if someone had clicked the radio off and only the clank and hiss of the radiators remained. Could this really be her saying such things? She saw her mother's eyes grow round, breasts sag backwards under the vacuum-like suck of air; but there was nothing in her, Mary Agnes, now to stop the outpouring.

"My dancing made me a foreigner in my own home. And by the time I was nine, a commodity like money, something to keep everyone's hopes up. But it spoiled everything and stole our family from us and made my brother hate me. Once that happened, something inside wouldn't let me try hard, even if I wanted to sometimes. You kept pushing me, but I stopped letting myself, so far as I could, get better at it when I was nine or ten. I had to. I was losing everything I cared about."

The confession was a pull, a snag in the fabric of both parents' eyes. Dread washed into her father's face as she turned to him.

"It wasn't your drinking, but that you treated me like a figurine. How could I be anything else, then? The two of you made a ghost of me. And Julian died to me by the time I was ten. I think now that when I entered the Order, I wanted to get away from both of you, from ballet, to keep it from eating up every penny--." She stopped, hearing herself.

"Santas Anna e Maria," the mother threw an arm into the air, "I've listened to just about all I care to. You at least owe us respect as your parents. But perhaps the fourth commandment doesn't apply to someone in a habit. You went into the Order and didn't have a vocation? Even with the scholarship, the Order wasn't free, if you remember. And you just wanted to get away?"

"Yes. No. I was--."

"The child is mad," Angelica Adelli hissed at her husband. "I don't understand a word she says. Who oiled her feet every night as if she were the king's own pig?"

"I wanted you to see me," Mother Adelli jabbed her fingertips against her chest, "Mary Agnes. I didn't want to be a ballerina if it meant not having a mother."

"Madonna mia," Angelica Adelli threw her head, "Who do you think spread her legs in the hospital? Who sat in those cold dark theaters night after night and kept after you so that your cursed laziness didn't ruin everything?"

"It wasn't lazi--."

"Everyone told me, 'Angelica, you could have been a movie star.' But how, with brothers and sisters to take care of, with parents who couldn't speak English and washed other people's floors? Your father had even less, but he pulled himself up. He could have been a professor, your father, but he decided he'd rather drink." And with her eyes she scarred her husband long and wickedly. "You and Julian had to be our hope. But Julian wouldn't stay home, or keep his hands off the bottle, either. Like father, like--."

"There was nothing at home for Julian! Home was all about me." Why couldn't her mother see it?

"And why didn't you do anything about that, Mary Agne--."

"Hey, don't drag me into this fairy tale," Lorenzo Adelli broke in, twisting in his seat to face his wife. "Just remember we didn't have our children in the public schools."

"Only because you were teaching at St. Rita. And what will we be living on so grandly when you retire, the royalties from all those great books you never wrote?"

"Please don't fight." Mother Adelli held out pleading hands. "Can't you see dance cost all of us every ounce of good feeling we had?"

"Oh, don't be so self-centered, Mary Agnes. We fought about plenty besides you, didn't we Lorenzo? But if we made dance such a misery, why didn't you stop? You danced twelve years."

"I really don't know," Mother Adelli puzzled. "You were counting on it, I knew that. And my body was happy when I danced, but always reaching further, further. I dreaded what would happen to us if I got even better. So when the experience came of God calling me, it was a relief. At last I knew what to do. Now it seems that may have been a mistake. I am so sorry."

The mother sat like a block of wood; the father glanced at his daughter, then studied the thick joints of his fingers. Then the rumbling, and the cough clattered over the desks.

Angelica Adelli glared at her husband wiping his mouth with a crumpled handkerchief. "Have you heard what your daughter has been telling us?"

Gingerly, he touched his daughter's face with his eyes. "I can't believe you could have danced better than you did, Pretty Feet; or that you held back."

The mother jammed her arms into her coat while her purse swung in crazy arcs.

"We're getting out of here, Lorenzo."

The father hesitated, then rose as well.

"Please," Mother Adelli rushed toward them, "Mama, Pop. Oh, please don't leave like this."

"You've made fools of your father and me, Mary Agnes. A wild animal would have more gratitude."

"But I am grateful. It's just--."

But her mother's back was vanishing through the Study Hall doors. Her father turned on the threshold.

"I didn't know, Pretty Feet. I was trying to do the right thing."

She stared at the emptied doorway, heard them climb the stairs, tread the corridor above. How could she have made the mistake of saying all that? She flew up the stairs to come even with them in the foyer. The mother halted to face her.

"Is that how you've felt all these years?"

Mother Adelli dropped her eyes. "Yes, Mama, it is."

Down the stairs to the etched inner door the mother marched, then out the front. The father wavered, then followed his wife.

Mother Adelli couldn't think what to do. Her parents were being torn from the book of her life; she could feel the ripping away in her body.

Then down the stairs herself to push open the heavy door to spring out into the cold where the sun, beginning now to set, threw lancets of pale rose over the earth.

"Wait," she called, hurrying toward their shrinking backs.

Trotting alongside her mother, she pleaded the confusion her life had been. "This has all only come clear these last days. Please, let me make it up to you."

Too soon they were at the commuter platform and the tiny North Shore train grew large, larger, then rattled to a stop. The conductor swung off, a flashlight in his fist.

"Boaarrrdd." He fixed the yellow beam upon the throbbing threshold.

Angelica Adelli looked at her daughter, at the pocketed red eyes, the twisted mouth. This one could have been a *diva*. She raised her hand in a stopping motion and stepped aboard the train.

But the father gathered his daughter into his arms, habit and all. "When it's darkest, God is never far away, figlia mia," he whispered through her veil.

She clung to him. "I may have to leave the Order, Pop." She blurted it out, surprised.

He pulled back, searching her face.

The conductor stamped his feet. "Boaarrrdd."

Lorenzo Adelli sat opposite his wife. The train car jerked forward. Leave the Order. And do what? He leaned at the scarred window to hold in his sight for as long as possible his only child as she waved her white flag of a hand. The rocking train rounded the bend and he knew one thing: There was nothing on earth to compare to his daughter.

He rummaged in his pocket for a cigarette, wishing to God it was a drink while in the darkened window, his wife's face of stone jolted above the railbed.

The train shrank around the curve, and despite the terrible weight pulling everything within her toward the center of the earth, something small rose up to walk with her on the wobbling highwire. It was the knowing that her wounded father, who could not help her now--or perhaps ever--would never close his heart to her.

Three

Friday evening. Table lamps lit the Community Room. Outside, the wind moaned through the trees and rattled the doors to the sun porch while Reverend Mother Gregory and Reverend Mother Crewelman stood before their religious community. Then Reverend Mother Crewelman signaled for silence with her clapper, about to take into her own hands the reins for the Convent of the Sacred Heart at Lake Forest, Illinois.

"It is my duty and privilege," she gazed upon the obediently silent gathering, "to announce the retirement of Justine Gregory, our beloved Superior, who has lavished upon us such devotion these fourteen years, and who will now join our sisters in Montreal." She gave her shocked audience a moment to register their loss, to let the woman have her moment. She went on when the patter dissolved. "It will now be my privilege to step in as your Superior, at the directive of our Vicar General."

Silence. Then, "God be with you, Reverend Mother Gregory, God be with you, Reverend Mother Crewelman." The Community managed applause again, and Reverend Mother Crewelman inclined her head and the heady sense of over-lordship took hold. "The Rule of Silence is suspended while we enjoy refreshments."

On cue, *Soeur* Josephine, with *Soeur* Katherina trailing behind, wheeled in the chiming dessert plates and the plain cake done up in a hurry.

But no Religious mistook this for a celebration. Reverend Mother Gregory was yet a number of years this side of retirement, they reminded one another with their looks. Only in an emergency would the Vicar General step around elections, they met one another's eyes. This must relate to the girl's death, a temporary arrangement, they picked at their cake. Silently, Mother Adelli promised herself to learn about leaving from her former Superior whose eyes neither hid her suffering nor pressed it upon others.

Now, coffee pot in one hand and teapot in the other, *Soeur* Josephine, passed among the nuns. Mother Adelli felt a rush of affection for this Working Sister with her perpetual odor of scouring powder. "I'm leaving too," she wanted to whisper as the brown hands lifted the teapot upright, "and I will miss your kitchen and your kindness. I will miss your pure spirit. I will tell others how you helped me." This working sister lived the surrender Mother Concepciòn spoke of, the life that she, Mary Agnes Adelli, grasped in yet an indistinct way she must live as well. She pursed her lips to the scalding tea.

"May I have a word with you, Mother?"

Mother Adelli rattled her cup to the table and stood.

Reverend Mother Gregory's face looked tired and sallow in the lamplight, but her eyes were calm and direct. "I will be gone by tomorrow night. Perhaps thirty minutes, in the library?"

"Of course, Reverend Mother."

She sat to her tea again, and the untouched cake. Helene's death had cost Reverend Mother Gregory her career. Whatever the former Superior had to say to her, she, Mother Adelli, was flesh open to the strap. The lacerations of words and looks had actually become comforting: At least she could pay something back to those her mistakes had damaged.

The sound of the clapper again. Every voice hushed and head turned to where Reverend Mother Crewelman stood in all solemnity weaving her fingers together for her additional remarks.

Reverend Mother Gregory went about the library turning on the desk lamps with their shades of emerald green glass. She would not again have the pleasure of seeing them all lighted together against the tall umbered library stacks, its aisles dark and narrow like private parts of the body. Young Mother Adelli stood in the doorway, her face abraded by guilt and grief. Of course such feelings were to be expected, but what use they served after the fact was beyond the Superior.

"Have a seat, Mother. A wonder, aren't they?" The Superior gestured to the lamps. "Like the life-energy of green things."

The younger nun smiled faintly.

Across from the tables, tall windows framed the diagonally drifting snow. At the other end of the room, a great dictionary sat open and precarious upon its stand. The Superior glanced up over the door--forty-five minutes to Compline.

"How are you feeling, Mother Adelli?" she dipped an oar.

"As if my skin were gone," the younger nun raised her hands and let them fall, "and all that I am is visible to everyone. And no way to protect myself."

The Superior nodded. "A painful state, but one of value." She noticed the young nun's habit and wimple loose now from her loss of weight.

The younger nun's eyes traveled to the window. "What I have caused stalks me--the father, his family, my family, my students, you my Superior, our Community--." She pressed her fingertips into her forehead.

"Such thinking is of no use now. You must stop it." Reverend Mother Gregory drew her grey eyebrows together. "No one can carry so much responsibility and remain sane--and it is arrogance, however well-meant, to try." She tugged at her veil caught on the chairback. "What happened was the action of a natural force. Anger is such a force, like weather. The girl was angry, and unless something stopped her, it was inevitable that--." She held her large head very still suddenly and stared at Mother Adelli. "Is that what the duck was about? Trying to stop the anger?"

Mother Adelli nodded. Relief stung her eyelids.

The Superior turned her head and, leaning it against her fist, gazed long into the muted perpendiculars of the stacks. She tapped the table absently with a finger. "It almost seems He let us stay trapped in our narrow concerns until the deed was done." She turned to Mother Adelli. "We might ask, if God could have stopped this death and didn't, what--."

"All she wanted was her father back. And what kind of punishment is death for a child's prank? And why wasn't someone alerted somehow when He could see she needed help?"

The quick labored breathing of the younger nun, the measured push and pull of the older one; the silence between. The smell of paper, of wood, of the electric lights.

"And if He wanted a death so badly, why didn't He take me?" Mother Adelli mopped her face with her knuckles. Knowing Who it was she reviled, she could not look at her Superior, turned shoulder and head away.

As outdoors lights came on, shadows of falling flakes laid a dark lace on the inner sills. Head propped upon a fist, the Superior watched the snow, her eyes moving back and forth. "So unseasonal, this. A winter before winter. But so beautiful, too--like a baptismal dress." She pulled upright, freed her veil again.

"There is something I must tell you, Mother."

Mother Adelli, still paralyzed by her blasphemy, did not move. The Superior waited, studied the backs of her hands.

"Turn around Mother Adelli."

The younger nun rotated her body, eyes locked to the wood grain of the table. Reverend Mother Gregory's fingers stole to the base of the lamp.

"It is not necessarily within the Superior's province to monitor students' problems or their emotional lives," she started. "Others have that responsibility. Better Superiors do it, nonetheless. However, I chose not to." She looked long and steadily at the younger nun. "But it was indeed within my province to handle erosion or a crisis when it was brought to my attention."

Mother Adelli lifted her eyes.

"You came to me several times. I ignored your difficulties because I didn't want to take the time to think about them, and because I wanted my name clear of the girl so that it would not become through her a barrier to the father. You seemed to me ready to handle the discipline problems that come with wider authority. Your record that way since March was superlative, and I felt the experience with the Rhenehan girl was germane to your future in the Order. All this became convenient reasoning on my part.

"You ask why no one stepped in. To do that, each person would have had to be different than they were at that time. To wish something had been different is wishing snow flakes were cherry blossoms. And actually wishing is not the problem; pretending is."

She leaned toward Mother Adelli. "I should have recognized the unusual difficulty of this child and intervened. I was aware that you were working with Reverend Mother Crewelman, and since the problem did not improve but got worse, it was doubly imperative that I attend to it. But I did not. I have given the matter much thought. You brought everything you could to the situation. I want you to know this."

Mother Adelli shook her head. "I hesitated, told half-truths, made excuses because I did not want to earn your displeasure or compromise my trip to Rome. That cost a life."

Reverend Mother Gregory patted the table. "May have, Mother Adelli; it may have cost a life. I am responsible for the unrepaired fence and for ignoring your calls for help. Then there is the run in the ravines that brought the pipe to her attention. You had never had any trouble there, and though I was not entirely in agreement with it, the activity seemed no more dangerous than field hockey. And there is the father's part. And the girl's nature. Only God knows what actually cost her life."

A great sigh shook Reverend Mother Gregory's body. She spread both hands on the table. "I have come to believe we humans can exercise perfect judgment only in retrospect. Each must settle her account as best she can, and it is wrong to take on more than one's due. Give yourself time, Mother Adelli; and meanwhile, offer up your suffering for whatev--."

The library door banged open and overhead globes blared down. Reverend Mother Crewelman stood with her pale hand on the switch.

"Oh, beg pardon," she said to her former Superior, but with eyes of property upon Mother Adelli. "I heard voices and couldn't imagine--." She made no move to leave.

"Good evening," Reverend Mother Gregory returned. Mother Adelli was on her feet.

Then the dictionary, open at "zodiac," in a sudden release of restrained energy flipped its remaining pages and would have leapt to the floor had not Mother Adelli plunged to the rescue.

"Words have been the undoing of many a prominent leader," Reverend Mother Gregory remarked dryly, never taking her eyes from the new Superior's face.

Reverend Mother Crewelman raised her chin and said nothing. She had only given Reverend Mother D'Gagnier the situation as she saw it, as was her duty. The clock ticked. She shifted her eyes to the younger nun steadying the great book.

"Your family was here. You had a good talk, I trust."

"Thank you, Reverend Mother. I--." Mother Adelli fell silent, coloring. Her mother storming off, the wound in her father's eyes.

"I was just saying to Mother Adelli, Reverend Mother Crewelman, that it is clear she did not get the support she needed dealing with that exceptionally difficult girl; and that she was by no means to take total responsibility for what happened."

The new Superior blinked and brought a cold gaze keenly around to Reverend Mother Gregory.

"Those of us who repeatedly extended ourselves to Mother Adelli instructed her in detail on a proper course of action. I don't see what more we could possibly have done."

Reverend Mother Gregory laughed out loud. Why the waxy old pelican was quick as lightning. She would be good with the Alumnae Association and Bishop McCaw.

"What more could we have done? Why, nothing at all with the eyes and ears we were using then. We would have needed new organs altogether, Reverend Mother Crewelman."

A puck of air burst from the new Superior's lips. She elongated her horseface and pulled herself taller.

"My eyes and ears were excellent at that time, thank you, and are excellent now. Did you want overhead lights?" Her hand was on the switch.

"We prefer the lamps."

"As you will."

The sudden dousing of the overheads, and rise of the soft green glow, flurry of long black skirts and door banging.

Reverend Mother Gregory shook her head. "This Community is in for lean times, I'm afraid. We must pray for that woman. Sit down, Mother Adelli." She gestured toward a chair. "What about your visit with your parents?"

Mother Adelli poured the story out. Reverend Mother Gregory settled back to let her fingers roam the base of the lamp. Beyond the window, the snow was nearly horizontal now.

"Let me see if I heard you correctly. You wanted your parents to devote their efforts and money to you as a dancer, but you did not want them to be in any way proprietary over you or the results. Is that right? Don't you find that a bit selfish?" She stroked the base of the lamp.

"Well, that's certainly what my mother would say," Mother Adelli stiffened.

"I don't hear in your voice now the repentance you say you reached after their visit." The Superior paused her fingers, then let them roam again.

"I am repentant, but they were ruining my life, running everything. Actually, I didn't have a life."

"You were under eighteen. Aren't parents supposed to direct the lives of their minors?" She ran a forefinger up the perpendiculars to the shade, then back down.

"They made an object of me. We had no family life. Everything was about dance, whether I wanted it to be or not."

"You are breathing so I assume you had a life then, as now. And you certainly had a family life; you just didn't have the family life you preferred. The arguments in the kitchen, your angry brother--wasn't that a family life?" Her fingers, without eyes, found the base again.

Mother Adelli closed her mouth.

"Is there a reason you should have the family life you prefer?" The Superior cocked her head. "Did your brother have the family life he preferred?" Her fingertips stroked the curves of the base. "Did your mother or father have the family lives they preferred? Have you heard of anyone who has had the family life he or she preferred?

"Mother Concepción."

"Mother Concepción lost her family at fourteen. Is hers a better story? Do you see how your attitude is childish, demanding that your parents feel only the way you want them to feel about each and every detail that touches upon your life?" She walked herself forward a little on the seat of her chair and laid both arms on the table. "I wonder whether you ever really wanted to be a dancer."

Mother Adelli pushed her chair back and stood.

"I have already been through this, Reverend Mother. I don't see what is wrong with wanting a mother and father to love you for yourself. Doesn't everyone need that?" She looked down with a dark face. "Sometimes I wanted to murder them for leaving me out in the cold while they basked in the glory of 'their ballerina.' I was the one who practiced and practiced."

"And you were the one getting the applause. Be truthful. Praise to your parents was for your performance." The Superior's voice cut a meticulous edge. "Perhaps what you hated was your parents keeping you from getting every bit of the applause for yourself."

Mother Adelli sucked in her breath. She held up both hands and began to back away. "I must leave. I am afraid I will forget myself, Reverend Mother. What you say is grossly unfair. Please excuse me."

The Superior reared back in her chair and a smile blazed across her face. The green of the lampshade crawled up to her chin.

"Must you fly into a storm to avoid saying that when you were a child you thought, felt and acted as a child, as St. Paul says? What else do children know except their own needs and wants? We all want all of whatever we love. God makes us that way, I believe, to entice us into life. It is everyone's story, one way or another." She leaned her chin on one hand and put the other on her hip like a washerwoman, curled its fingers. "But it must have made you furious to have your mother take so much credit, to pick your pocket in broad daylight and spend the money in your face."

Mother Adelli hesitated; her face contorted. Then she laughed, laughed for the first time since her student's death--bent over and laughed hard and long, let it peter out and dropped weakly into her chair.

"She would show me off like a circus pony, or the Christmas pie." More laughter, then choking, her eye rims grew red.

The Superior smelled the self-pity. "And what do you think your mother was feeling as she showed you off like her prize pony?" She reached back and freed her veil.

Her mother's tense tired face. Her father next to his wife in the theater; his adoration from the dark audience. Herself, nine years old, a snowflake wearing a tiny tiara and twirling, arms raised, fingers uncurling. As the music swelled and she trembled high onto her toe before the rapt audience, the applause came on like a cloudburst.

Now, for the first time, she saw it; her hands flew to her solar plexus. She was what her mother and father salvaged from the wreck of their marriage. She was the work they did together.

"My dancing was the one thing they had between them. I never recognized it before," the young nun murmured, still caught in the vision.

Satisfied, the Superior said nothing. Now forgiveness could begin. She glanced at the clock. "Oh, Lord," she sat up straight. "I told Mother O'Rourke I would have a word with her before Compline. Do you mind--?" She looped her hand at the room.

"Certainly, Reverend Mother." Mother Adelli stood.

Reverend Mother Gregory turned at the threshold to hold Mother Adelli for a moment in her gaze. "Did you really want to be a dancer?" she asked; and before the younger nun could reply, stepped across the threshold.

Mother Adelli closed the door and, turning off one lamp after another, realized with wonder that she was without the pain of the death, that on top of or beneath the debris within, there stood as if at the horizon a thin clear line like a slip of sky. Was it to do with her parents?

She glanced at the clock, shrank from going to chapel. The very idea of God still riled her. Why hadn't He just broken her neck before something happened to the girl?

Working across the room, in her mind Julian appeared in his bedroom on Granville, tossing a tennis ball against the door. Thump, thump. On the wall hung a crucifix, his Loyola pennant, a poster of the Paulist Choir at Symphony Hall, and a photograph of a redwood forest in northern California.

"I don't know what God says to murderers," he turned, grinning to where she saw herself seated at his desk; "but now I know what murderers say to God."

"You think I'm a--."

"I think you're a human being."

"He's in charge. Why didn't He save her?"

One, two, three tosses of the ball. Julian shrugged.

"It's His game."

Children often died in accidents, disobeying their parents. The younger brother of a student in Omaha died in an old refrigerator, hiding like Helene. What about babies left in the fields in ancient Rome and still today in China? What about Suzanne Degnan? She saw the scythe move over the field. It cut the green shoot along with the dry stalk. It was His field. Helene was His field. She was His field. Each person was His field. Still, she hated death. What kind of a God makes death? She pulled out a chair and sat motionless. The hands of the clock moved, moved. After a time, she stood to finish turning off the rest of the lamps.

In chapel, the Community waited for Reverend Mother Crewelman. Mother Adelli lowered the seat of her prie dieu. She had meant to tell Reverend Mother Gregory she'd decided to leave the Order; now it was too late. Now she must do the thing alone. Reverend Mother Crewelman arrived short of breath and Compline began.

Mother Adelli rose mechanically, turned the pages of her breviary, bowed to the altar, to her sisters in the Order. After ten minutes, her body freed itself from her mind to respond to the rise and fall of voices in prayer, and unexpectedly her imagination began to choreograph the chanted psalms as a dance sequence like one from *Giselle*.

Giselle. She was seventeen, felt the stage tremble under the applause for her, the *ingénue*. She knew she could have it all if she wanted.

"For He shall deliver thee from the snare of the fowler, and from the deadly pestilence," her Community sang.

But it was as she knelt with the others that all came clear suddenly. The terrifying power of her own talent was what had made her flee to the cloister. God had only said to give Him her life. It was she who chose the cloister.

She climbed the stairs to the dormitory and crept onto her cot. In Helene's death she had met the face of God-- not the God of her childhood, or the God of her calling, nor of her novitiate, but a God Who brought terror and death. She closed her eyes. This was not a God she understood.

Then, drifting into sleep, she remembered her college science class junior year when they studied the medusa-- how, deadly injured, it would sink to the ocean floor where its body would fold in upon itself and be absorbed. It was then the root-like stolons appeared, then lengthened and became polyps again, growing the new medusa.

Four

"Well, Mother Adelli," the new Superior drew her shoulders back in a way that elongated her neck, "have you given thought to your future?"

It was 10:00 a.m. Saturday morning. Reverend Mother Crewelman sat at Reverend Mother Gregory's desk; to her right, a stack of manila folders. Her eyes swept the young nun. In four hours, Justine Gregory would be gone; but there was still the matter of this woman to be decided.

Mother Adelli met her Superior's eyes, but her memory was fixed on another Superior in another room, ten years earlier.

"What do you want from us?" Reverend Mother Wilber, the Superior at Albany, had asked the traditional question smiling at her, barely eighteen then and rehearsing her answer the fourteen hours on the train from Chicago.

"To serve God as a member of this Society."

Reverend Mother Crewelman did not smile, but tapped her fingers on the desk.

"Well, Mother?"

Mother Adelli blinked. "I have decided to apply for release from Vows, Reverend Mother."

"Pardon?" the Superior leaned forward.

"I said I wish to be released from Vows, Reverend Mother."

Reverend Mother Crewelman's eyes widened. She tugged a handkerchief from her sleeve, then poked it into place again.

"Well, this is surely the last thing I expected."

"And the last thing I expected, Reverend Mother."

She didn't like the young woman's tone of voice, as if she was to be the decider of the next steps--and after the death and chaos she had caused.

"Well, it is totally out of the question." And the Superior erased the idea with a sweep of her hand.

Mother Adelli's eyes widened. "But I must, Rever--."

"Thanks to you, any of us any time could be called to court and to the witness box. You will go nowhere. You are a danger to yourself and others. And I will insist that you be reassigned here where we can keep an eye on you." The cords of her wax-colored neck strained against the skin as she spoke. "And how would it look to a judge if you left the Order while this matter of a death remained unresolved? How might that influence the favor of his decisions?"

Mother Adelli drew her rosary into her lap. "I'm afraid those are things I hadn't thought of."

Reverend Mother Crewelman took a folder from the stack and leaned forward. "Time is a carpenter's tool, Mother Adelli. Too soon mountains become hills, then plains, then," she gestured horizontally, "everything disappears into something else, including who did what, when and how. You will misremember, then broadcast it-- no matter who it maligns. You can see we have an obligation to think ahead for you." She flapped the folder open.

For a Religious of ten years to apply for release just before Final Vows was a scandal, and would run wildfire all the way to Europe. To suffer it any time, much less on her first day as Superior was unspeakably galling, shameful and unfair.

"Since I cannot know who I might harm and in what way, Reverend Mother," the younger nun spoke up softly, "from this day on, I will never speak of what happened again, except to a Superior or confessor. I give my you word on that--and with all my heart. I wish no one further harm."

"But a word you obviously cannot keep. I witnessed those tears of yours long before the girl's death; yet you did not change." Reverend Mother Crewelman set down her pen, narrowed her eyes. "You think you can leave all this behind you. No. What you will leave behind are the lessons you have failed to learn; and those will follow you, Mother, believe me. For once, you will do what you are told, or how can you be saved?"

Mother Crewelman picked up her pen, wet her finger and turned to the folder. The tick of the clock. Slap, slap from the corridor. Someone dusting the floor. Yes, her superior was right. She, Mary Agnes Adelli needed salvation. But who could give it to her, lost as she was? And who could keep her from harming others?

"Apparently you did well enough at Albany and Omaha. But here no one knew you. As we mentioned in your Chapter of Faults, you did not take your thoughts to anyone."

Mother Concepción knew her. And Reverend Mother Gregory, now. *Soeur* Josephine. Some students, in their way. Rosary beads slipped through Mother Adelli's fingers.

"Your irresponsibility toward the girl shows your great disregard for our Society. Some have made great sacrifices to be here. My father was a graduate of Columbia, and the name of God was anathema at home. When I entered the Order, he disinherited me. He did not even send for me when he was dying." She threw a cold look of triumph at Mother Adelli.

But Pop would call for her, surely; and she would come, no matter how difficult, how far.

The new Superior swiveled in her chair. "All great saints are single-minded in their obedience. I vowed to protect our disciplines; it has not made me popular." She pressed her long fingers together, turned and shook them at Mother Adelli, "Had I been Superior these past months, that girl would be alive; there would be no suits, no settlements. Things will change now. There will be no more," she waffled her hand, 'shim sham.'" She stretched her neck, raised her eyebrows. "And we will be the ones to decide whether you remain in the Order, Mother Adelli; not you."

Mother Adelli started up, the pocket rosary falling from her fingers. "But Reverend Mother, I must be allowed--."

"You will stay here. You will bury this thing and start over." The Superior tugged the handkerchief from her sleeve.

Bury it? It seemed she must eat, drink and sleep it, breathe it until it became flesh of her flesh. Helene's life and death would be a music playing deep within her now until she passed. Such were the offices of Memory, its work of mercy to those in grief. This was how she would honor, expiate and leave nothing behind.

"You are ill, Mother Adelli. And it is dementia itself to think you can make a sane decision." The Superior dabbed at the corners of her mouth. "That is why you have Superiors."

Demented. Yes, a cripple who couldn't keep the Rule, or even seem to tell the truth.

"And it would be sinful now to throw away all the effort and expense of your training and rehabilitation, not to speak of the investment your parents have made." The Superior closed Mother Adelli's folder.

Her parents. Now she knew that lies buried in childhood would one day push up green through the hardest of rock. To try to protect herself was futile; there was no way to out-maneuver the Great Will. She searched her Superior's face, saw in it the uphill climb.

The sky out the window was all swiftly moving clouds; and the room, where it deepened behind the Superior's desk, dropped into a lively shadow land. Reverend Mother Gregory would have lit the lamps to warm it. Oh how she wished for her, for her counsel now. She leaned toward her new Superior.

"In these last few days, Reverend Mother, I have discovered that my vocation to the Order was tainted from the beginning. So to stay here is now against my conscience."

The Superior barked a laugh. "That famous conscience of yours, the one that led to the decision about the duck?"

"Reverend Mother Gregory helped me to see the resentments I have held against my family. And I have discovered my responsibility in the choice I made to leave ballet. In this way I have found some peace." And grief, oh more grief. "I thought I had a vocation, but I find instead I was hiding from problems I couldn't--."

"I will tell you when you find peace." Reverend Mother Crewelman leaned far forward; her words slashed the air "And let's not be childish. We all bring problems with us. My mother called me once a week for years, weeping that my father would not utter my name."

Mother Adelli sat back. Her face filled with compassion. "I didn't know. You have suffered to be here."

"I don't parade my crosses for public admiration, Mother. You like to think yourself special; it glares in your Chapter of Faults. Running from problems, were you? And just what do you think you are doing now?"

Yes, running as if her skirts were on fire. Running anywhere except back to the mistake. The older woman's face was the color of uncooked dough. She searched beneath its surface for doors, found them closed and locked, as usual. And here again was the disturbing undercurrent of pleasure she often sensed the Superior found in the spiritual suffering of others.

"Release from Vows takes a year or more. Did you know that? It must be cleared at the Vatican. And our request will hardly be momentous. You will wait in line, as any humble Religious ought. There will be forms and more forms back and forth, months on end, and a great deal of writing for everyone involved. It is selfish to make work for so many over feelings that will change with your mental condition."

The fragrance of leather from a reading chair drifted onto the air. Mother Adelli let it wrap around her, and a feeling of reverie crept upon her as she sat silent, listening to the abstract scratch of the pen's nib. When she finally spoke, it was to no one but herself.

"I worked so hard in the Novitiate, and everything there was pure joy. When I took First Vows and pinned a black veil to my wimple, I felt a visible blessing from Heaven descend upon me." Like handling the charms on a bracelet, she touched upon those days. "I grew to love teaching. After nine years I was named Mistress of the Third *Cours* here. Then Helene came with her troubles. Though Reverend Mother Gregory was never easy to talk to, I tried to bring my difficulties to her. I wanted the girl to be happy." She raised her eyes to her Superior. "Usually I brought difficulties to you only when I was so ordered because our conferences left me in such despair." Could she be saying such things to this Superior?

Reverend Mother Crewelman looked pleased, even proud. "Yes. Despair scours the soul. I keep my charges in despair as much as possible. It is the first rung on the ladder of sanctity." She pressed her lips together. "My task as your Spiritual Advisor was to see that every flaw, no matter how small, was rooted out." She wiped her mouth. "But you speak of finding peace, Mother Adelli. With a death on your conscience?"

"I see her coming from her alcove or reaching for something on the *Goûter* cart; and then hear her cry for help, see her blue under the frozen leaves. It is only God's law against killing myself that has kept me from that."

Reverend Mother Crewelman stiffened, sniffed, pulled her face into her wimple. Aflare of pity ran through her against her will, knocking on closed doors. Well perhaps, after everything died down, she could quietly let the woman go her way; but certainly not in this, her first year of leadership.

Beyond the gates, a truck ground its gears. The Superior skipped through a folder, checked it off. She dug her pocket watch from under her cape and set it on the desk.

Mother Adelli watched the Superior's eyes race across a page. The clock ticked. In these moments of reverie, suddenly she saw it all so clearly.

"It is obedience that I have been hiding behind all my life. As long as I was obedient, I didn't have to make decisions or become responsible, or even develop a conscience. Those things belonged to my parents, to my Superiors. Now I see that I am responsible whether I want to be or not, and whether I am obedient or not." She straightened. "Following my Superiors did not keep me from being responsible; following them in the future will not keep me from being responsible. I wish--"

"Fulfilling the Vow of Obedience is not being responsible? Surrendering your life to God is not being responsible?" Reverend Mother Crewelman jolted forward, her horsey mouth gaping.

"Surrender is what Mother Concepciòn tried to tell me about; it has cost me a great deal to understand it even a little bit."

"I appreciate the authorities you consult." the Superior tossed her head. "Mother Concepciòn was daft for who knows how many years." She sniffed long, flattening her nostrils. "You say it is God's will for you to be out in the world, alone, with no guides--you who carry the price of a life!"

To think that the frailties of her mind with its back and forth could have cost a life. She swallowed, let the slurry of nausea pass. She had this one small place inside, clear as a drop of water; and she must protect it as if it were a flame in the wind, for she would not walk that old broken path again if she could help it.

She looked up. Before her was her Superior imprisoned in her work. She'd had no Helene to drop her like pottery on stone. Who could help those in authority? And how many religious were forthright about their Superiors, about the effect of their demands in the Chapter of Faults? She never had been.

"The mistake that caused me to come to the Order was hidden where I couldn't reach it," she went on, "God planned or allowed such a thing. Sometimes that is the only explanation that makes sense to me."

"Lord, but you are a dangerous fool." Reverend Mother Crewelman slammed down her pen. "Now you try to make God responsible for what is entirely your fault. You admit you have been wrong before. How will you know when you are wrong again and in danger of Hell, with a mind so riddled with contradiction and confusion?"

"God must help me. This path is wrong for me. I must leave it and look for the right one. Otherwise how can I ever find my way to Him? However long the papers take, I must start them. How can I know if a vocation to any Order is right unless I leave? What else can I do that's honest?"

"No Order will take you after this." The Superior settled back smug in her chair. The woman didn't know what she was saying moment to moment, must not be allowed to get out there where she could blather whatever came into her head. But then the wasted and hungering face suddenly made her stomach wrench; her voice softened. "We are the right path for you, Mother Adelli. We will help you. You are unhinged from the girl's death. You are safe with us."

The small buttons down the front of Mother Adelli's cape rose and fell. Helene's death had unhinged her, yes; but from the past! She let her eyes drift to the window. Two crows in a racket of bowing dusted themselves with snow. She felt almost peaceful now---as if some emergency had passed.

"I don't really know now whether the spiritual experiences I had were meant to bring me to this or any Order," she went on; "I don't know what such experiences mean, or if they even amount to a vocation."

The Superior gazed curiously at this young nun, wasted in the chair. "When we finish, I will order a sedative from the doctor. Before dinner, go to the infirmary to get it. And sleep there tonight. Mother Spencer will keep an eye on you."

Mother Adelli tilted her head, let her eyes rest on the corner of the desktop just where the wood turned and gathered light. If "vocation" meant "a call to do God's will," then she had that; but how did a person find out what a life was meant for? The familiar flash of panic. She drew her eyes into her lap searching for that one clear space she had found before. After a moment, she brought them up.

"My decision is still to apply for release from Vows."

"Denied. Your are under obedience to me."

Mother Adelli held her peace.

Reverend Mother Crewelman closed a folder, reached for another. "You are in need of medical and psychological help. The subject is closed. Now, I have work to do."

Mother Adelli straightened in her chair. "The Church acknowledges conscience as the only and final judge in any matter, Superior. I will be forced to take my appeal directly to Reverend Mother D'Gagnier. I cannot stay here against my conscience." She stood.

"I will NOT have you bothering her. I forbid the use of the telephone. I forbid you to leave the building. Go and prepare your office for your replacement. See that your Study Hall is straightened. Look to your dormitory and linens. Don't bring this new woman into a mess."

"Then I will have to go into the neighborhood for help."

Reverend Mother Crewelman stopped marking, saw it all--the peaked face at the door, the stammered explanation, the scrawled phone number of the Convent as assurance the charges would be accepted, the quizzical looks, later the neighborhood dinner party with its gossip.

"Do you hold nothing sacred--this Community, this Order? Are you that selfish?" Reverend Mother Crewelman exploded.

Mother Adelli felt her heart pound at the base of her throat. She turned and walked toward the door, opened it and walked through.

"Mother Adelli, come back here." Reverend Mother Crewelman's voice leapt after her down the corridor, repeated past the windows and offices to the elevator. "Come back here. Mother Adelli."

The elevator car was on the third floor. Mother Adelli eyed the stairs, then turned her body to stone, ready to face her adversary. Black skirts churning, Reverend Mother Crewelman bore down upon her.

"All right. I will speak to the Vicar General," the Superior hissed through her large yellow teeth. "We don't want you here anyway."

Mother Adelli pushed the button to call the car. Reverend Mother Crewelman spun away, then turned back.

"You are to go to San Francisco. Reverend Mother D'Gagnier has made that decision for you. You will live with our Community at Lone Mountain and attend the Jesuit university there. I don't know how your request for release may effect this arrangement." She gritted her teeth. "Now I must call her. You can be sure she will hear my opinions on all of this."

The woman narrowed her eyes. "I cannot believe you would be so selfish as to pursue such a path when we are so susceptible to an injury just now that you have caused. Lacking everything else, evidently you lack loyalty and feeling for your Community as well." She dug for her handkerchief. "I can see that no effort or extension of good will means anything to you. Mother O'Rourke will have Vicar General's reply by dinnertime. Show the woman from New York whatever she needs to know. She will be here by three."

They stared at one another for a moment.

"And I pray for your soul," the Superior snarled, then stalked away, handkerchief bulging in her hand.

Mother Adelli watched the elongated torso move down the corridor. She had never noticed before how the Superior's body slanted and her arms swung like pendulums with her stride.

As she pulled the elevator gate aside, the repressed fear knocked her knees loose so that she tottered against the gate holding on to it until the tremor chattered through.

The new woman was middle-aged and stocky. She had little to say and few questions as they toured the grounds and building. Mother Ryan did not want procedures. She had headed the Third *Cours* in Tarrytown for eight years. She found everything in order except for the sports closet. "I'll see the girls put this to rights immediately," she dusted her hands.

There was little for Mother Adelli to clear from her office except a few holy cards and a photograph GeeGee had taken just before the Day of Recollection. Helene stood outside at the Minims' Door squinting into the sun. The bow on her uniform collar was upside down. Mother Adelli swallowed, slipped the picture into her pocket and let her stinging eyes sweep the space one final time. She closed the door and gave the key to the new woman.

Mother Ryan immediately wanted to rearrange Study Hall. Where could the custodian be found on a Saturday? Then Mother Adelli closed that door too, but not before her eyes drank in for the last time the late afternoon light luminous in ribbons and patches over the old wooden desks. She searched hungrily for a sight of Helene, for the rage of red hair over a book, her square shoulders hunched, a freckled cheek dimpled around a closed fist, one foot tipped onto its side and the other stacked on top.

Mother O'Rourke took Mother Adelli aside at dinner to inform her she was to catch the sleeper to San Francisco the next afternoon. A single compartment was reserved for the two nights and three days. The limousine would carry her to the station. And there were two messages from Reverend Mother D'Gagnier: A University of San Francisco catalogue waited for her with Reverend Mother Gillespie at Lone Mountain, and that the papers to Rome she requested would be started. Might she see her parents in Chicago on her way to the train? The secretary tilted a sympathetic head; No, but Mother Adelli must call her family immediately.

She held the receiver against her ear and listened through the linen of her wimple, heart pounding. Her father's voice, then he stepped away.

"She's not ready, Pretty Feet. You know how she is." His breathing was heavy, his speech thick. He had been drinking. "Write to me from San Francisco. I can send you a little money if you need it. When you get settled, I'll come out. We'll do the town, eh, Pretty Feet?"

At lunch in Cloister the next day, they heard John of the Cross.

Then there was only the one black bag to snap shut and the small briefcase to lift with her other hand. As she passed through the foyer and struggled with the heavy front door, a blue sedan pulled around the driveway in the falling snow. GeeGee, dropped off early, started up the steps as Mother Adelli came down. The girl turned to stare at the Mistress of the Third *Cours* who passed her without a word and with downcast eyes.

The school limousine pulled up. Mother Adelli felt the round eyes of her student, as always filled with questions. She pulled back from entering the car's door and turned, but neither time nor words could be exchanged in that little moment held softly between two worlds spinning so rapidly apart. She lifted her hand.

GeeGee, snow settling upon her tam o'shanter, dropped her plaid overnight bag at her feet to wave in return, uncomprehending. Her eyes followed the broad car as it ferried her Mother Adelli through the stone gate, down the road to disappear into the loose weave of winter.

Mother Adelli looked into the rear view mirror to see GeeGee become a doll, a smaller doll, a pink dot; then to see the red-tiled roof disappear beneath the treetops, until only its white cupola and cross were visible under the drifting heavens; then Nature filling up even that space with branches black and tangling against the low grey background.

Turning to the limousine window, she saw the long grass teeming, reaching and turning in step with its partner Wind, and watched them separate to turn and reach again and again. Then, at an energetic pull--familiar and everlasting—feel her Self pass between the grains of the window pane and into the wonder of that wordless, restless and eternal movement to join that which her body in some way had never left.

Meanwhile the limousine strove onward through the snow to whatever would come next for the small passenger in her black garb who, the driver noticed, rested her chin on fine small hands, and seemed to take an interest in nothing--nothing at all--but that wind-driven field.

Epilogue

Walk to the well.
Turn as the earth and the moon turn,
circling what they love.

Whatever circles comes from the center.

Rumi

ACKNOWLEDGEMENTS

This novel began in Andy Alleghretti's fiction writing semicircle at Columbia College, Chicago. It took hold in its own right under the coaching of novelist Betty Shifflet and continued full force with John Schultz, the   inspired creator of the Story Workshop® approach to writing where this amazing "way in" helped me realize that my dream of being a fiction writer was not only possible but imminent.

Equal thanks must go to my wonderful editor and a fiction writer with his own following, Mark Paxson who opened the way to publication not only for this and other books, but for my first Kindle venture,"3/Chicago". His patience, steadfastness, generosity and good will have introduced me to a new world of publication, greatly various and by its nature communal. My gratitude also to Pam Jones for her proofreading, deep reflection and steadfast support getting the story to its final station.

Others one time or another, have read the text and been fueling stations along the way. Among them are my sister Martha Abbate, Chicago historian Jean Spaay Hunt, Patricia Novak, Jaime O'Reilly, Mary Watson, Carolyn Sabin, the women of the Chicago Dinner Party Project who gave me "start up" money for my first writing office, Ceci Sommers, Anne Schultz, John Starrs, Doris Jorden, my workshop directors at Columbia College, Christina Maynard, Mark's mother, Diana Paxson, and wife, Irene Paxson, my high school friend, Judy Huber Greenley, and a phalanx of others, whose names ought to be here too.

Cover photography and interior art is the work of Barat College alumni Kate Oelerich (Kate Oelerich Photography, Winnetka, Illinois), who stepped out of her normal portrait speciality to provide images of our beloved building and its architecture which housed, years apart, The Convent of the Sacred Heart for me (1945-50) and

Barat College, class of '68 for her. Kate also brought Emily Connolly into the final work on the book.

Emily Connolly (Emily Connolly Imaging, Indianapolis, Indiana) with her stunning cover designs and book interiors furthered the story to palpable dimension for its readers. Great thanks to both for their outstanding work.

And to the many participants in my workshops here in Sacramento, Chicago and elsewhere who see to it that I stay dedicated, sharp, and loose. Their loyalty to their own futures as writers gives me a writing community that keeps inspiring me to press on no matter what.

ZOE KEITHLEY, born in Chicago, was a boarding student in the Third *Cours* from 1945-1949 and in First Academic as a commuting student, 1949-1951. She graduated from Trinity College, Washington D.C., continued studies at New York University, University of Iowa, California State University, Chico, and finally at Columbia College, Chicago where she stumbled into the famous Story Workshop® approach to writing

photograph by Fiona Renton

conceived of and led by John Schultz. It was in those workshops that writing began to flow mightily for her with a plethora of short stories and a first novel. Through the Chicago Teachers Center, she brought her writing training to teachers in Chicago's public schools. Retirement returned her to Northern California where her children and grandsons live, and where she continues leading workshops and writing fiction and poetry.

A Pushcart nominee, chapters of *The Calling of Mother Adelli* have appeared in *North American Review, Emergence II & IV and Best of Hair Trigger.* Keithley's fiction has won or placed in *American Fiction, Zoetrope.*

Made in the USA
San Bernardino, CA
23 April 2014